LIGHT
for the Journey

Robert T. Gamba

Order this book online at www.trafford.com
or email orders@trafford.com

Most Trafford titles are also available at major online book retailers.

Printed in the United States of America.

ISBN: 978-1-4251-1723-8 (sc)
ISBN: 978-1-4269-8021-3 (e)

Trafford rev. 08/20/2012

 www.trafford.com

North America & international
toll-free: 1 888 232 4444 (USA & Canada)
phone: 250 383 6864 ♦ fax: 812 355 4082

Light for the Journey

John 1: 5
And the light shines into the darkness, and the darkness did not comprehend it.

As we walk through the experience of this life, we will quickly discover that the path is not an easy one. There are heartaches, disappointments, and sorrows along the way. However, there are also the great promises of God that are given not to take the experiences away, but to bring us through them with confidence, by the power of His guiding light of love and wisdom.

There was a lighted star, which guided the wise men to the newborn Christ in a small town on what seemed to be an ordinary night. The merchants were counting their sales for the day, the shepherds were tending their herds, and the stars filled the sky with the glory of the Creator. There was one star in the sky that was different on that night, which even attracted a small crowd of shepherds.

God also gave the light of a pillar of fire by night to lead the Israelites out of bondage from the land of Egypt and into the promise land of blessings. This must have been some sight in the darkness of night, as a flame hovered over them like a helicopter with a giant floodlight.

God has also given us a light, the light of His word, through the power of His Spirit to all that believe, which ignites our souls with the fire of faith. Of course, there is a pending factor to whether we can apply the light of His grace to our everyday lives. God instructs us to follow His lead, and if we decide to follow our own, then we cannot walk in the light of God, but will stumble in the blindness of our own pride. After all, God is all-knowing! If we actually think that we can direct our lives better than the Creator of all life can, then we are still stumbling in the darkness of ignorance. There is no question that ignorance will leave a soul in a state of insecurity and unable to see the plan and purpose God has for our lives. For God does have a purpose for every one of us, along with many tasks of faith that are used according to His plan and not ours.

Some of the prophets of old were blinded by their own insecurities, forgetting that God is the Creator and Sustainer of all things. Although they heard the word of God, some failed in faith, as we all have, seeing their assignments as impossible for them to accomplish, forgetting that it was God doing the work and not them. Therefore, it is faith in what God declares that enables anyone to run the course of His purpose by grace, and not with our limited strength. Moses, Jeremiah, Jonah and many more, after hearing the word from God, protested and told God, 'You have the wrong man for this job.' Failing to understand at first that all God desires to accomplish in our lives is by His strength, wisdom and power. This leads us to some very important questions about the path that we are on and how well is our own spiritual vision. If we are not on the right track, God's track, and are running with the heavy weights of regret, complaining, and an unforgiving heart, then we are running in the darkness of doubt and unbelief, which gives birth to fear. Moreover, we will discover that running on the track of God's purpose is only half of the equation; the other half is how well we run on it with the wisdom from the light of God's mercy through faith. This is by no means insinuating that God's gift of salvation is merited on how well we perform. On the contrary, we cannot even enter the race of faith unless we have been born from above. We simply cannot perform for a gift, because then it is a wage, something that is earned. We are given the ability to enter on God's path and are guided by His light, not because we have earned it, but because it was given as a gift and we accepted it. Of course, there was a price, a cost that needed to be paid for the penalty for sin. However, we did not posses the wealth to pay the price for our eternal redemption. Although eternal salvation is a gift to those that believe, it cost the pure, sinless blood of Jesus Christ to pay for it. That was a price that was paid in full, which is hard to fully comprehend now, but we will when we see Him face to face.

The lighted path of eternal life is in the redemption of the cross. What does God say about this path? Jesus said many things about the road that leads to the Father.

A young man came to Jesus and asked, *"What good thing shall I do that I may have eternal life?"* A good question and it is interesting how it appeared that the one who asked it had his sights on the eternal riches of God instead of the temporal treasures of this life. We find out later in the conversation that this was not the case at all. Jesus begins by telling him to *"keep the commandments,"* obey God. We all know that no man has ever fully kept the commandments of God, except one Man, Jesus Christ. Therefore, how could we reach the goal of eternal life by keeping the commandments of God? The one that asked the question answered quickly and boldly to the statement by Jesus as he responded, *"All these things I have kept from my youth."*

However, the first, foremost commandment is to *love the Lord your God with all your heart, mind, and soul*, even more than all earthly possessions. We then see from the next couple of verses that the young rich man never really had a true understanding of the very first commandment of God. For God is not looking for earthly treasure; He does not desire silver or gold from us. God is looking for our love, not the mere pennies that we call riches, that compared to the riches and glory of God are worthless. Now this is not to say that the young rich man was a thief, murderer, or a fornicator. He might have attempted to obey all the commandments below the first, but by not obeying the first, he broke them all. Therefore, this young rich man knew that he was missing something, as he asked Jesus:

Matthew 19: 20

"What do I still lack?"

We can clearly see that though this young rich man appeared to be an upstanding, devoted believer in God, maybe a good church member, he lacked the reason for keeping the commandments. The reason why we should try to please God is because we love Him, although He loved us first. The motivation for obeying God's word should be love and not for obligation. If we do it for any other reason, we are missing the very purpose of our existence. For this purpose, we were created, to know and love God and each other. If we obey the first commandment, which is to *love the Lord, your God with all your heart,* the other commandments will be easier to obey. This should certainly raise some questions in our own walk through this short experience. I know it has in mine. Although this young rich man was considered a good and decent citizen, he was indeed blinded by the temporary riches of this life. Therefore, he was in the darkness of error, although his life appeared to be one of high moral values. He was probably respected by many people who thought they knew him. Jesus knew that he lacked the most important part.

Matthew 19:21
Jesus said to him, "If you want to be perfect (lacking nothing) *go, sell what you have and give to the poor, and you will have treasures in heaven; and come, follow Me."*
We need to take a step back and realize what was taking place in this conversation. The light of God's love was shining into the heart of this young man, revealing the lack, the emptiness that he had been struggling with his entire life. This lack, the emptiness of the heart is a life that is lacking the love of God; therefore, it is a heart that is searching for something, or somebody to fill it. The empty heart will try almost anything to fill the lack that only God can fill. We can easily see this in the present age, the race to buy bigger, newer, and the most recent updated version from a materialistic society, trying desperately to fill the void in their hearts. This void, the lack of God's love, can never be filled with gold or silver, bigger cars, boats and houses, but only by surrendering to God, then He will fill our hearts with His love that will take us through eternity. The true purposes of our lives are in the desires of God's heart and His desire fills our hearts, since His desire is to love. Remember that Jesus extended this same offer to all the apostles as He did to this young man as He said, *"Follow Me,"* and they abandoned all they had to follow Him. They might not have been as rich as this young man, but they did have possessions that they quickly left behind at the offer of Jesus. This lesson of the rich young ruler is the light of God's wisdom that reflects in our own souls, revealing our own measure of faith in the invitation to follow the King. It brings two important questions to the surface of our existence.

The first, which is the most obvious, is do we value our possessions more than our relationship with God? Most of us would quickly say that God is more important then anything else in our lives. Of course, this is a very easy thing to say when God is not making any request or demand to leave something behind, or give something away that we care for.

The second question, which goes much deeper into our reasons and motives for all we do, is the same question the young man had for Jesus. *"What do I lack?"* The young man seemed to have it all together. He had high moral standards, a respected position in the ruling class and wealth that has always been a speculation of God's blessing in one's life. However, with all that, including his youth, there was a lack, a space and a void somewhere in his soul. It was the first commandment.

We will also never be able to fulfill the first commandment of God without knowing the Creator on a personal level. How can anybody really love someone that they do not know?

Therefore, the lack, the emptiness in our hearts, will never be filled no matter how many things we buy, or even how much good we attempt to do, because only God, through His mercy of revealing Himself to us, can make us complete, lacking nothing. Once we know Him, we love Him, and true love is priceless.

The young rich man appeared to be on the right path, with the best intentions. However, we can see that his heart was with his material possessions and earthly riches with a mask of religion. Moreover, many men in history have fell victims of disasters with the best intention.

Jesus tells the church of Ephesus in the book of Revelation that they had labored with good works, as the young rich man, whose name was not worthy to be mentioned. The church was keeping the commandments two through ten. Jesus praised them for their labor, patience, and endurance. However, then Jesus rebukes them in saying:

Revelation 2: 4

"Nevertheless, I have this against you, that you left your first love."

Some theologians will say that the church in Ephesus was simply backsliding back into the world, that they lost their first zeal for the Gospel. However, I believe that the *first love,* which Jesus refers to, is the same first love that was lacking in the young rich man. The church was beginning to wear the same costume of religion, and their first love was like an oil lamp running out of oil. They began to go through the motions of love, but lost the passion. As the young rich man had a void in his life, the church in Ephesus was also beginning to *lack one thing.* Jesus told them to repent and do the *first works.*
Matthew 22: 37, 38
Jesus said to him, "You shall love the Lord your God with all your heart, with all your mind, and with all your strength. This is the first and great commandment."
When Jesus extended the ultimate offer to leave all these worthless possessions behind, to do the work of God and walk with God into the glories of eternity, the young man walked away saddened. This is not to judge this young man, but rather it is for us to look in ourselves, and to know what is our response to that very invitation in our daily decisions. Although God may not be asking us to physically give away all our possessions, but rather give them second place in our hearts and let Jesus Christ occupy the first. For it is in the first place in our hearts, the place where our first love lives, where we can fulfill the first commandment of God and do the *first works.* That is to *love the Lord God with all our hearts, with all our minds* and with all our possessions. Moreover, one day, whether we like it or not, we will leave all our possessions, even our own bodies behind. Then, these few years here compared to eternity will seem like a blink of an eye. However, without the light of God, we will never perceive this now, but will be blinded by the earthly possessions and pleasures of this short life. Gaining a few short years here with our possessions and missing eternity with God, would be like settling for a toothpick compared to owning a multi-million dollar home. The problem exists because in the darkness, due to sin, the toothpick is all that is seen. Our physical eye then blinds our spiritual vision, missing the light of God's wisdom.

Daniel 5: 23
And the God who holds your breath in His hand and owns all
your ways, you have not glorified.
Without the light of faith in Jesus Christ, we will never be able
to trust God, or glorify Him, even by seeing the wonder of His
creation as a testimony that He is the Almighty. For the
physical creation testifies of God's goodness, grace and power,
but sin blinds the spiritual eyes, preventing us in seeing the
Creator, even through His creation.
Romans 1: 20
For since the creation of the world His invisible attributes are
clearly seen, being understood by the things that are made, even
His eternal power and Godhead, so we are without excuse.
Although we cannot see God with our physical eyes, we see the
creation, which is a reflection of God. And with the light of
God's wisdom that is within our spirits, by His Holy Spirit
according to His word, we should realize that only God could
have created such a perfect universe. The blackness of shame
from sin blinds even the best intents and is given to such
synthetic theories like evolution. God reminds us that we are
without excuse since creation itself testifies that He is God.
The invitation that was given to the young rich man is
extended to us every day with every choice we make.
However, by ignoring the light of God's word to direct our
every step toward eternity, we use the standards of men as our
point of reference and lose our insight for the eternal.
Psalm 119: 105
Your word is a lamp to my feet and a light to my path.
As the responsible owner of a new automobile is careful to
check the routine maintenance guidelines in the owner's
manual, much more we should be in the owner's manual for
our eternal souls, the bible. We know that the owner of the
vehicle that does not follow the required maintenance
procedures, mandated by the manufacture, will severely
shorten the operating expectancy of the vehicle.
Jesus said that He is the light of the world, and His words are
the light of life. Without the power of His word, there is no life,
no light, and no hope for redemption, sanctification, or the
restoration of our spirits. It is the light of Christ, the word of

God, through the Holy Spirit, that brings us through the journey of this short earthly life, and brings us to our eternal destiny.

John 8: 12

Then Jesus spoke to them again, saying, "I am the light of the world. He who follows Me shall not walk in darkness, but shall have the light of life."

We no longer need to stumble in a non-purpose existence of darkness, not knowing the eternal outcome of our souls. We do not have to wait in a fearful expectation of death, and wonder what lies beyond when we encounter the failure of our physical bodies. We no longer need to be a slave of the deceitful lies of sin that impairs our spiritual vision, and prevents us from perceiving the Glory of God. We are invited, as the young rich man, to follow Jesus Christ, because in Him alone lives the light of all life, by the sacrifice on the cross.

2nd Peter 1: 19

So we have the prophetic word confirmed, which you do well to heed as a light that shines in a dark place.

The prophetic word of God, the Holy Scriptures that was given to men as a light, is in the same sense as we would use a road map to find a destination to a place that we have never been before, but once we arrive there, it will be home. For those that believe, the destination home is in the full manifestation presence of God. Without a map, a clear directive on how to travel to one location to another, we can only guess, or ask opinions on how to reach our destiny. This is where the error of man has stumbled in the darkness of his own pride, assuming that by his own merit and wisdom he can reach the destination of God. We cannot! The Inner Light that brightens the path to God was darkened the moment Adam and Eve stepped out from the garden. However, God did not give up on His beloved possession, He had a plan. God continued to speak to men, through men, to lighten our paths to our eternal destiny to the presence of God as the gospel was preached to the prophets of old, and recorded for our benefit.

Hebrews 1: 1 & 2

God, who in various times and in various ways spoke in time past to the fathers by the prophets, has now in these last days spoken to us by His Son...

All Scripture is from God and the Gospel of Jesus Christ being the completion of the road map, the finished work that clearly leads us directly to the end of the journey and into the everlasting presence of God.

The Gospel is the final Divine Light, the mystery of God's redemption for mankind revealed, given by God to lead us out of the darkness of ignorance and into the knowledge of His marvelous love.

The epistles of the apostles are also Holy Scriptures that explains in deeper detail the Gospel of God's redeeming power. The Old Testament also gives a witness to the Gospel, as it was foretold to the prophets repeatedly. For the Gospel of Jesus Christ is the completed work by God for the remission of our sins. It is the final battle that ends the war over our souls.

Hebrews 6: 19

This hope we have as an anchor of the soul, both sure and steadfast, and which enters the Presence behind the veil.

It is the light of hope in Jesus Christ that can sustain us through any shipwrecks of this life, even our departure from these earthly shells, which will happen to all of us one day. This journey is short, and the time is near for the Lord's return. The word of God is our light and without it, we are reduced to blinded opinions that are rooted from the guilt and shame of sin. We can look at the world today and see the darkness of greed that has led a generation to feast on selfishness, and in a consistent search of new pleasures, a different high that will satisfy their emptiness *(lack)*. However, for all those that have been born into the light of His mercy, have an anchor, a steady position by the power of God's word. The word of God is our lenses that pierce through the hopelessness of this generation and shines the light of hope through a darkened sphere.

Hebrews 4: 12

For the word of God is living and powerful, and sharper than any two-edged sword, piercing even to the division of soul and spirit,

and joints and marrow, and is a discerner of the thoughts and
intents of the heart.
Psalm 119: 105, 74, and 81
Your word is a lamp for my feet and a light to my path.
...I hoped in Your word.
...I hope in Your word.
I hope and pray that this book might help the light of Christ,
which is the word of God, by the power of the Holy Spirit, shine
in your hearts and encourage you that He is continually
leading us into the light of His presence. The word of God is the
only key that can unlock the door of knowledge, through the
guiding of the Spirit, by the surrender to Jesus Christ as Lord
and Savior. The surrender to Christ is the first step, since
Christ paid the price for our eternities; therefore, we are
eternally grateful. Unless we have surrendered to His love,
entrusting Him with every detail and aspect of our lives, we
can never know Him as God.
2nd Corinthians 4: 6
For it is God who commanded light to shine out of darkness, who
has shone in our hearts to give light of the knowledge of the
glory of God in the face of Jesus Christ.
God's light of mercy and grace that has shone through the
birth, life, death and resurrection of Jesus Christ for the
redemption of man brings us to eternal salvation by invitation.
Once accepted, God lives in the heart of every believer by faith,
a light unto our spirits by His promise.
Joel 2: 29 & 32
...I will pour out My Spirit in those days.
That whoever calls on the name of the Lord shall be saved.
This is the true light for our journey, which is able to take us
through even the darkest moments of this short earthly stay.
As the moth is drawn to the flame, so our hearts draw near to
His word, as His warnings and promises ignites our spirits
with the light of His wisdom and love. Once the light of His
word is in us, then we are lights among a darkened world, as
we reflect the glory of Christ, and glorify His work according to
His greatness, and not our own. Moreover, the light of God's
love will consistently guide us in the direction of home, and
shines through us as a testimony of His mercy for all to see. As

Jesus waits for us with open arms, and receives all that believe upon His name with no shadows of partiality or condemnation, He sees the light of faith that is planted in the soil of our hearts, which grows into a tree of everlasting life, deeply rooted in His promises.

Luke 11: 35 & 36, Philippians 2: 15, Matthew 5: 14-16

"Therefore take heed that the light which is in you is not darkness. If then your whole body is full of light, having no part dark, the whole body will be full of light, as when the bright shining of a lamp gives you light."

"...In the mist of a crooked and perverse generation; among whom you shine as lights in the world."

"You are the light of the world. A city that is set on a hill cannot be hidden. Nor do they light a lamp and put it under a basket, but on a lamp stand, and it gives light to all who are in the house. Let your light so shine before men, that they may see your good works and glorify your Father in heaven."

\

Salvation According to John

John 21; 24
This is the disciple who testifies of these things and wrote these
things; and we know that his testimony is true.
1st John 1: 1, 2
...Concerning the Word of life – The life was manifested, and we
have seen and bear witness, and declare to you that eternal life
which was with the Father and was manifested to us...
With all the different views, and all the different faiths on the
basic Christian belief of salvation, we need to establish the
truth in our hearts concerning God's plan of mercy for the
world. There would be no sense in building on the doubts of a
double-minded person that is uncertain of God's plan for
eternal redemption. Therefore, before we move any further,
we need to settle the issue in our hearts and minds that eternal
salvation is a gift from God that cannot be earned. To establish
this truth, we need to turn to the writings of a man who heard
the message of salvation firsthand. We also must trust that his
testimony, along with the other Scriptures, was handed down
to us by the direction of the Holy Spirit, and not by the
fumbling of man's own incompetence. The Apostle John makes
this clear by the power of God and not by his own power, that
all is written in truth, testifying as an eye and ear witness to
the great salvation for us in Jesus Christ. After all, what would
be the gain for any of the apostles to lie about the chain of
events in that they testified? It was because of their testimony
of Jesus Christ that they had to endure imprisonment,
whippings, death threats, and eventually death. Most of us
today would cave in under that kind of brutal persecution.
Now concerning this salvation, it begins with accepting Jesus
Christ as Savior and Lord in faith, which is the first act of
obedience toward God from the heart, even in a rebellious
state. Once this decision has been made, only then are we
empowered to resist and overcome the darkness of ignorance,
as the light of the Holy Spirit enters our hearts, even in the
most hidden, less obvious places in our lives. We need to
establish these truths right from the beginning, that this is

God's way of salvation as He teaches us through His word, because it is His plan for our lives, here on this earth and for our eternities. This decision will begin to change the very structure of our everyday life, because we are now able to see the light of God's word in faith.

John wasted no time in establishing the deity of Christ as he opens the Gospel, laying down this foundation of truth, so that we may believe and be established in God. What better place to start than confirming the truth of Christ Jesus and building our faith upon that Rock, knowing that once our faith is structured in this word, we cannot fall into the sand of doubt and unbelief.

John 1:1

In the beginning was the Word, and the Word was with God, and the Word was God.

Some so-called Christian religions have even misinterpreted the very first verse, leaving them in error for all the Scriptures. Staying on course, remember that this chapter is not a detailed study of the gospel by John, since that would need to be composed of many books and years of research. This also is an interesting thought as here we see the writings of an uneducated fisherman, in that the highest levels of educated scholars study because of the overpowering wisdom that is revealed in them. Could an uneducated fisherman really have written this on his own?

Moving along, we do want to capture the true meaning of our eternal salvation from the messenger who wrote it and witnessed it firsthand. The very first verse must be established in our hearts and minds so we will not doubt, but realize that all the promises recorded in this gospel are originated from God. *The Word,* Jesus Christ *was with God and is God.* Jesus is the Son of God, who the Hebrews, during His earthly ministry interpreted this as God the Son. This is why that statement brought such objection and anger among the religious leaders of that day, as they pointed their fingers at Jesus and screamed, *"You being a Man make Yourself out to be God."* The Hebrew priest understood the claims that Jesus clearly made and they hated Him for them. However, for the believer, the deity of Christ must be the true foundation of our faith if we are attempting to have any understanding in the eternal gift of salvation that God wants us to receive. *Jesus, the Christ, God with us,* is the one doing the teaching in all the Gospels, and through the power of the Holy Spirit, men recorded these teachings. We have picked John's Gospel because it teaches the most about our eternal dwelling. We need to trust that these are the words of God, written through a common fisherman with little or no academic training. This man could have had less than a sixth grade education, yet the words in this book can send scholars in deep studies for years. This is a brick of truth that needs to be set in place so we can build a house of faith within us, based on what John recorded about God's wonderful gift of salvation for you and me. The Scriptures are a supernatural, accurate record of our history from God's perspective. Moreover, since He is the Creator of all life, all planets, and all the solar systems, I think it might be a good idea to hold His view of truth in high value, because God is the only truth.

The apostle quickly brings us to the forerunner of Christ; a man named John who paved the way for the divine Life as he testifies:

John 1: 29

"Behold, the Lamb of God who takes away the sins of the world."
Let us begin to build our faith on the foundation that God, through the death and resurrection of His Son Jesus Christ, took away all our sins on the cross. Whether we choose to believe this or not, it is still true. Truth is reality! It does not change based on opinions or viewpoints. It is not by our charity, our so-called sacrifices that do not add up to a hill of beans, or our church membership that saves our souls from eternal separation from God. Rather, it was God's sacrifice! His charity to us and His love for us that caused this great manifestation of our eternal salvation made known. Jesus takes away our sin by the power of His blood and not by our powerless efforts that are stained with our own sins. This would be like trying to clean something with a dirty rag. No matter how hard you rub, scrub, and rinse; the dirt will simply not be removed, but will just be re-mixed around in different locations. The blood of Jesus is the only holy, pure, stain-

removing agent that did what not all the soiled rags could ever do, clean up the mess. I realize that we all have egos that are quick to justify our actions, or prove to others and God that we are worthy to receive a place in heaven by the power of deeds. Forget it! It is simple, God is holy, and we are not! God gives the gift of eternal salvation to all that are willing to receive it, not to those that have earned it because we could never earn it. The Holy Spirit begins to establish this early in the first chapter.

John 1: 12

But as many as received Him (Jesus), to them He gave the right to become children of God, to those who believe in His name.

God says here, *as many as received Him, to those who believed in His name.*

This word sets the mortar around the stones of faith, used to build our house of trust in God. We receive Him by faith. We believe Him by faith and not by our works, or by our so-called good deeds, and certainly not by what religious group we might belong to. Moreover, to those that truly receive Jesus Christ in faith, He gives a right. These rights can be slightly compared to the rights of becoming a citizen of a free country like ours, as we do have legal rights as a citizen. However, the true legal rights that God speaks about are the rights of a family member. This is a birthright, more than just a member of a group or a citizen of a country, but part of His family.

John 1: 12 & 13

He gave the right to become children of God...

Who were born, not by blood, nor the will of the flesh, nor of the will of man, but of God.

Here we see the rights of a family member, born into a family, inheriting a family name, which is Jesus, but not by our own will. This is one reason why God places so much importance on the earthly families, because they are examples of our spiritual family. They also are bonded together with a commitment of a covenant and births, which brings forth birthrights. Therefore, John records that there is a second birth that occurs by faith in Jesus Christ, which brings us into the family of God, as our first birth brings us into an earthly family. The second birth is not in the natural, *by blood.* It is not the will of man, *nor the will of the flesh*, meaning by our physical actions, *but of God.* It is the supernatural birth of our spirits, which automatically brings us into a position of reconciliation with God, through faith in Christ. This re-birth, or born in the family of God, is explained throughout this gospel, but is certainly highlighted in the third chapter when the Lord is explaining this to a high ranking Pharisee named Nicodemus. What is interesting about this conversation is that the Pharisee is thinking in the natural, good deeds and good works, while Jesus is teaching in the supernatural, that which is born of faith. Faith in Jesus Christ is the supernatural power of God, given by God, given to everyone that is willing to receive the truth of the gospel. This is not the same requirement as given in the Old Covenant by Moses, where works were required to be in good standing with God because no sacrifice was found worthy enough to erase the sin of man. For no one could ever completely keep the laws of that covenant, not even Moses. There was no eternal redemption in it. It did however redeem those that lived by it with temporary blessings from God in the natural world, since good works coincide with natural law. On the other hand, the New Covenant, which was given through the blood of a sinless Man and not through the blood of animals, far exceeds the old with an eternal redeeming pardon. This is the grace in that the apostle witnessed as he sees the risen Christ from the dead. Knowing, that through His death and resurrection, we also are raised in a new hope and in a New Covenant, with a new life in Christ Jesus.

As the law knowledgeable Pharisee comes to Jesus by night with what I am sure was a long list of questions concerning His authority and teachings, Jesus stops him dead in his tracks with one sentence.

John 3: 3

Jesus answered and said to him, "Most assuredly, I say to you, unless a man is born again, he cannot see the kingdom of God."
Whatever list of questions the Pharisee had for Jesus were thrown out the window when hearing the above statement. I can image the puzzled look on the Pharisee's face as his jaw dropped at what Jesus was saying. However, this is how John began recording the very first chapter as he writes, *"Who were*

born, not of flesh." He lays the groundwork down from the beginning that there is another birth, not in the natural, but in the supernatural power of God, within our spirits. We are born into the household of God, as heirs, as real family members. No longer separated by the divider of sin, no dividing veil between our hearts, we are His children and He is our Father God! What is this birth? What are the requirements for becoming a child of God? The Pharisees question was one of shock and confusion as he asked:

"How can a man be born when he is old? Can he enter a second time into his mother's womb?"

The Pharisee, a teacher of Judaism, which was a highly respected position in the Jewish culture, did not have a clue to what Jesus was talking about; he was blind to the kingdom of God. After all, Jesus said, *"Unless you are born again, you cannot see the kingdom of God."* That certainly gives a good description of the Pharisee's spiritual vision, or the lack of it. The apostles, especially John, being shown by God, explains to us how to become a child of the living God without doubt and without leaving us in an unsolved mystery as whether or not we are saved for eternity. We need to look at what John recorded when Jesus taught on the eternal salvation that was and is and will be offered to all men until He returns as the King of all kings. Another good starting place is perhaps my most favorite and well-known verse that was given to us through the apostle. Jesus, still talking to the Pharisee as he listened in wonder, gives us a jewel of a promise and even explains to us why we can have this gem.

John 3: 16

"For God so loved the world He gave His only begotten Son, that whoever believes in Him should not perish but have everlasting life."

Jesus not only gives us the answer on how to be born again, a child of God, which includes everlasting life in the kingdom of God, but also gives us the answer to why we can have it. We need to forget any religious interpretation of this verse and simply read what it says. For God so loved the world that He gave. God began the act of redeeming us by the power of His own love toward us by giving. Eternal salvation from God is not merit through a reward process, as though God is keeping score, or a list of credible deeds, versus a list of our sins that would automatically cancel out anything that we might classify as good. God gives us eternal redemption because of His love for us, and the key words here are 'He gave' and 'so loved.' We did not give to Him, He gave to us, therefore, our redemption is not earned, but simply received as only any gift can be. Again, as we read in the first chapter of John, to those who believe, whoever believes in Him (Jesus Christ) becomes a child of God that will live with God for eternity. The key that unlocks the entrance door into the forgiving heart of God is believe, which is faith in the Son! There is no other entrance, since Jesus Himself taught that He is the only way and the only door to God. Any other so-called door will lead us only into the darkness of error, and in a fog of uncertainty and doubt. Once we begin to depend on our own so-called righteousness for eternal salvation, we miss the loving gift of God's grace through the sacrifice of His Son, given by His love and not due through the wages of our conduct. Moreover, since we have all sinned, and the wages of sin is death, then we are spiritually dead from the sin we inherited, even from Adam and Eve. There is a dead spirit in all those who do not believe, which is blind, deaf and dumb concerning the love of God, which resembles a physically dead corpse in the natural.

Jesus goes on to give us the same formula for becoming a true child of God, and inheriting the promise of eternal life in the kingdom of God without doubt. However, before we move on to the continual teaching of Jesus concerning the gift of eternal life, the apostle records the testimony of John the Baptist as he begins to see the clear plan of God's redemption for all people.
John 3: 36
"He who believes in the Son has everlasting life; and he who does not believe the Son shall not see life, but the wrath of God abides on him."
Here again we see that faith or no faith in Jesus Christ is the deciding factor. John's spiritual vision was 20/20 as he sees the kingdom of God unfolding. The Pharisee that came to Jesus by night could not see it. The Jewish rulers could not see it, because their faith was not in God, but in their religious rituals

that had drifted further away from God's reasons to perform them, which pointed to Christ. None of the so-called custodians of God's people could see the kingdom of God because of their own blindness of pride, greed and selfishness.

As Jesus moved across the country, He preaches and teaches the good news of God's plan for salvation and explains how to enter the kingdom, He comes to a well in the region of Samaria. There at the well, tired from walking for miles in the hot sun, He sits and sends the disciples into the town for food. As he rested, a Samaritan woman approaches the well to draw water. Jesus asks her for a drink, she denies and the conversation moves into the eternal.

John 4:10

Jesus answered and said to her, "If you knew the gift of God and who it was who says, 'Give Me a drink,' you would have asked Him, and He would have given you living water."

Jesus does not change His message throughout the gospel as He tells the women the same formula we heard from the first chapter. Again, the first and foremost ingredient in understanding the eternal life that waits for all those that are willing to accept it, is that it is a gift of God through the redeeming blood of Christ. Jesus does not teach that eternal life is a reward, a wage, or a payback that we classify as good works. God gave His Son as a gift. Then we come to the question, how we can receive this gift of God. Jesus said, "If you knew the gift of God, you would have asked Him..."Therefore, someone must be told about the eternal salvation of our spirits in Jesus Christ, which is the responsibility of the church. Once told, the next step is to believe and then ask in faith. Jesus taught, "Ask and you will receive..." This is where God then gives, because we ask. Hear, believe and ask is the simple formula. Jesus goes on to reinforce His statement by saying:

John 4: 14

"But whoever (anyone), *drinks of the water that I shall give him will never thirst. But the water that I shall give him will become a fountain of water springing up into everlasting life."*

Jesus continues the same message as we move through the gospel. The apostle clearly understood the gift of God as he repeats the formula of eternal life throughout the book.

However, we need to take a footnote on the division between
the spirit and the flesh, the natural and the supernatural to
further build the structure of faith.
John 3: 6
*"That which is born of flesh is flesh, and that which is born of the
Spirit is spirit."*
John 4: 24
*"God is Spirit, and those that worship Him must worship Him in
spirit and truth."*
John 6: 63
"It is the Spirit that gives life, the flesh profits nothing."
It is only when we are born a spiritual birth into the family of
God, which we are then able to live in the Spirit and worship
God in spirit. For in the acceptance of the eternal sacrifice of
Jesus Christ, there is forgiveness for all our sins, eliminating
the wall of separation that prevented us in entering the Holy
presence of God because of our unholy nature. Our natural
shell of flesh is still unholy and corrupted from the inherited
sin of Adam, the death of our bodies being the evidence of that
truth. However, our spirits are made alive to God once
redeemed by the blood of Christ, therefore, it is in our spirits
that we are able to see the kingdom of God and worship the
Creator. For to *worship God in Spirit and in truth* is to obey the
truth of His word by the power of His Spirit, and not by our
own will power. We cannot obey *the truth* of His word unless
the desire comes from within our spirits, which are birth from
the Holy Spirit of God. This is why Jesus told the woman that
there would come a day when the veil of separation between a
Holy Creator and an unholy creation will be torn down. That
day was the day of the cross, when God nailed our sins to the
wood, paying the price of eternal separation from God. Jesus
Christ is the only way that anyone can worship the Father in
Spirit and truth, since He is the doorway by the sacrifice of His
own blood on the cross. This can only be achieved through the
acceptance of His sacrifice through faith. There is simply no
other way as Jesus Himself taught: *"I am the way, the truth and
the life, no one comes to the Father except through Me."*
Jesus continues in town after town, day after day, teaching the
same message, giving the same testimony of God with the

evidence of supernatural signs. No matter how the questions are asked, or whom it is that is asking the question, Jesus remains true to the same message that they heard from the beginning.

John 6: 28

Then they said to Him, "What shall we do, that we might work the works of God?"

No matter how many times Jesus explained to them the formula for eternal life with God, they returned to the works of the flesh, looking for some way that they might be able to justify themselves before God. However, Jesus again points to the true salvation, witnessed by John, which is eternal salvation through faith and not through works of the flesh.

John 6: 29

Jesus answers and said to them, "This is the work of God that you believe in Him whom He has sent."

Jesus repeats the same message, that it is not with the soiled by sin deeds of the flesh that can pardon our errors before a Holy God. It is only through faith in Christ that our sins are washed away as white as snow. Believing in Christ is the only way that we are able to be reconciled with the Creator and inherit a birthright in the family of God.

Jesus moves on to another town, but the continuing debate goes on. Every time Jesus taught in a temple, He was challenged with questions and with the same two points of arguments. The questions were always a hopeful scheme to entrap Him in His own words. This is the same method a lawyer will use when examining a witness. The lawyer will attempt to discredit his or her character, so the jury will have doubts whether their testimony is true.

The first question in opposition was the question of His authority and deity. This was a consistent battle between Jesus and the religious leaders of that day. From healing on the Sabbath to even when He was hanging on the cross, the leaders questioned His deity.

The second was the way to eternal life with God. These Pharisees were the lawyers, trying to discredit Jesus before the people, but never could. Jesus always made them look foolish, and this frustrated the Pharisees with a burning hatred toward

Him. However, Jesus never strays from the same message, but continues with the same teaching that He started from the beginning.

John 8: 25

Then they said," Who are you?" And Jesus said to them, "Just what I have been saying to you from the beginning."

As the miraculous signs of healing became daily occurrences, and the crowds are growing everyday, Jesus continues to teach about the light of God's love and the darkness of sin. He demonstrates the awesome power of God's forgiveness, and the love and compassion that God shows us in our every day lives, even in the small ways. Nevertheless, He never strays from the message of God's gift of salvation.

John 8: 24

"Therefore, I said to you that you will die in your sins; for if you do not believe that I am He, you will die in your sins."

Jesus taught that there is only two ways to leave this life, and one way is to enter eternal life with Him. The other way leads into an eternity of separation from God, which is described in many verses as a living hell. Whether the theologians want to argue what is symbolic and what is not according to the translation of the Scriptures, separation from God is not a good place to be. We can clearly see the evidence of that in this life, how some have distant themselves from God, failing deep into the slavery of their own sin, leaving themselves with sick and perverted minds.

John 8: 34

Jesus answered them, "Most assuredly, I say to you, whoever commits sin is a slave to sin."

There is no liberty in sin, only bondage to the very act that steals our peace, our love and our very lives. Sin is also blinding; it prevents us from seeing the will of God, as it separates us from His purpose for our lives. We read in the Old Testament, how sin was and still is so serious in the eyes of God, that it could only be covered, but not removed by the blood of an innocent animal. The wages of sin is death, and since blood is the life of every creature, once blood had been sacrificed, then sin was covered. Sin was not removed by the sacrifice of the innocent blood of an animal, because there was still a conscious of sin in the people.

Through Christ, the wages of our sin has been paid by whom John the Baptist identified when he saw Jesus walking and declared, *"Behold, the Lamb of God who takes away the sins of the world."* This is the message that John and the apostles preached that turned the world upside down and should do the same in our little worlds.

As Jesus continues to travel from town to town, teaching the message of salvation, He receives bad news about a friend *being sick*, which became fatal.

John 11: 14

"Lazarus is dead."

It is here in John's record of events that again we see the clear message of God's salvation as the questions are hurled toward Jesus when He arrives at the house of Lazarus. His sisters wondered why Jesus could not have saved their brother from this fatal sickness. Those that looked on asked, *"Could not this Man, who open the eyes of the blind, also have kept this man from dying?"* The body of Lazarus lies in the tomb now for four days. This certainly convinced all that he was dead. As Martha, the sister of Lazarus tells Jesus, *"Lord, if you had been here, my brother would not have died."* Jesus then tells the true gospel of God's wonderful salvation as He looks into the eyes of a grieving sibling. The rising of Lazarus from the dead was not just to flex the power of God's strength over death, but it was a neon sign, a flashing red light used to proclaim the greatest news in the history of humanity. God was glorified in the miracle as He manifested His power to restore life, even to a dead corpse that was rotting after four days in a cave, but the message of salvation was the purpose of the miraculous sign. Jesus answers Martha, and should certainly answer our doubting minds as He tells the simple and plain truth of the gospel.

John 11: 25 & 26

Jesus said to her, "I am the resurrection and the life. He who believes in Me, though he might die, he shall live. And whoever lives and believes in Me shall never die. Do you believe this?"

This is where the tire meets the road, what separates the believers from unbelievers. This is the very core of God's plan to rescue a dying humanity from the grave of sin. Every truth of God concerning the forgiving, restoring, resurrecting and redeeming mercy toward man, must all point to the above statement of Jesus! Every eye in heaven and earth need only to look to this verse and answer the question that has changed the lives of countless people in the course of history. The merciful salvation of God toward man will never and could never be based on the poor performance of humanity. Even our best intentions fall far short from the requirement of redemption.

Among every so-called religious leader, every great man that stood for truth and righteousness, Jesus Christ is the only Man that could ever make this claim. Jesus is the salvation of God revealed in a physical, bodily form, as the blood of His own body was spilled on the altar of a cross, never to be sacrificed again. The Apostle John, led by the Holy Spirit, brings the message of God's mercy to us, in that all that believe may stand firm in the word that Jesus spoke. If we leave this life with only memories of a brief experience by the grace of God, without the eternal sacrifice of Christ that cleanses us from all sin, then we have lost all, and have forsaken the only lifeboat able to save us from a raging sea of judgment. No matter what we think we have gained in the material possessions of these short moments, if we lose eternity, we have lost it all. If we have traded the gift of life eternal for the mere pennies of the temporary pleasures of sin, we will die in judgment and exist in eternal regret. Jesus, the direct representative of the Godhead, taught repeatedly that it is through Him and Him only that we may cross over from the land of bondage from sin, as Egypt was to the Hebrews, to the promise land of God's redemption. Jesus himself, being the payment for all our sins, the only dry land in which the waters of judgment have been parted for us to pass through. Any other so-called path will only drown those that walk in the ocean of transgression as the Egyptians found out. It is God that made the path through the waters that saved the Hebrews, and it is God that made the path of mercy that leads all that believe safely through the sea of death, and into the promise land of eternal life in His kingdom.

John 3:18

"He who believes in Him is not condemned; but he who does not believe is condemned already, because he has not believed in the name of the only begotten Son of God."

Through faith in Jesus Christ, we have passed through the judgment of condemnation and into the eternal freedom of pardon by grace.

Romans 8: 1

There is therefore now no condemnation to those who are in Christ Jesus.

We that believe now live in the declaration of mercy, no longer condemned by the law. Faith alone being the key that unlocks the cell of shame and releases us into the forgiveness of His love. This is the true gospel, as Jesus taught it and John recorded it. If we took the other three gospels, and all the epistles written to the church for clarification and edification, we will see the same simple message proclaimed repeatedly without change, for Jesus Christ is the same yesterday, today and forever.

1st John 5: 1 – 5

Whoever believes that Jesus is the Christ is born of God, and everyone who loves Him who begot also loves him who is begotten of Him. By this we know that we love the children of God, when we love God and keep His commandments. For whatever is born of God overcomes the world. And that is the victory that has overcome the world – our faith. Who is he who overcomes the world, but he who believes that Jesus is the Son of God.

Eternal salvation, given by God and received by faith, overcomes the world through Jesus Christ. For He is the Light of the gospel, and the Light of hope that the apostle witnessed, taught and preached with no shades of gray. Whoever believes has the Light of hope in them, which can shine on others, so that they may be saved.

Ephesians 5: 8

For you were once darkness, but now you are the light of the Lord. Walk as children of light...

The Seed of Light

Genesis *1: 11*
Then God said, "Let the earth bring forth grass, the herb that yields seed, and the fruit tree that yields fruit according to its kind, whose seed is in itself, on the earth;" and so it was.
We can clearly see from the order of nature what God sets in place from the beginning. After the initial creation of the earth, God creates plants that will duplicate themselves by the amazing power of a self-contained seed. This is a good place to point out that nature itself testifies of this order of reproduction after *its own kind.* As the evolutionist will maintain the argument that out of nothing came something, nature tells us that it all comes from a seed of life that reproduces only after *its own kind*, except for the first of any kind created by God Himself. You know the silly question, 'What came first, the chicken or the egg?' God created the chicken, and then the chicken produced the egg.
If we look at the testimony of nature, we see that living things make duplication of themselves, *according to their own kind*, by means of a seed, which they carry in them, as we do also. Can a living thing duplicate itself by another seed? Can we find tomato seeds in a potato? Can we find orange seeds in a grape? When God created birds, fish, creeping things and cattle, He commands duplication through a seed.
Genesis 1: 21 – 25
So God created great sea creatures, and every living thing that moves, with which the waters abound, according to their kind, and every winged bird according to its kind.
Then God said, "Let the earth bring forth the living creatures according to its kind..."
And God made the beast of the earth according to its kind, cattle according to its kind, and every thing that creeps on the earth according to its kind.
Living things, including plants are able to duplicate through their seed, *according to its kind* and not unto another kind, since the seed carries the blueprint for the reproduction of life. God created the living seed in every plant, animal and human

to duplicate life. This is the principle law of nature, because without the seed of life in every living thing, life would not continue. When it comes to the living human being, there is the natural seed of life that enables us to reproduce ourselves, just as the rest of nature, but there is also another seed. This seed is not natural, but supernatural; it is spirit, which is born of God. This seed is the light of God that shines through us and resides in us for eternity; it is the spark of true life.

John 1: 4

In Him was life, and the life was the light of man.

This seed of God, that gives birth to our spirits is eternal and not given to us to reproduce like the natural. God is the only one that can produce this seed. God gives a birth from His Spirit to our spirits, which is referred to by the Holy Spirit as *born again, born from above, or begotten to a living hope.* This seed is the light from our Creator, the life of His very nature that is intertwined with our spirits, resulting in a union. For without God's seed in us, we are spiritually dead, which means separated from God, unable to pass through the veil of separation that divides an unholy creation from a holy God.

John 3: 3

Jesus answered and said to him, "Most assuredly, I say to you, unless one is born again, he cannot enter the kingdom of God."

1st Peter 1: 3, 23

...According to His abundant mercy has begotten us again to a living hope.

...Having been born again, not of corruptible seed, but incorruptible...

1st John 5: 1

Whoever believes that Jesus is the Christ is born of God...

1st John 5: 4

For whatever is born of God overcomes the world...

There should be no doubt that a re-birth experience can and does take place in the spirit, whether it does or not for you will hang in the balance of faith, or a lack of it. The Scriptures tell us that we must be born anew to even see the kingdom of God, no less enter into it, and that it is according to God's mercy that a re-birth can take place. Once born from above, one has the incorruptible seed of the living God for eternity. Remember that a seed can only reproduce *according to its kind*. Therefore, we are transformed into the likeness of Jesus, as Adam was before he sinned, as God spoke; *"Let Us make man in Our image* (kind), *according to our likeness."* Adam was not God, but like God, different from any other spiritual being, created directly from the seed of God with an outer shell of flesh. There is no other place in Scripture where God states that He will create another living being in His likeness. Before Adam's sin, he was a complete spirit man with no inner or outer conflict, and in total harmony with God and himself, as God intended. Now since the fall of humanity came by one man, so the rise of humanity also came by one Man, this is the re-birth of our spirits, by the living seed of God. This re-birth can take place through only one avenue, and that is by the narrow path of faith in Jesus Christ. Why through only one way, which is faith in Christ? Every man from Adam to the present age has sinned against God, except for One. How could anyone pay the debt of another when he himself is in debt? However, if someone could come into the world, that had no debt of sin, He could pay the debt for all. Jesus has no sin; therefore, He alone was able to place Himself as a sacrifice for the sins of others, canceling the debt of sin against us, bringing us back to the original state of Adam, well almost. Remember that in the beginning, Adam did not have a conflict within himself because his mind and spirit were in harmony, which I believe was a perfect, glorified body of flesh. However, our fleshly mind now knows sin from the seed of Adam; therefore, they decay from the seed of death, for *the wages of sin is death,* also resulting in a consistent battle of the fleshly mind against the spirit. Though our spirits are birth by the seed of God, our mind is not, bearing the seed of Adam, resulting in an inner conflict of good and evil. For we are born of the seed of Adam, according to the flesh, this is in the natural with sin. Therefore, the believer in made of two natures, which are in conflict with one another. Moreover, the believer that is not dominated by his or her spirit, which is born of God, is in more of an inner conflict then an unbeliever, and will certainly have no inner peace of spirit or mind. For an unbeliever yields to the flesh, satisfying the flesh's desires without question. The conscience of sin becomes a mute sound, dominated by the voice of a selfish will.

It is interesting to note how Adam had all that we could ever ask for or imagine. He was placed in the paradise of the Garden of Eden. Looking at some of our conservation parks today, we can only dream of the purity of Eden, full of the rich resources of healthy air, food and water. The sheer beauty of the virgin landscape must have been stunning. We can only imagine what the night skies must have looked like as Adam fell into his evening rest. The animals were under his domain, which means that they obeyed his words. If he told them to come, they came, to go, they went. Not only was Adam free from shame, since there was no sin, there was no guilt, so his mind was truly free of any past errors that could haunt him in the late hours of the night. Adam had perfect sleep, a perfect diet, and was at peace, but in charge of his surrounding, and besides all that, he had a perfect mate. God hand tailored Eve just for Adam, so we can rest assured that she was perfect for him. To sum it up, Adam lived in a perfect world, and most of all, he had a close intimate relationship with God. There was no fear of condemnation or judgment in him. He had no shame, no guilt, no lies or deceit in his mind; no blindness from the selfishness of sin, he was free, as free as anyone could possibly be. With all of this, I am amazed that after being warned by God not to eat the forbidden fruit, they were willing to sacrifice that perfect life that they shared with the Creator. Now if the devil can deceive two sinless people, with a perfect life and with a deep relationship with the Almighty God, I must conclude that deceiving us is like taking candy from a baby. Look at the sharp contrast of the lives that we live compared to the first blessed couple. Our paradise has turned into polluted cities, full of unnatural toxins that are destroying the air and water supply. Hate, murder and theft in all levels of society are just common news and every day occurrences. This is where the mercy of God stepped in. God understands our frail, contaminated nature. Sin is embedded in us like a colored stain on a white cloth. Our fleshly nature is drawn to sin because of all the generations from Adam to the present that have been slaves to its call. However, once born from above by

the living Spirit of God, we are *new creatures in Christ.*
Although the old sinful nature continues to wage war against
our new spirits, the living God will live within us, if we allow
Him first place in our lives, and He has overcome sin, the
world, and even death.

Colossians 9: 10

*...Since you have put off the old man with his deeds, and have put
on the new man who is renewed in the knowledge according to
the image of Him who created him.*

Once we have accepted God's gift of grace in our hearts with an
open confession, receiving the sacrifice of Jesus Christ on the
cross that paid for our every error, we then are reborn with a
new inner man from the seed of God, *according to His image,*
like the seed that reproduces *according to its own kind.* Our
spirits are re-birthing and renewed daily through the
knowledge of His word; therefore, we begin to live according
to God's *likeness and image.* This was God's plan from the
beginning, as when He made Adam and Eve, they were created
in His *likeness and image.* In other words, we are able to take
on the attributes of God according to the seed of His Spirit that
He has placed inside of us. However, remember that there is
one technicality this time around. Unlike Adam and Eve before
they disobeyed God, we still have an old man nature that
causes a battle with our spirits. Our carnal minds are still
programmed to sin, or should we say that sin is in our hard
drives, still present in our thought patterns. This is not to say
that we all commit the most obvious sins like murder, adultery
and stealing. However, deception, gossip, self-centered greed
and a gross error of judging one another still reigns in our
nature. This is where the conflict of the new man and the old
begin to clash. Those that have not received the sacrifice of
Christ for the atonement of their sins are also in an inner
spiritual conflict. It is not the same conflict as with the spirit
filled man or woman, but with God Himself, since sin still
reigns in their lives, so rebellion against God still reigns,
making themselves enemies to the only Savior that can save
us.

Colossians 1: 21

And you, who once were alienated and enemies in your mind, by wicked works, yet now He (Jesus), *has reconciled in the body of His flesh through death.*

We can clearly see that the prior state of our nature, before we are reconciled through the death of Jesus Christ, is alienation from God, actual enemies of God. This is a rebellious state against God, which is the true definition of sin. Moreover, in this rebellious darkness, though there is no inner conflict between the old man and the new; there is also no inner peace, because there is a spiritual conflict against God, who is the Author of peace and all life. Nevertheless, all those who set their faith in the Lord Jesus Christ as their Savoir and Lord, no longer are in conflict with God. God can and will impute His peace into every believer, if we grow in the new man, in the knowledge of our Savior through His word, then the new man, the re-born spiritual child of God will dominate the old sinful nature and lead us closer into an understanding of His love.

Colossians 3: 9 & 10

Do not lie to one another, since you have put off the old man with his deeds, and have put on the new man who is renewed in knowledge according to the image of Him who created him.

Though our sin nature in the flesh is not destroyed, since we still live in these earthly shells, we have an inner peace in our spirits, in the inner man where sin rules no more and where we bear the image of Christ. Jesus tells us that we now have His peace within us.

John 14: 27

"Peace I give to you, My peace I give to you; not as the world gives do I give to you."

Romans 5: 1

Therefore, having been justified by faith, we have peace with God through our Lord Jesus Christ.

Ephesians 2: 14 & 17

For He (Jesus) *is our peace...*

And He (Jesus) *came and preached peace* (peace with God), *to you who were far off and to those who were near...*

Where there is forgiveness, there is peace and in the forgiveness of God, there is the complete pardon for our every trespass that brings forth a birth of hope from the rich mercy of God's love toward us. Where there is no forgiveness, there is a hole of emptiness, where the seed of God's love is missing. In that place, there is nothing but a dark cold space of blackness where God's light has chosen to be shut out and begins to be filled with resentment and bitterness. Even if we might see certain people we know put on a mask of fulfillment and inner peace apart from Christ, God reminds us that those without Him have no peace and a false sense of righteousness and security.

Psalm 14: 1 & 17
There is none righteous, no, not one.
And the way of peace they have not known.
Romans 3: 23
For all have sinned and fall short of the glory of God.
Isaiah 5: 6
And all our righteousness is like filthy rags.

God plainly tells us that by our nature, the nature we inherited from Adam and generation after generation of sin, we do not seek God on our own. We all seek a life of self-gratification, blinded by our own desires, as some religious leaders did in the days of old, even in the days of the earthly ministry of Christ and as some still do today.

Jeremiah 23: 16
They speak a vision of their own hearts, not from the mouth of the Lord.

Whatever costume of goodness one might put on, like a formal tuxedo or an evening dress, falls far short of the redeeming power that is needed to erase our errors so God's peace can live in our hearts. We either were in this state at one time, or are still in the darkness of our self-centered flesh. No matter how we perceive the one in the mirror, or others, we have all fallen from the righteousness of God. Moreover, in that fallen nature, there is a void of God's light of love, which is the only true fulfillment of life that can give us true peace. For in the light of the knowledge of God's love, there is an assurance that by His grace and the abundant richness of His mercy, we have been redeemed by His sacrifice on the cross, with no fear of judgment. Therefore, our so-called self-righteousness is seen for what they are, *filthy rags* and we then realize that it is God's light of grace that saves the lost soul from the judgment of sin. The final result, peace! It is the peace of God. This peace is the relationship between the Creator and His creation that Adam and Eve had so carelessly lost for a bite of the forbidden fruit. However, from that point in time, we see a promise of the Seed of God, through the woman, that will bridge the relationship that collapsed.

Genesis 3: 15
"And I will put enmity between you and the woman, and between your seed and her Seed; He shall bruise your head, and you shall bruise His heel."

God speaks to the serpent, the devil and makes a promise that from the Seed of the woman will come, as the Apostle John testifies; *"That was the true Light, which gives light to every man coming into the world."* Moreover, the Apostle Paul also taught; *"Now to Abraham and his Seed were the promises made. He does not say, "And to seeds," as of many, but as of one, "And as to your Seed," who is Christ.*

Jesus Christ is the Seed of Light, who has bruised the head of Satan by the ultimate sacrificial offering on the cross. The Seed of the promise, who destroyed the wall of separation between the Creator and His creation, built with the bricks of sin and the mortar of guilt and shame.

Matthew 12: 46
"I (Jesus) *have come as a light into the world, that whoever believes in Me should not abide in darkness."*

For before the Seed came in the flesh, there was no sacrifice holy enough that could break the chains of imprisonment in the cell of transgression, the prison of sin and the darkness of rebellion against God.

Galatians 4: 4 & 5
But when the fullness of the time had come, God sent forth His Son, born of a woman, born under the law, to redeem those who were under the law, that we might receive the adoption as sons.

Here we see the fulfillment of the promise from the beginning in the garden, to the letters of Paul, God's redemption and salvation plan for all our errors from Adam to the present time. The Seed of Light that was planted in the earth, and on the third day arose from the grave, is now planted in the hearts of all believers.

John 12: 24

"Most assuredly, I say to you, unless a grain of wheat falls into the ground and dies, it remains alone; but if it dies, it produces much grain."

The grain produces *according to its kind*; as we read in Genesis, all of creation re-produces *according to its own kind.* Adam was created from the seed of God as a living soul, being made in God's *image and likeness.* Although we still have the seed in our bodies to re-produce according to our own kind, the Seed of God's light was lost due to the darkness of sin, which brought forth death. However, since our original construction was created from an image of God, God was able to incarnate in the form of a Man, satisfy the charge of the judgment of sin that was against us, and restore the light of His life back into the human race. This is the re-birth of hope in all who are called back in a relationship of eternal life with God. In the Spirit, we are born of God's Seed, Jesus Christ. He is the Seed of the true Light.

2nd Corinthians 4:6

For it is God who commanded light to shine out of darkness, who has shone in our hearts to give the light of knowledge of the glory of God in the face of Jesus Christ.

John 1:7 – 9

The man (John the Baptist) *came for a witness, to bear witness of the Light that all through Him might believe. He was not that Light, but was sent to bear witness of that Light. That was the true Light, which gives light to every man coming into the world.*

John 8:12

Then Jesus spoke to them again, saying, "I am the light of the world. He who follows Me shall not walk in darkness, but have the light of life."

1st John 1: 5

This is the message which we have heard from Him (Jesus) *and declare to you, that God is light and in Him there is no darkness.* John the Baptist said that he was a witness of the Light, the true Light that came into the world to give life eternal to all that are able to receive it. Jesus testifies; *"I am the Light,"* and anyone that follows Him will live in the light of God's redemption of mercy and eternal love. The Apostle John also bears witness that *God is light*, and the light that came forth from God into the world is Jesus Christ. Again, we see the Holy Spirit testify of the deity of Christ, as *the light of the world*; *God is light.* No other place in Scripture or in any other belief is a man called light. Many false teachers and so-called prophets might have claimed to see the light of God, but no man could ever claim to be the Light, since that would be a claim of deity. Jesus made this claim, therefore, Jesus is either telling the truth, since He also testified that He is the truth, or He was in a gross error concerning His own identity. Of course, this would make no logical sense, since Jesus openly testified to be the Christ, the Savior of the world. Jesus was not confused about His own identity. Therefore, if any other so-called religion testifies that Jesus Christ was just a prophet, or an angel, or just a messenger from God, they do not understand the claims that Jesus made concerning His rightful place in the Godhead. *God is light,* and *Jesus is the light* that came from God into the world as a blood sacrifice for the remission of sins, Jesus is the *light of life, the light that came into the world* of darkness! Who could make that claim besides God alone?

1st John 8: 12
God is light and in Him is no darkness at all...
Psalm 27: 1
The Lord is my light and my salvation.
Everyone that believes upon the Lord Jesus Christ has the light of eternal life residing in their hearts, being born from the Seed of Light, since a seed can reproduce only *according to its own kind.* This birth brings the light of hope to all those that eagerly seek Him in faith. The Apostle John testifies that *God is light*, as David sings: *"The Lord is my light."* John the Baptist testifies that Jesus is the *light that has come into the world.* The testimony of these men, who did not know one another, all proclaim the same message that God is the light of life in the creation and redemption of man, and that Light entered the human race through the birth of Jesus Christ.

2nd Corinthians 4: 3 & 4
But even if our gospel is veiled, it is veiled to those who are
perishing, whose minds the god of this age has blinded, who do
not believe, lest the light of the glory of Christ, who is the image
of God, should shine upon them.
The Apostle Paul, who was an educated Pharisee in the Law of
Moses, testifies that without the light of Christ in our hearts,
we are blinded by the god of this age and in total darkness
concerning the gospel of God's love. Those that abide in this
darkness are perishing into an eternal separation from God.
This life is void of God's light of love, which is Christ Jesus.
For in the presence of the Light, there is vision, there is clarity
of understanding and knowledge in the spirit, because it is by
the Spirit of God that He is revealed. When we are in the
manifestation of God's presence, which is through the avenue
of His word, our paths are lighted by His glory. This is not to
say that our short-term, temporary futures here in this life are
revealed, but our eternal futures with God, forever beholding
His glory are guaranteed through faith, and seen afar off. The
Holy Spirit through the heart of an apostle tells us to put on
God's light, like a floodlight that causes the darkness of fear to
disappear. For where light is, darkness cannot be. God is not a
God of fear, confusion or uncertainty, but wants us to be
secure in His love. It is in the darkness that all sexual
immorality, extortion, slanders, gossips, murder, and even
murder with the tongue, is passed through the ones that live in
the ignorance of pride. However, in the light of God there are
the works of the Spirit, manifestations of His love, which live
through the lives of those that have been born of God. True
love gives birth to the fruits of giving, sacrifice and even long
suffering. Where there is love, there is a positive hope in every
breath, because hope brings confidence, which is faith in what
God has already promised for our good, by His word.
Therefore, where God is, in His presence of holiness, there can
be no darkness of evil, but only the light of His being which is
the very essence of His divine love. God does not merely shine
His light upon us, but He is the Light that shines in us and lives
through us by His grace. Therefore, we are not as the moon
that only reflects the light of the sun, but the Light Himself

lives in us, through us as the Holy Spirit is bonded to our spirits in a union of His love.

Ephesians 5: 14

"Awake, you who sleep, arise from the dead, and Christ will give you light."

Isaiah 50: 10, 51: 4 & 5

"Who walks in darkness and has no light? Let him trust in the name of the Lord."

"I will make My justice real as a light to the people. My righteousness is near, My salvation has gone forth."

Romans 13: 12 & 14

The night is far spent; the day is at hand. Therefore let us cast off the works of darkness, and put on the armor of light.

But put on the Lord Jesus Christ...

The Promise of Life and Death

Hebrews 9:27
Just as man is destined to die once, and after that to face
judgment...
Revelation 20:14
The lake of fire is the second death. If anyone's name was not
found written in the Book of Life, he was thrown into the lake of
fire.

Revelation 20:12
Another Book was opened, which is the Book of Life.
God also tells us about a book. Although He tells us about other
books, the Book of Life is the one that we should fully
understand, because the Book of Life is recording the names of
people who will inherit eternal life with God. All those who
truly believe, who have confessed with their mouth and
believed in their hearts will have their names written in the
book.
Daniel 12: 1
"And at that time your people shall be delivered, everyone who is
found written in the book..."
 Now this second death is not the same as the first death,
although they do have one thing in common, separation. The
first death will separate our spirits from our bodies. The
second death will separate those who do not believe in God,
from God. All those that have their names written in the Book
of Life will be in paradise, in the presence of The Lord for
eternity. Eternity is forever!
Daniel 12: 2
"Some to everlasting life, some to shame and everlasting
contempt."
Everlasting is an endless amount of time, timeless! It is hard
for us to comprehend this truth, since we are so pre-occupied
with the rather short stay here of seventy or eighty years. It is
like trying to understand that space has no end. This short
circuits our brains, how the emptiness of space could endlessly
go on and on. This is a good reminder of how limited our
understanding really is, compared to the magnitude of God's

wisdom and knowledge. After all, if we cannot even understand the things that He has created, how can we think that we can fully understand the Creator? However, God's eternal, unconditional love can be known through what He has done and what He has promised in Christ.

Luke 23: 43

And Jesus said to him (the thief that was crucified next to Him), *"Assuredly, I say to you today you will be with Me in paradise."* Those who believe will live forever with God, free from death. However, to those who have rejected the Son of God, will be cast into a lake of fire, a lake of burning sulfur and this is called the second death, tormented without rest. Of course, you can read the words yourself in the Scriptures. How can this be for real? Just look up in the sky and see how the fire of the sun just keeps burning and burning. Heat so intense that if the earth's orbit would move just a little bit closer, we would burn like a sheet of paper set on fire. If God created the fire of the sun, the intense explosion of gases that are bound in a planet form, I am sure God has no problem creating a lake of fire. Some theologians could very well argue that this lake of fire is only symbolic of being out of the presence God; either way, we can know that it is not a good place to spend eternity. For the Scriptures clearly shows us that in the separation from God, there is torment. We can even see this in this current life, tormented souls that hurt and kill others and even themselves. Even so-called successful people are without peace and tormented apart from the security of God's love. Although someone might gain all the material riches that they thought would satisfy their souls, they are still empty shells with just more possessions. Moreover, all those that do not believe will depart from this life without the redemption in Jesus Christ, with no material possessions, no luxury of pleasures, but with a tormented emptiness that will never end.

Revelation 21: 8

"But the cowardly, unbelieving, abominable, murderers, sexually immoral, sorcerers, idolaters, and all liars shall have their part in the lake which burns with fire and brimstone, which is the second death."

The book of Revelation explains the reality of God's eternal judgment, and His grace. God also spoke to the prophet of old concerning *a book of remembrance.*

Malachi 3:16 & 17

A scroll (a book), *of remembrance was written in His presence concerning those who feared the Lord and honored His name. "They will be mine," says the Lord Almighty, "in the day when I make up my treasured possession."*

Here, in the above Scripture we find an awesome promise from God. God gives us His word that He will remember those who honored Him. God tells us that once our names are recorded in His Book, we are His possession, redeemed and washed clean by the blood of Jesus Christ, who was given as a sacrifice for the sins of all humanity.

Philippians 4: 3

...And the rest of my fellow workers, whose names are written in the Book of Life.

Therefore, we know that while there is judgment for all those that refuse the redemption for sins in the sacrifice of Jesus Christ, there is also grace for all those who have accepted the *free gift* of God's love. The key words that are stressed in the Scriptures are the words *free gift.*

Romans 5: 15, 16, 18 & 6: 23

...The free gift...

...The free gift...

...The free gift...

For the wages of sin is death, but the gift of God is eternal life in Jesus Christ our Lord.

Although the gift of eternal life with God is given freely to all those that are willing to accept it, there was a price that was paid for it. We did not, nor could not pay the price for the redemption of our own sins. However, Jesus could and did, since He fulfilled the judgment of the law, taking upon Himself the full penalty of our sins, *for the wages of sin is death.* Jesus fulfilled the wages of sin on the cross, since He Himself had no sin.

John 11:25
Jesus said to her, "I am the resurrection and the life: he that
believes in me, though he were dead, (first death of our physical
bodies), *yet shall he live* (never to experience the second
death).
The first death is guaranteed for every one of us that live on
this planet until the Lord returns. We have no idea when our
last breath in these bodies will be. I know we hope that we will
be here long enough to raise our children, maybe even see our
grandchildren, and maybe even see retirement from a lifetime
of working. The truth remains that we do not know when God
will call us out of the world.
There is another guarantee that God gives according to the
promise of life.
2nd Corinthians 1: 22
...Who has sealed us and given us a guarantee.
Ephesians 1: 13 & 14
...Having believed, you were sealed with the Holy Spirit of
promise, who is the guarantee of our inheritance, until the
redemption of purchased possession, to the praise of His glory.
The guarantee is the Holy Spirit, who has sealed us in the hope,
and given as a down payment for us to know without doubting
that our redemption is written in stone. Where there is no
hope, no faith, there remains the fear of the unknown. It is the
spirit of faith; the light of hope given by the Holy Spirit that
brings us through the fears of this life and into the assurance
of God.
The man named Job went through the trials of losing
everything that a person could lose, as his friends consistently
questioned his faith, insisting that the misfortune he
experienced was a result of his sin. However wrong they were
about Job, God did give these men some insight in His love. For
where there is true repentance there is a light of hope. It is the
light of faith that shines through the darkness of our trials and
fears, and surrounds us with the security of God's love.
Job 11:17 & 18,
Though you were dark, you would be like the mourning. And you
would be secure because there is hope.

God wants us to know with certainty that we live in the
security of knowing that the promise of life eternal is a reality
of faith, which is the helmet of salvation, a guarantee that
should not be questionable. It is not through a blind faith that
we can live in the certainty of God's promise, but it is through
the eyes of our understanding that we see Jesus our Savior and
know that we will be with Him forever. Jesus told His disciples
that though they will no longer see Him physically, they would
see Him through the eyes of their inner beings.

John 16: 16

*"A little while longer and the world will see Me no more, but you
will see Me, because I live, you will live also."*

It is by the power of God's abundant love that releases the
scales of ignorance from our understanding, so we are able to
see those things concerning the kingdom of God. God alone
gives the light of knowledge in the heart of those that seek Him
by faith, through His word.

John 3: 3

*"Most assuredly, I say to you, unless one is born again,
(conceived by the seed of faith in Christ), he cannot see the
kingdom of God."*

We did not earn eternal life in paradise with God; it is not by
our own power or strength that achieved this goal. God's gift of
life, in the eternal, as well as in the temporal, is given out of the
matchless abundance of His mercy and love. No one is an
accident of the birth in the natural, as well as in the spiritual.
God alone gives life, although we have the natural seed within
us to reproduce after our own kind, it is God that gives the
spirit, and our physical body without the spirit is dead.

Hebrews 12: 9

*Shall we not much more readily be in subjection to the Father of
spirits and live?*

When Jesus was resurrected from the dead, He showed
Himself in the flesh and not as a ghostly spirit. It is here again
that we see that we are made of a two-part nature.

Luke 24: 39

*"Behold My hands and My feet. Handle Me and see, for a spirit
does not have flesh and bones as you see I have."*

We see that there is a definite distinction between the physical body and our spirits. As the power of electricity gives working force to those things that are manufactured, designed to draw electrical current to perform, so our physical bodies are dependent on our spirits to maintain life. The Spirit of God creates life to our spirits, and our spirits give life to these empty physical bodies.

Genesis 2: 7
And God formed man of the dust of the ground, and breathed into his nostrils the breath (Spirit), *of life; and the man became a living being.*

John 6: 63
"It is the Spirit who gives life; the flesh profits nothing."

Job 12: 9 & 10
Who among all these does not know that the hand of the Lord has done this, in whose hand is the life of every living thing, and the breath of all mankind?

Therefore, this is the hope, the hope of certainty, the hope in God's word, which is not a hope of just wishful thinking. God is as sure as the beat in our hearts and the breath in our lungs. We can rest in the security of God's promises that although the outer man decays, the inner man is renewed, and will grow in the knowledge of God everyday, if we are willing to listen to His word and remain steadfast in His love.

2nd Corinthians 4: 16
Therefore, we do not lose heart (our hope). *Even though our outward man is perishing, yet the inward man is being renewed day by day.*

We can see that throughout the Scriptures the Holy Spirit reveals the reality to us that we are made up of an outer man of flesh, bone, blood and tissue; and an inner man made of spirit. We also see that the two, though they both live together, are very different. One is seen, the other unseen. One is temporal, the other eternal. One is life, and the other destined to die. One came from the dust of the earth, the other from God. One can see in the spiritual, the other is blind to it and both wage war against the other. Therefore, let us establish the fact that we are two in one.

2nd Corinthians 2: 6 & 7
For it is God who commanded light to shine out of darkness, who
has shone in our hearts (our spirits), *to give the light of*
knowledge of the glory of God in the face of Jesus Christ. But we
have this treasure in earthen vessels...
God's light of knowledge, revealing the greatness of His love
toward us, illuminates the soul of all those that come to Him. It
is the very light of God's love that comes into our spirits and
ignites the flame of faith causing the darkness of sin to flee like
an injured enemy. For this very purpose Jesus came, *to set the*
captives free from darkness, so we might live in the light of His
will. Moreover, all that believe on His name, though in the
flesh, can live according to God in the spirit. This is the
promise and power of His love toward us!
   Revelation 22: 1
And he showed me a pure river of water of life, clear as crystal,
proceeding from the throne of the God and of the Lamb...

As we see there is a lake of fire, a place of darkness, and a place
void from the love of God, we also see a pure river of life that
flows from the throne of God. Yes, we have a choice between a
lake of fire and a river of life. Moreover, the only entranceway
to the river of life from the lake of fire is by the cross of Jesus
Christ. There is no other bridge that can be crossed, but that of
the cross. Our bodies are dying every day. We know deep
inside that one day will be our last moment in these shells, we
just do not know when. Though we might gather many earthly
possessions and riches, and have many pleasures while we
remain in this flesh, the day will come when we leave here and
we will leave with only our spirits and the promise of life, or
without the promise. The theologians can argue until they are
blue in the face about times and seasons, about the first and
second resurrection. However, this we know without a doubt,
our bodies will die, and our spirits will move on to the lake of
fire, or to the river of life. Whatever one we will be in, we will
be awake and aware of our surroundings.
The well-known man named Job, who was a man of great gift
of life. faith and understanding, knew where his earthly shell
came from and who it was that preserved his inner man, his

spirit. Job knew that he was made of a two-part composition. He was a spirit, dressed in a uniform of flesh, as we are. Therefore, when the present uniform is removed, the spirit remains alive, because it is the spirit that lives forever.

Job: 8: 11 & 12

Your Hands have made me and fashioned me, an intricate unity...

Clothe me with skin and flesh, and knit me together with bone and sinews? You have granted me life and favor, and your care has preserved my spirit.

The promise of life is in the dwelling of the spirit, given by the Spirit of God. Life is not in the abundance of our possessions, as our possessions are composed of dead matter, or in the level of our intellect, because our intellects are limited to the things that are seen. We will simply not find the promise of life in anything else, but by His word. God reveals the promise of eternal life through His word, sown in our spirits, by the power of the life, death and resurrection of Jesus Christ, since He is the Author of all life. We cannot work for it, purchase it, create it or obtain it through empty, lifeless means. Life can only come from life, as a seed that comes from the prior cycle of regeneration. A living seed cannot come from a dead stone. God has laid the path to Himself, paved it with the blood of His Son and sealed it with the power of His Spirit. God did the work through the sacrifice of Jesus Christ, leaving us with the simple choice of accepting or rejecting His gift.

Romans 6: 23

For the wages of sin is death, but the free gift of God is eternal life in Christ Jesus our Lord.

There should be no doubt that our spirits will leave these earthly bodies. There will come a day when every one of us will experience this act of death, when the physical body stops functioning and begins to decay. The Scriptures tell us repeatedly that as our earthly bodies remain on the earth, whether in decay or ashes, our spirits move on.

Ecclesiastics 12: 7

Then the dust (our bodies) will return to the earth, and the spirit will return to God who gave it.

It cannot be any clearer, as revealed to us in the above Scripture; however, God goes on to give us many more examples of life and death. Let us put aside the fact that the early followers of Christ were willing to die for what they believed, because many people have been willing to die for their beliefs. Others have sacrificed their lives to the emptiness of greed, power, and revenge, even to false gods. The early followers of Christ were willing to give up their earthly lives rather than to deny Jesus Christ. However, this act alone does not prove that they were any different then anyone else that was willing to die for their cause. The difference between those who are willing to die for a cause and those that are willing to die for the sake of Christ is simple. Those that are willing to die for Christ are also willing to live for Him. The true followers of Jesus Christ are continually presenting themselves as living sacrifices, vessels of life that can be used for the glory of God in this life. The Christian has the witness within their hearts, which is the Holy Spirit, who testifies to their spirits that the promise of God is true.

The separation of the spirit from the body, which is the death of the physical body, is not the death of the spirit!

Jesus gives us a great insight into eternal life after these bodies die. Jesus tells us about two men, a rich man with no name mentioned who lived a life of luxury, and a beggar named Lazarus. Every story and parable that Jesus presented was truth, since He is the Truth, in which I believe were all based on true stories. There are many times in the Scriptures when someone's name is not recorded, as in the case of Lot's wife. It could very well be that some of these people's names are also not recorded in the Book of Life, which is one of the requirements to live with God for eternity. The story that Jesus tells us reveals the separation of body and spirit in detail, giving us great insight to our eternal destinies.

Luke 16: 19 & 20

"There was a certain rich man who was clothed in purple and fine linen and lived in luxury. But there was a certain beggar named Lazarus, full of sores, who was laid at his gate, desiring to be feed with the crumbs which fell from the rich man's table.

The two main characters are men that lived different lives. One man that needed the mercy of the other and one man that refused to give it. Years go by, although it is not mentioned when both men died, we can assume that the beggar Lazarus died first being sick from a lack of nutrition, and his body full of open sores, which the dogs would lick. Even the dogs had more mercy on Lazarus than his own fellow man. Lazarus is also listed first to die, the death of his physical body, but his spirit was carried to the place were the spirit of Abraham rest. Again, we see a clear division, a separation between our temporary physical bodies and our eternal spirits. Remember the person that is telling this story! Jesus Christ is the Truth. Therefore, every word that came out of His mouth was truth. The story is not only some symbolic message about the greed and selfishness of the rich, it is the truth of the eternal destiny of two men.

Luke 16: 22

"So it was that the beggar died, and was carried by the angels to Abraham's bosom. The rich man also died and was buried."
Jesus taught that many would sit at the table with Abraham in the kingdom of God, while some will be left out with weeping and the gnashing of teeth, meaning in the torment of regret. We see that the next few verses will expose the judgment of God, where the rich man will spend an endless eternity in punishment. The judgment is not a non-existent state, where the spirit has no idea what is going on. The rich man saw for a brief moment the rest of Lazarus and felt all that was happening around him.

"Then He (The rich man), *cried out and said, "Father Abraham, have mercy on me, and send Lazarus that he may dip the tip of his finger in water and cool my tongue; for I am tormented in this flame."*
Our spirits, even when separated from these outer shells, are very much alive, able to see at times, able to hear, speak and feel. The Scriptures do speak of the outer darkness of judgment and the blackness of darkness that is reserved for punishment. Therefore, vision must be limited in judgment, because separation from God is a state of spiritual darkness. The torment of God's judgment is real, and the pain is not only

the pain of regret, but also the pain from a burning flame that has no end. As Lazarus rested in the peace of God with Abraham, the rich man with no name was sentenced to a place of torment.

Luke 16: 24, 25, 28

For I am tormented in this flame.

But now he is comforted and you are tormented.

...Lest they come to this place of torment.

It is the rich man's spirit; the inner part that lives forever, that is tormented right now. In the rich man's case, he is doomed in a real place that God had reserved for rebellious angels named Hades or Hell. Jesus tells us that there is such a real place of darkness, regret, and torment.

Matthew 24: 41 & 46

"Then He (God) will also say to those on His left hand, 'Depart from Me you cursed, into the everlasting fire prepared for the devil and his angels.'

"And these will go away into everlasting punishment, but the righteous into eternal life."

The spirits of both Lazarus and the rich man lived on, but in two different places. Jesus tells us that both places are real, and there is as well, a great gulf fixed between them. If the two places were not real, then there could be no separation between them. Nothing cannot be separated from nothing. This defies even the laws of physics, as any scientist will also tell us.

Luke 16: 26

"And besides all this, between us (Abraham and Lazarus), and you (the rich man), there is a great gulf fixed, so that those who want to pass from here to you cannot, nor can those from there pass to us."

There is nothing symbolic about this verse, for it is simply stating with clarity that between two places there is a great separation. The two places are real, Abraham and Lazarus are real in the spirit, and so is the rich man as his spirit is in torment this very day. Jesus taught repeatedly about life after this short stay in these fleshly bodies, and spoke clearly concerning the eternal life of our spirits, since life comes from

the Spirit of God into our spirits. Jesus also taught about a
resurrection, when God will restore our mortal bodies with
immortality to all that believe, and will return back to the
earth, were Christ will reign. For where ever Jesus is, there is
our home, as we will behold His glory in the presence of God.
The Apostle Paul, who was not only willing to die for the sake
of the Gospel, but was also willing to partake in the sufferings
of Christ as he was beaten, whipped, stoned and imprisoned,
received great insight concerning life beyond these bodies.
2nd Corinthians 5: 6 - 8
*So we are always confident knowing that while we (our spirits),
are at home in the body, we are absent from the Lord. For we
walk by faith, not by sight. We are confident, yes, well pleased
rather to be absent from the body and to be present with the
Lord.*
The apostle explains, that all those who believe on the Lord
Jesus Christ should be rested, well pleased in this confident
hope, that when we, our spirits are separated from our bodies,
we will live in the presence of our Savior, Jesus Christ. Paul and
John both stressed the importance of this confidence, so we
are not carried away in the pursuit of the temporary pleasures
of this life, losing sight of our eternal treasure, which is eternal
life with Christ Jesus.
1st John 2: 25 & 5:11
*And this is the promise that He has promised us – eternal life.
And this is the testimony: that God has given us eternal life, and
this life is in His Son.*
God places the treasure of this confident hope in the promise
of eternal life, by the testimony of the Holy Spirit, in all of those
who are His. It is the treasure of God; by the witness of the
Holy Spirit that testifies to our spirits, which is the deposit of
our eternal treasure of living with Christ forever. Christ is our
treasure, manifested through the Holy Spirit, which is the very
promise Jesus gave to His followers, which includes all those
who believe today. The Apostle Paul understood this deposit,
which is a guarantee of the promise.

2nd Corinthians 4: 7
But we have this treasure in earthen vessels that the excellence of the power may be of God and not of us.
This is why true believers are in the world, but not of the world, since the world of unbelievers do not posses this confident hope, the treasure of Christ, through the Holy Spirit who assures the promise of God. Therefore, their only pleasure is in the temporary riches of this life, blinded of the exceeding riches in Christ Jesus that are waiting for all those that lay their hope in Him.
For just as the Holy Spirit is there to guide and influence all people that set their hope in Christ, there is also a spirit of anti-Christ, who is Satan, who leads unbelievers to death. Jesus spoke about him as the ruler of this world. He is the ruler because man has submitted his free will to him, resulting in becoming a slave to Satan, and not even aware of it.
John 14: 30
"I (Jesus) will no longer talk much with you, for the ruler of this world is coming, and he (Satan), has nothing in Me."
Jesus taught that there are evil spirits, fallen angels in this world. Nevertheless, Jesus also tells us about the Holy Spirit and promises us *that He will guide us into all truth, is a* Helper and Comforter to us, and will keep us in the truth on the journey home.
John 15: 26
"But when the Helper comes, whom I shall send to you from the Father, the Spirit of Truth who proceeds from the Father, He will testify of Me."
We who believe should rest in this promise, knowing that God cannot lie, as the Holy Spirit is joined to our spirits in an eternal covenant union in the love of God, by the power of His grace.
1st John 5: 10
He who believes in the Son of God has the witness in himself.
It is not by our power, our so-called good behavior, or our so-called righteous acts. God clearly tells us that all of our so-called good deeds are stained with the blemish of sin. It is like wearing a light colored suit, stained with black ink. No matter how many times we clean the suit, or what shoes we wear, or

what fragrance we put on, the suit in still stained and is good for nothing except to be used as a rag. However, once the Holy Spirit has entered our lives, by the power of the blood sacrifice of Jesus Christ on the cross, we have a new suit. God creates a new spirit within us that is given by His power and not by our so-called good works. All of this is a testimony that our spirits live on beyond the limitations of our mortal bodies. The Apostle Paul, by the witness of the Holy Spirit, testifies that it is gain, far better to leave these bodies and be in the full manifestation of Christ, which will be our home forever, than to remain in them.

Philippians 1: 20 & 23, 24

For to me, to live is Christ, and to die is gain.

For I am hard pressed between the two, having a desire to depart and be with Christ, which is far better. Nevertheless, to remain in the flesh is more needful for you.

The Holy Spirit, through the life of the apostles, and through the lives of all those who believe on the name of the Son of God, clearly teaches that our spirits will remain alive forever. The apostle testifies by the power of God, according to the divine promise of eternal life, that to depart from these earthly bodies is gain, if we are to be with Christ. It is the very promise of God that Paul stood confident, in the eternal hope that was reserved for him and is reserved for us in Christ.

2nd Timothy 1: 1

Paul, an apostle of Jesus Christ by the will of God, according to the promise of life, which is in Christ Jesus.

The word of God continues to testify that our spirits live on, beyond these bodies, as we read the words of Jesus on the cross.

Luke 23: 46

"Father, into Your hands I commit My spirit."

We see again the separation of the spirit from the body, death, which Jesus experienced Himself on the cross. However, Jesus returned in His earthly body, glorified as He is now resurrected from the dead, and sits at the right hand of God. We see without a doubt that at the point of the death of our bodies, our spirits are separated from our bodies, but we go on. For it is in our spirits, the inner being that supplies life to these earthly shells of flesh. Jesus taught this repeatedly to His followers, and if we are followers of Jesus Christ, if we have accepted Him as our Lord and Savior, then we need to fully understand what He taught and promised. Even while Jesus was on the cross, He promised one of the men that was crucified next to Him, that on that day, they would both in paradise.

Luke 23: 43

And Jesus said to him, "Assuredly, I say to you, today you will be with Me in Paradise."

We know that within hours of this statement, Jesus and the criminal crucified were both pronounced physically dead. Therefore, it was not the natural body of the thief that was going to be in paradise with Jesus, but his spirit.

Then we come to the brutal stoning of Stephen, who was testifying before the counsel of the Jews. As the last few rocks were thrown at his head, he looked up to heaven and prayed:

Acts 7:59

"Lord Jesus, receive my spirit."

Stephen did not pray to the Lord to spare his mortal, earthly life; but prayed to the Lord Jesus to receive him in the spirit. Stephen was not afraid of the separation of the spirit from the body, but we can assume from his request that he welcomed it, as Paul stated, "to die was gain." This is not some bizarre suicide oath that was among the first followers of Christ, but it was a full assurance, a confident hope that when they left this earth, their lives in their spirit would be with Jesus. The Holy Spirit testifies in the Epistle of James that life is in our spirits and the physical body is a shell for the spirit to dwell.

James 2:26

For as the body without the spirit is dead, so faith without works is dead also.

God is not saying in this text that we must work for our eternal salvation in Christ. Rather, because we are saved, we can do the good works of faith. Salvation is a gift, which cannot be earned by deeds. The work for our eternal redemption was already paid in full, nailed to a cross! How could we ever think that we could add anything to that? God uses the example that the body without the spirit is dead to show the separation of

the two, and that faith is dead without the representing actions in our behavior. In other words, if we say we have faith in God, then we should act as if we have faith, not to say we have faith and then commit faithless actions. The body without the living spirit, given by God is dead. Although the reality of this fate seems to escape us in our day to day lives, it will happen to all of us until the Lord returns. We have witnessed this with loved ones and will continue to witness it throughout the rest of our stay here. We do not know when or how, but it will come our turn, and for some, it may be too late. Knowing this fact, we should all have an earnest desire to understand God's one and only plan for our redemption. Some will look down at the consistent warnings from God as we begin to see His word unfold before us. Others will simply not be interested in anything that cannot be seen, passing it off as mere speculation, or religious superstitions. For faith is the confident hope in God, who is unseen; if we could physically see Him, faith would not be required. Then others are too busy; they have no time for anything but work and the pleasures of this life. However, Jesus gives us a stern, clear warning concerning the way to His eternal kingdom.
Matthew 7: 13 & 14
"Enter by the narrow gate; for wide is the gate and broad is the way that leads to destruction, and many who go in by it. Because narrow is the gate and difficult is the way which leads to life and there are few who find it."
It is the eternal life with God, with our spirits now and later in resurrected bodies to live back on the earth that Jesus is speaking of when He uses the word life. Although many will choose to ignore the warnings of God, while having their eyes blinded by the lure of temporary pleasures and their ears tickled with empty philosophies, our spirits continue into eternity. We know that this physical body in temporary. However, the promise of life is in the spirit, and God assures us through the power of His word that our lives continue into eternity, far beyond what we can image because of our limited understanding. God promises us a life into eternity with Him!

2nd Corinthians 5: 1

For we know that if our earthly house (a temporary dwelling),
this tent, is destroyed, we have a building from God, a house (a
permanent, eternal home), *not made with hands, eternal in the
heavens.*

The Apostle Paul, through the light of the Holy Spirit, gives the
church a clear understanding of our eternal destiny. For
whoever's name is written in the Book of Life, these are the
spirits that God brings to the knowledge of His forever love,
which does not change as the seasons, but remains consistent.
If this earthly house, this tent, which is the current physical
body that our spirit lives in, is destroyed, dies from natural, or
unnatural causes, we have a building from God. The building,
the house from God is the eternal place, not made with hands,
but it is a place in His presence. This is the believer's confident
hope of knowing that God has prepared a home for all those
that are His. Jesus Himself testifies to this truth in the promise
of our eternal dwelling.

John 14: 2 & 3

*"In My Father's house are many mansions; if it were not so, I
would have told you, I go and prepare a place for you. And if I go
and prepare a place for you, I will come again and receive you to
Myself; that where I am, there you will be also."*

Jesus has prepared a place for us, a home with Him. Although
we do not know what we will see, or what we will be, we know
that Jesus will be there in all His glory and we will see Him as
He is. The attempts to explain the awesome presence of God in
heaven by the Apostle John and the Prophet Daniel are more
difficult to understand than someone from the dark ages trying
to understand the current computer technology. Even that
comparison is a poor example. The Holy Spirit guided these
men in writing what little they could identify of what they saw.
It is also interesting to note, that although these men were God
fearing and both had a personal relationship with God, when
they stood before the Almighty, they fell like dead men,
stricken with fear by the overwhelming massive power of His
presence. However, this we know; that God is faithful, He
cannot lie. Jesus taught repeatedly that if we place our trust in

His love, not in our own self-justification and not in the temporal things of this world, then we will be with Him forever! The reason why this is possible is that this was the very reason why we were created. Maybe some of us have forgotten what love is. *God is love.* God's love is perfect, not flawed, as ours by past hurts, self-satisfaction and insecurities. His love is pure and ready to give to all that call on Him. God actually wants to be with us because He loves us. I know this often confuses our reasoning, why the Almighty, perfect God would want to be with the likes of us, but it is true.

John 3: 16
"For God so loved the world that He gave His only begotten Son, that whoever believes in Him, should not perish but have everlasting life."
If for some reason, God only allowed us one verse to record the true meaning of His goal and objective, the above verse says it all. God wants us to be with Him to the extent that He sent His Son in the form of a man and actually became one of us. He then completed the task of paying the *wages of our sin,* which is death, even death on the cross.

Ezekiel 24: 12
"As a shepherd seeks out his flock on the day he is among his scattered sheep, so will I seek out My sheep and deliver them from all places where they were scattered on a cloudy and dark day."
Jesus has prepared a place for the spirits of those that call upon His name, that believe on Him, and promises that we will by no means be disappointed. Besides that, there is more! Jesus also tells us that some day our spirits will return to these same bodies, but these fleshly shells will be different from what they are now. Jesus taught about the resurrection from the dead, when our mortal bodies will put on eternity, never to cease functioning again. We should not be surprised that God can send the spirit back to the body temporarily or permanently. The famous resurrection of Lazarus, who was dead in the tomb for four days, which means the body of Lazarus was already decomposing, is proof of God's resurrection power. The gospels also testify that there were

other people that were raised from the dead by Jesus. John tells us that there were so many wonderful and supernatural things that Jesus did in His short three-year earthly ministry, that even the world could not contain the books if they all were recorded.

John 21: 25
And there are also many other things that Jesus did, which if they were written one by one, I suppose that even the world itself could not contain the books that would be written.
We do not really know how many people Jesus raised from the dead, but judging of the multitudes of people that Jesus healed, I would think that there were many. In the case of Lazarus, it is valuable for us to eavesdrop on the conversation between Jesus and the sister of Lazarus named Martha. We can draw a safe conclusion, based on the things written about this woman, Martha, that she was practical, organized, sharp, a hard worker and obviously understood some of the teachings from Jesus. When Jesus finally came to the house of Lazarus, He said to her:
John 11: 23
"Your brother will rise again."
Martha took this as a comforting word, like,' He is in a better place and you will see him again.' Martha answered Jesus in confirming that she well understood what the Master had been teaching, that on the last day there will be a great resurrection when our spirits will return to these bodies. Martha was paying attention during the teaching of Christ. However, Jesus response is one that we need to understand, because it further confirms that even if the body dies, the spirit lives on and that He, Jesus, is the only way to eternal life with God.

John 11:25 & 26
Jesus said to her, "I am the resurrection and the life. He (anybody), *who believes in Me, though he may die* (the death of the body), *he shall live* (in the spirit). *And whoever lives* (in the spirit), *and believes in Me shall never die. Do you believe this?"*
God has taught this repeatedly, that the first death of the body has no bearing on the life of the spirit. Our spirits move on to either the second death, which is the judgment of God without

Christ, or to an eternal pardon in Jesus, through Jesus and by Jesus, since He paid the price of our redemption on the cross. We have many options in this life concerning mates, careers, and leisure, but when it comes to our eternal destiny, we have only two. The choices: to leave here either with the forgiving, redeeming sacrifice of Jesus Christ as our eternal atonement for our sins, or without Christ. In that case, our sins remain with us and we cannot bring our sins into the dwelling place of God, which for this very reason, Satan was thrown out of heaven. It all comes down to the very question that Jesus asked Martha, *"Do you believe this?"* For there comes a time when we cannot find all the answers and our limited logic goes only so far, then we must answer the question by faith. Although Martha was a logical, realistic woman, she answered the question with a big *"Yes"* in faith.

John 11: 27
She said to Him, "Yes, Lord, I believe that you are the Christ, the Son of God, who came into the world."
Martha hit the bull's eye of faith! This is the beginning of our salvation, acknowledging who Jesus is, while the end is accepting what He did for us on the cross, which had not yet taken place at the time of this conversation. However, Martha makes a bold confession of faith, which made the heavens shake. Jesus goes on to call Lazarus out of the tomb, and he comes out alive! I am sure that it would have been interesting to hear Lazarus give his testimony. Though this might be the most well-known miracle, there are others recorded in the gospels. Luke records about a daughter of a certain ruler of the synagogue that died as her father came to Jesus for His help.

Luke 8: 41, 42, 49
Behold, there came a man named Jairus, and he was a ruler of the synagogue. He fell down at Jesus' feet and begged Him to come to his house, for he had only one daughter about twelve years of age, and she was dying.
While He (Jesus) was still speaking, someone from the ruler of the synagogue's house, came saying, "Your daughter is dead."
While Jesus was on His way to the ruler's house, someone from the house gives the father the bad news, *"Your daughter is*

dead." Jesus does not stop, but continues to the ruler's house, and once there, the girl was raised from the dead. Luke, being a physician, does not just say that the girl was raised from the dead, but explains how she came back from the dead.

Luke 8: 55

Then her spirit returned, and she arose immediately.

Since Luke was obviously an educated man in the science of the physical body, he makes it a point to record, *her spirit returned.* Luke understood that we are created of physical and spiritual matter. He also understood that once the spirit of a person leaves the physical body, the body is dead, which is exactly what James recorded. This physical life is temporal; the spiritual life is eternal. Therefore, there are no accidents of birth, since God is the only one that can give us a spirit, from His Spirit, only then are we created physically and spiritually.

Job 34: 14 & 15

If He (God) *should set His heart on it, if He should gather to Himself His Spirit and His breath, all flesh would perish together, and man would return to dust.*

Jesus told the Pharisee named Nicodemus, who came to Him secretly to question Him in the night concerning the kingdom of God that life is in the spirit. Jesus knew exactly what was on his mind, so before the ruler could even get started with whatever he had planned to say, Jesus cuts him off and says, *"You must be born again."* Jesus was not talking about a natural birth, but a spiritual, so here again, we see a clear division between our natural flesh and our spirits. The birth, which Jesus speaks of, is not the birth of our flesh, but a re-birth of our spirits. Nicodemus wrestled with this, asking, *"How can a man be born when he is old? Can man enter a second time into his mother's womb and be born?"* The Pharisee was thinking in the natural, and Jesus was talking spiritual. This religious ruler could not comprehend these words. Jesus goes on to tell us that unless one is born of the Spirit of God, they will never see the kingdom of God, no less enter into it.

John 3:3

Jesus answered and said to him, "Most assuredly I say to you, unless one is born again, he cannot see the kingdom of God."

Therefore, the re-birth of the spirit comes forth, born through the birth canal of faith, by the power of the death and resurrection of Jesus Christ. It is in our spirits where our eternal destinies are secured. For our bodies are still under the curse of death, bound by the sin of Adam. While the spirit of the true believer has been re-born from above, released from the curse, our physical bodies will still decay and die. Since it is written, *"For in that day that you* (Adam and Eve), *eat of it* (The forbidden fruit), *you shall die." The wages of sin is death*. The sin of Adam and Eve brought death to their spirits, to their physical bodies and to ours as well, as we are brought forth through their natural seed. Although the death of their spirits, separation from God began that day, the death of their bodies began gradually. As the years went by, and man's sin increased, so did the wages of death. However, through the sacrifice of Jesus Christ, the wages of death has been paid in full, resulting in an abolishment of the separation between God and man. Our spirits are then re-birth as heirs into the family of God, and our physical bodies will also be re-formed, resurrected from the decay of sin, into the eternal grace of God, by faith. The Holy Spirit also tells us that Jesus went into the prison of spirits from former days and preached the gospel of hope.

1st Peter 3: 19
...By whom also He (Jesus) *went and preached to the spirits in prison, who formerly were disobedient when once the Divine long suffering waited in the days of Noah...*
Their flesh was dead, but their spirits were, or still might be in a spiritual prison. If our spirits lay dormant, in a comatose state, then Christ would not have been able to preach to them. All the statements in the word of God tell us that our spirits remain alive, aware and understand what is happening to them. Our lives are in our spirits, for our spirits are the source of life, and our physical bodies being the containers for our spirits. Those that believe otherwise are deceived and shortsighted, even blind to this spiritual truth. God gives us a crystal clear promise that when all is said and done, there are only two different places where we will live our eternities.

Two very different places as we read this truth throughout the Scriptures.

Matthew 25: 32, 33, 41, 46
"All the nations will be gathered before Him..."
"And He will set the sheep on His right hand, but the goats on His left."

"Then the King, will say to those on His right, 'Come, you are blessed of My Father, inherit the kingdom prepared for you from the foundation of the world."
"Then He will say to those on His left, 'Depart from Me you cursed, into the everlasting fire prepared for the devil and his angels..."
"And these will go away into everlasting punishment, but the righteous into everlasting life."

All nations, meaning everyone will stand before Jesus Christ. Jesus will set apart the unbelievers from the believers in the final judgment. Then King Jesus will give those on His right His kingdom, a place in paradise, in the very presence of God, where there is no more pain, no tears, no sin and in a glorified, resurrected body. Jesus promised that where He is, those that place their trust in Him will be also. Then there are those on His left. These souls have turned away from God's gracious offer of mercy. While God gave all He had to redeem the human race from the error of sin, some would simply rather be in the sin of being their own god.

Hebrews 12: 9
Shall we not much more readily be in subjection to the Father of spirits and live?

There are many people who I have spoken with about Christ, that have been turned away from God because of certain religious organizations, and the television evangelists who preach one message and live another. Some religious leaders claim to take an oath of poverty, while they live a lavish lifestyle. Others preach new revelation from God, and if you want that new message from the Lord, all you have to do is send in your contribution to receive it. People have been discouraged from the lack of truth from these religious leaders and begin to justify themselves, based on their own opinions.

However, this is a legalistic view, which leaves the person in thinking that God will justify them by their good behavior. God tells us that even our best intentions are soiled with the stain of sin. This is why we needed a Savior! If we are depending on ourselves, reasoning, 'As long as I am a good person, I will not be judged by God,' then we are declaring ourselves, as our own savoir, and God will never accept that. This is why Jesus came down from the throne of glory to save us from the judgment of our own sin.

Jesus tells us repeatedly that there is a real place of judgment, everlasting punishment, and everlasting fire.

John 5: 28 & 29

"Do not marvel at this; for the time is coming in which all who are in the graves will hear His voice and come forth – those who have done good, to the resurrection of life, and those who have done evil, to the resurrection of condemnation."

The basic infant birth of faith in obedience to God, which is the only real good we could ever do, is accepting His offer for the sacrifice of our sins by the death and resurrection of Jesus Christ, for we are saved by His grace and not by our own merit. Without this first step, there can be no other steps. We cannot earn this sacrifice, since we did not, nor could ever have done the work for our redemption on the cross. However, by accepting the sacrifice of Christ, we are obedient to God by the working of faith, understanding that we have sinned, and in need of a Savior and willing to place God on the throne of our lives, even above ourselves. We need to understand that our spirits will live on into eternity and will be in only one of two places. For there are only two ways to leave this world: In Christ, forgiven of our sins, or without Christ, taking our sin with us. Of course, we must remember that God is the only one that can open our eyes to the truth. God alone can bring us to the cross of Christ, we cannot save ourselves.

Matthew 25: 46, Hebrews 2: 9

"And these (all that reject the sacrifice of Christ and die in their sins), will go away into everlasting punishment, But the righteous (All that have accepted the sacrifice of Christ, and have been forgiven for His name's sake), into everlasting Life."

...That He (Jesus), by the grace of God, might taste death for everyone.

The Apostle Paul, who had received great insight by the Holy Spirit concerning the mercy of God, gives us a glimpse of the place where we already have a citizenship and are heirs to the promise of eternal life. Whether Paul had received this knowledge in a vision, or it was seen through the eyes of his understanding, it is a great benefit for all those that believe because it confirms again that our spirits live on.

Hebrews 12: 22 - 24

But you have come to Mount Zion and to the city of the living God, the heavenly Jerusalem, to an innumerable company of angels, to the general assembly and the church of the firstborn who are registered in heaven, to God the Judge of all, to the spirits of just men made perfect, to Jesus the Mediator of the new covenant...

Notice that the Holy Spirit begins by stating that we have *come to Mount Zion, the city of the living God, the heavenly Jerusalem.* Though our spirits have not arrived there yet, we have already come with an eternal reservation because of God's grace on us, through Jesus Christ. For all those that place their trust in the sacrifice of Jesus Christ already have their names written in the Book of Life, therefore, our eternal destinies are sealed by the redeeming power of His blood. The work of our salvation was completed; finished on the cross! We are not in a secured place within the kingdom of heaven by our sin stained achievements, but by the pardon of grace. We see the outcome of accepting the invitation of God, as all those that believe, along with an unaccountable number of angels, are gathered around the throne of the Most High. God says that every believer in Christ Jesus is there, the church of the firstborn who are registered in heaven. The church, which is the body of believers, is a tabernacle not made with dead mortar and brick, but with the living stones of spirits, has already been registered, checked in, and reserved for paradise. This is what the true child of God has come to in the presence of the Almighty God, the Judge in all His glory. We also come to the *spirits of just men made perfect.* Here again we see Scripture testifying that there are spirits of men in the presence of God.

He does not say that the men are there in the fleshly shells of bone and marrow, but they are there in the spirit. The complete text is telling us that we also are there, connected in the Spirit, registered, reserved in a place where the Creator dwells. This is all possible because who it is that is there with us, the one who paid the price for our admission. We have come to *Jesus the Mediator of the new covenant* and to *the blood of sprinkling that speaks better things that that of Abel.* Jesus is there; risen and glorified, representing everyone that has placed his or her trust in Him, representing the new covenant that was sealed by His blood. We have come to God with Jesus, by Jesus, in the company of millions and millions of angels and spirits that were once here as we are now. If the spirit of a man or woman does not live on, then there could not be a place where we have already come to in the spirit as outlined by the Holy Spirit to the Apostle Paul. There is a place; it is a place that Jesus has prepared for those that believe in Him, it is the very place where Jesus is.

John 14: 3
"And if I go and prepare a place for you, I will come again and receive you to Myself; that where I am, there you may be also."
Revelation 22:1
And he showed me a pure river of water of life, clear as crystal, proceeding from the throne of God and of the Lamb.
It is there, at the pure river of water of life where Jesus has prepared us a place. Jesus makes no error in His promise that all those that trust in His sacrifice, trust in His name, trust in Him, will be with Him, where He is. Many people say God can do anything, but they are wrong! God cannot sin, He cannot lie! Therefore, we can rest assured that every word that has been entrusted to the prophets, apostles and writers of the Scriptures are true by divine intervention and direction. God gives us His word, and we can take that to the bank of eternity. We all know the testimony of the Apostle Paul, in which he was struck down by the brightness of God on a Damascus road. Paul testifies that it was Jesus Christ who spoke to him and gave him the instruction for his ministry. When Paul stands before King Agrippa in the Book of Acts, Paul tells the story

himself, testifying that it is by faith alone in Christ that can redeem our spirits. God, through the power of His love, transforms us from the kingdom of darkness, to the kingdom of light. This is the promise, sealed, signed and delivered to humanity.

Acts 26: 17 & 18

"...To whom I (Jesus), now send you (Paul), to open their eyes, in order to turn them from darkness to light, and to receive forgiveness of sins and an inheritance among those who are sanctified by faith in Me."

This is the true liberty, the true freedom that is in Christ Jesus and sealed with the promise from God. That we who believe are free from the powers of darkness and have inherited the kingdom of light. This liberty in faith is a freedom from sin, since we have received forgiveness for all our sins, past, present or future. Though we face the promise of physical death that will no doubt come to these mortal bodies, we also have the promise of life eternal in the spirit and one day in glorified bodies, where sickness, pain, sorrow, and death are no more.

John 14: 18, Revelation 7: 9 & 10

"I will not leave you as orphans, I will come to you.

After these things I looked, and behold, a great multitude which no one could number, of all nations, tribes, people and tongues, standing before the throne and before the Lamb, clothe in white robes, with palm branches in their hands, and crying out with a loud voice, "Salvation belongs to our God who sits on the throne, and to the Lamb."

As time passes by, we will all come to the realization that all we see, all we have and all could plan in the natural will end one day. Many will point here and there, but the truth remains of one real God, who by the power of His love sent His Son for the forgiveness of sin, as a one-time offering.

Crossing Over

Exodus 14:21
Then Moses stretched out his hand over the sea; and the Lord
caused the sea to go back by a strong east wind all that night,
and made the sea into dry land, and the waters were divided.
There have been many sermons preached about this event in
history. We know that Moses certainly had the faith at this
point in the exit from Egypt to stretch out his hand to the sea,
so that God could make a path where there was no path. God
placed this light of faith in the heart of Moses and had this
planned before the Israelites ever stepped one foot off
Egyptian soil. We also read in the beginning of the chapter how
God said He would harden Pharaoh's heart.

Exodus 14:4
"Then I will harden Pharaoh's heart, so that he will pursue them
(the Israelites)."
Therefore, God hardened Pharaoh's heart to pursue God's
chosen people, and then placed the light of faith in the heart of
Moses to make a path, where no path was before to avoid their
capture. Is God the King of Hearts? Judge for yourself, since
God clearly tells us that the Pharaoh acted upon the things that
God placed in his heart, and Moses had enough faith to stretch
out his hand to the sea. Did God take away the free will of the
Pharaoh and Moses to execute a spectacular plan for the
liberation of the Israelites? God did not take away free will
from Adam and Eve, who were sinless before they ate the
forbidden fruit. God did not create us as robots, since robots
cannot love. However, since God is the Creator of all, even our
spirits, He certainly rules over the hearts and minds of men,
which mean all things are subject to His purpose, and not ours.
Why did God have the Israelites exit the land of Egypt in such a
spectacular way? There were other ways that the Israelites
could have walked on dry land to bring them to the place of
God's promise. However, God's purpose was to erase all
doubts in the hearts of the Israelites concerning His power and
His love for them, so they all would know that they could trust
Him every step of the way. We can certainly learn from their
experience.

Exodus 6: 7
"Then you shall know that I am the Lord your God who brings you out from under the burdens of the Egyptians."
God wanted no delusions in the hearts of the Israelites that it was the one and only living God who had intervened in the hardship of His people. For the Scriptures testify that God had sworn to Abraham, Isaac and Jacob, that He would give them many descendants and a land for them to live. When God makes a promise, He wants it to be clear that He will make that promise happen, by His power and His actions. It is an interesting note here how Jesus also promised; *"I will build My church and the gates of hell shall not prevail against it."*
The problem with so many organized religions today is that the leaders attempt to build the church, when God clearly said that He would do it by His power, according to His will and glory, and not man's.

Exodus 6: 8
"I swore to give to Abraham, Isaac, and Jacob; and I will give to you as a Heritage: I am the Lord.'"
The Scriptures tell us that the Israelites started out with confidence. By this time they had already witnessed the power of God and were beginning to activate their faith. However, we will see that the Israelites allowed the fire of faith to die by worry and doubt later in the journey. Their failure is a great lesson for us, since our journeys closely resemble their experience as we travel to the eternal land of promise.

Exodus 14: 8
And the children of Israel went out with boldness.
Two important facts arise out of the onset of this event that we need to draw from, and will give us a great perspective on God's deliverance.
The first is that God begins to set the chain of events by placing certain things in our hearts. He planted faith in the heart of Moses and hardened the heart of the Pharaoh. We need to realize that when God begins to move in the situations of our lives, He starts within hearts, our hearts and the hearts of those around us. Sometimes we fail to notice the work of God in our hearts and only expect to see an outward manifestation of His power. We need to look on the inside first, and then we

will see an outward move of God. God moves through faith! As many will say, 'Show me and then I will believe.' God tells us, 'Believe, and then I will show you.'

The second is that once we activate our faith in what God has already promised, we can walk out of our own captivity of bondage by His power with boldness and assurance that God is able to perform all He has said.

We can certainly learn from the Israelites' experience, that God will part the waters of danger in our lives, but we still need to walk through the dry land, through the narrow path of faith. There will be many times in this life in that the only way we will be able to reach the other side of God's best will be to walk through parted troubled waters. In other words, faith needs to be tested. The Israelites took the first steps of faith and walked out of the natural and into the supernatural move of God, and they did it with boldness. Faith gives birth to boldness, a confident pressing into the rich mercy of God in Christ Jesus. Do we want to cross over to God's best that He has planned for our lives? Do we want to live in the promised land of His blessings that are flowing with the milk and honey of His love? Then it is going to take some steps of faith, and some boldness, even in the midst of what looks to be an impossible situation. Another interesting note in the parting of the Red Sea is the Scripture tells us that *the Lord caused the sea to go back by a strong east wind all night.* This might have been the darkest night in the move of the Israelites. The Red Sea was before them and Pharaoh with his army was behind them, the Israelites had their backs against the wall. They begin to question the plan of Moses, forgetting that God was in control. Ever been in a place like that in your life? Have you ever come to the road in your life that has a brick wall in front of it and you're thinking to yourself, I am in real trouble now. While we will experience dark nights of opposition that will test our faith to the limits, we need to remember that God is stronger than all our darkest nights. While the Israelites were tossing and turning in their sleep, God was busy at work in the night making a path where there was no path before. When the Israelites finally awakened, it must have been like Christmas morning to a young child. They awoke to see a supernatural move of God that should have ignited their faith like a nuclear explosion. God was working in the night to provide the Israelites a way to safety. God works the same way in the lives of every believer. Just when things get the darkest, when it seems that maybe, somehow God had taken a nap and forgot the situation that we are in, we will discover that He has been working through the darkest nights of our lives. However, there is a requirement; somebody has to believe God. In the case of the Israelites, Moses took the lead and activated his faith as God had promised to deliver the Israelites out of bondage. It is also going to take faith in our lives to see the super manifestation of God part our troubled waters. However, although Moses had taken the lead role of faith, the children of Israel were still going to have to take steps of faith through the path of dry land in the middle of a raging sea. They had to make a decision whether or not they were going to the other side by trusting God to keep the waters parted. Moses had brought them to the path of faith, now they needed to walk through it. This is the same in our lives, as a minister of God's word can take us to the path of deliverance, but we are going to have to take the steps of faith to walk through it. When we face the dark moments of our lives, we need to look at them through the eyes of faith, confident that God is working with *a strong east wind* of love to make a path of deliverance. Moses gave the people the best advice that anyone could give in troubled times.

Exodus 14: 13

And Moses said to the people, "Do not be afraid. Stand still, and see the salvation of the Lord which He will accomplish for you today."

If we follow the advice of Moses, we will also see the salvation of God bring us through the times of trouble, for God will make a path for us to walk through the sea of threat. Moses gives us the example to follow, in the middle of danger and fear; he rises above the questions of doubt and places his full trust in the mercy of God. Moses did not give in to the fear and doubt that opposed him, but rather he surrendered to the leadership of God Almighty! There may come some times in our lives when even the ones closest to us will speak with the words of fear and doubt in the middle of a situation that appears hopeless. We can listen to the news programs that broadcast the sins against God and humanity, and that attempt to inform the viewers with truth. However, this negative information is filled with the same fear and doubt that attempted to blind the Israelites when facing the journey to the promised land. God had promised Moses and the Israelites that He alone would deliver His people out of bondage and into a land of hope. *Exodus 3: 17*

"And I have said I will bring you up out of the afflictions of Egypt..."

God has also promised those who have placed their faith in Him through Jesus Christ that He will bring them through the afflictions of this life and into the victory of His love now and also for eternity. However, there is a crossover, a crossing from doubt to faith, from uncertainty to confidence and from death to life. For if we now stand on the shores of threat and uncertainty, we will need to cross through the waters of unbelief to the coast of hope, faith and blessings.

 Psalm 119: 166

Lord, I hope in your salvation, and I do Your commandments.
There is also a great divide between the physical and the spiritual, the natural and the supernatural, the death of separation and to the reuniting to His glory. There is a sea that divides faith from doubt that God has already parted by the birth, death and resurrection of Jesus Christ, so we are now able to cross over. The Israelites also had a divine path cleared for them that would lead them to the land of promise. However, they could never enter that land because of the doubt that eventually drowned the fire of their faith by the troubled waters of unbelief. The inner sea of their hearts, which was filled with worry and doubt, was a much larger sea to cross than the Red Sea.

As the Israelites had been given the assurance of God's promises to receive a land flowing with blessings, they never saw beyond themselves, beyond their own journey through the wasteland of sand. They had never visualized the land that God had promised because their minds were blinded by their own fear and sin.

Jesus has promised that one day we, all those that believe in Him will cross over from this life to eternal life with Him, leaving behind these shells of flesh for a time. It is then, when we reach the other shore of the journey that we will see our loved ones that have already gone ahead. Moreover, Jesus Himself will be waiting to greet us in to life eternal, where fear, tears and death will be no more.

1st Thessalonians 4: 17
And thus we shall always be with the Lord.

As the Israelites would never have been able to reach a destination that they themselves could not see, so we also need to see with spiritual vision the promised land of life eternal. The Hebrews had never really believed the promise; so, it was impossible to bring them to the land of promise. Those who do not believe the promises of God will never be able to travel through the waters that divide glory from judgment. If we only see our current circumstances and lose sight of the other side, where God's glory is waiting for us to enter into, then we will remain in the desert of hopelessness. Without spiritual vision, we will never see the manifestation of God's promises for our lives. For God's blueprint of eternal salvation is built on faith. Are we willing to look beyond this life and into the promise of eternity with God? Faith is a confident hope and without hope, we are simply empty vessels of flesh, waiting to die in the desert of uncertainty. Jesus consistently taught the importance of faith; the developing of faith and acting on the faith that has been nurtured inside of us. Jesus marveled at strong faith and questioned weak faith. Faith is the fuel, the combustible substance that ignites the hearts of men, and moves the Spirit of God. If we had no gasoline for our cars, it would still look like a car, we would still posses the car, but the car would remain dormant. Without the fuel of refined oil, the car is unable to function as to perform the task of providing transportation. The auto will sit there, stripped of its intended purpose. This is why God told us through the Apostle James that *faith without works is dead.* If our actions are not fueled by the igniting power of faith, as the car without gasoline, our actions are dead, the auto will not move. We really need to understand that God is not talking about the principles of the world, in that some people appear to succeed through deception and greed, in which no faith is required. Jesus taught about the requirements of faith in the kingdom of God, faith in obedience being the only requirement, but it needs to be the driving force in all that we do. Every time we obey the word of God, it is fueling our actions with faith.

Does this mean that if all our actions are in faith, we will know all the mysteries of God? Jesus gives us a great insight on the seed of faith.

Mark 4: 26, 27

And He said, "The kingdom of God is as if a man should scatter seed on the ground, and should sleep by night and rise by day, and the seed should sprout and grow, he himself does not know how."

The farmer plants the seeds by faith in good soil, knowing that the ground will cause the seed to grow into a crop. The farmer may not know how the earth changes the seed into a living plant or tree, but he knows that it does and plants the seeds by faith, which is the hope of things unseen. Therefore, can we say that this is blind faith? Once we have seen God work in our lives, in which we all have; then it is no longer blind faith, but faith standing on the word of God and also seen through our past experiences by His power.

God will not settle for the back seat! We will either trust Him fully in the driver's seat of our lives, which truly makes Him Lord and God of all we are, or we will remain in the driver's seat ourselves, making ourselves our own god.

As David went against Goliath, the small young boy told the big man that he had seen God deliver him from the mouth of the loin and the claws of the bear, so watch out Goliath! The parting of the Red see should have been enough of an experience to carry the Hebrews through the desert and into the promised land, but they were quick to forget this supernatural move of God. We also must be sure to remember all the supernatural interventions of God in our own lives. This is not to say that we can base our faith only on past experiences. Faith grows by planting the word of God in our hearts and minds, believing that what God did in times past,

He will do the same for us. However, remembering past experiences of God's work in our lives will also strengthen our faith. This will also help us in times of temptation and tribulation, reminding ourselves that God delivered us before and He can do it again, just as He did for David.

Now works that are not planted in faith, but in deceit, greed and selfishness might appear to be successful in the natural, but the growth that these seeds will produce is a harvest of the weeds of bitterness, resentment and confusion. If we plant weeds, we should not expect a harvest of wheat. It only took one weed of doubt, one act of disobedience for Adam and Eve to reap a harvest of shame, guilt and separation from God.

Genesis 3: 13

And the Lord God said to the woman, "What have you done?"

Adam and Eve crossed over from the obedience of faith in God, enjoying the heaven-like surroundings in the Garden of Eden, to the disobedience of doubt that caused them separation from God and the heavenly surroundings of God's blessings. They traded a lie for the truth, forsaking the wisdom of God, and believing a fallen angel, which since then, we all have done. They traded the blessings of God for a curse, life for death. This is why we need to trust God carefully in His commands to us, because we sometimes do not realize the consequences that will follow our actions and how it will affect the people around us. Adam and Eve needed to trust God, and we also need to trust God in His instructions to us by faith, though there are some things that might seem harmless to us, yet they could be damaging to our lives. Adam and Eve crossed over to the cursed land of disobedience, and brought humanity with them, so we have inherited their nature of rebellion toward God. Therefore, we needed someone to cross us back over to God's blessings in obedience, for we all have fallen captive to sin, as Moses led the Israelites out of captivity.

Romans 3: 23

For all have sinned and fall short of the glory of God.

Now Moses, who led the people of God out of the land of Egypt, was a shadow of God's master plan for the redemption of man. God promised His people that He would take them out of a land of bondage, to a land of freedom and blessing. Though

Moses could not take on himself the sins of the people for their redemption, following God's instructions, he was able to lead them out of the land of bondage through intercession on their behalf. For Moses was a link, a bridge of hope that could carry a stiffed neck, disobedient people back to God. However, Moses had also fallen short of God's glory; therefore, he could only take them so far.

Numbers 20: 12

Then God spoke to Moses and Aaron. "Because you did not believe me, to hollow Me in the eyes of the children of Israel, therefore you shall not bring the assembly into the land which I have given you."

We can see that every man has failed God, and has at some time rebelled against His instructions that is given by the power of His love. Any action contrary to the word of God is unbelief; the opposite of faith, for faith is in the obedience to God's word. Moses and Aaron failed to bring the assembly into the promised land because they also failed to believe God. How could we ever cross over, back to the favor and blessings of God, for since the beginning all men have failed to live in complete obedience? God had a plan!

Romans 5:19

For as by one man's disobedience many were made sinners, so also by one Man's obedience many will be made righteous.

Adam sinned in an act of disobedience against God and brought the inherited curse to all of us that are from his seed. However, Jesus Christ, who lived in complete obedience to God, sacrificed His obedience for our disobedience. Since He lived the perfect life, and there was no sin found in Him, Jesus was the only Man who could reverse the curse, by the sacrifice of His obedient blood.

Romans 5: 8

But God demonstrates His own love for us, in while we were still sinners, Christ died for us.

Anyone who believes in their heart, and confesses with their mouth that Jesus is the eternal sacrifice for their disobedience, and yields to His Lordship, has crossed over from death to life, from the captivity of error, to the liberty in the knowledge and salvation of God. For the sacrifice of Jesus Christ was so perfect, just as He is perfect, that by believing in Him as our Savior and Lord, we are forgiven for His name's sake. Our spirits are now back in the place of obedience to God; however, our minds still need to be renewed daily. It is now in our minds where the crossing over from self-centered, captive to sin living, to Christ-centered life in the kingdom of light that will need to be traveled by faith. As Moses and his company had to fight through the barriers of the enemies to cross over to the land of promise, we also need to cross over, press in with an obedient mind through the roadblocks of our enemy. Simply committing to attend a two-hour service on Sunday will not renew our minds. Our minds now need to be renewed, refueled by the word of God daily so that our minds and spirits (which have already been reconciled) will be in one accord, instead of an internal battle between the spirit and the flesh. Sunday service is important in our walk of faith for many reasons, worshipping God is the first and foremost and standing in unity with the brethren is second. However, the Sunday service should not end on Sunday if we really want to cross over our minds and align our thoughts with the word of God. Knowing God's word and acting on it is the key that will unlock the abundance of God's blessings in our lives and align our actions with the will of God. Hearing and not acting on God's word will prevent us from crossing over to a unity of mind and spirit with God, which will result in a lack of God's peace within us.

Ezekiel 33: 32

"Indeed you are to them as a lovely song of one who has a pleasant voice and can play well on an instrument; for they hear your words, but they do not do them. "

God spoke to Ezekiel and explained to him that by someone simply attending your sermons; it will not bring them to the promise land of blessing. God goes on to tell the prophet that his preaching was like entertainment to the listeners, it tickled their ears, but did not penetrate their hearts. What causes this to happen? God gives Ezekiel and us the answer.

Ezekiel 33:31

"For with their mouth they show much love, but their hearts pursue their own gain."

We have all been guilty of selfishness and pursuing our own will instead of pursuing God and His will and purpose for our lives, according to His good pleasure and not ours. We have all sinned in this area and have lost sight of God's eternal plan. The Israelites that walked with Moses were led in circles through the desert of doubt and unbelief, never entering the promised land because of this very reason; it is called self-blindness. When all we can see is ourselves, we will never see or enter the promised land of blessings that God has ready to release to us. We need to cross over from self-centeredness, to Christ centered, for the promised land is in Christ.

Philippians 3: 7 - 9

But what things were gain to me, these I have counted loss for Christ. Yet indeed I also count all things loss for the excellence of the knowledge of Christ my Lord, for whom I suffered the loss of all things, and count them as rubbish, that I may gain Christ ...

A New Creation

2nd Corinthians 5: 17
Therefore, if anyone is in Christ, he is a new creation...
Whether we realize it or not, every day we are delivered over
to death in the natural. The clock ticks, the days on the
calendar race by, and before we know it, we are wondering
where the years went. As fast as the earth spins, so our earthly
lives race through the barriers of time. So then, what is the
purpose? To live here for a few short decades and then vanish
into the realm of nothingness, a non-existent, non-conscience
state of comatose.
James 4: 14, Isaiah 40: 6
*Whereas you do not know what will happen tomorrow. For what
is your life? It is even a vapor that appears for a little time, and
then in vanishes.*
*All flesh is like grass, and the loveliness is like the flower in the
field. The grass withers, the flower fades...*
Are our lives so meaningless, so shallow that we are destined
to taste only a morsel of life and disappear into the blackness
of nothingness? Even the angels in heaven ask:
Psalm 8: 4
"What is man that You (God) *are mindful of him...?"*
To paraphrase this statement they ask, 'why even waste one
thought on man, a self-centered lump of dust from the ground
that exist for a few moments?' There is no argument that our
earthly time is like one grain of sand compared to the endless
shoreline of the eternity of life. If this is it, then what hope do
we have?
Romans 7: 24
*O wretched man that I am! Who will deliver me from this body of
death?*
All the above portrays a rather hopeless perspective. The
apostles and prophets were correct in expressing our few
moments of life here on earth, and how the shadows of death
hang over us as a reminder that time is not on our side.
Ecc. 9: 2
One event happens to the righteous and the wicked.

No matter what might happen in the course of a lifetime, no matter how long or short our lives might be, the fact remains that we will all face death and this is certain, it is an absolute. Most of us will agree that death it is not a subject that we like to talk about. Some of us will stick our heads in a whole and ignore the unavoidable.

King Solomon had a lot to say in the Book of Ecclesiastes, through the inspiration of the Holy Spirit. He focuses on the vanity of life and the reflections of a selfish man that withheld no pleasure from him. Solomon boasted that whatever his eye wanted, he gave it. However, during the writings in the book, we see a rich, spoiled man that finally concludes that anything we do that is not done in faith in God, is all vanity.

Ecc. 9: 3

This is an evil in all that is done under the sun; that one thing happens to all.

The evil that sniffs our earthly lives away is sin. If it were not for sin, there would be no physical or spiritual death. It is the death of our physical bodies that God, through Solomon brings to light repeatedly as He reinforces that we are being slowly executed by sin (death), everyday.

Ecc. 9: 5

For the living knows that they will die; but the dead know nothing...

Some cults, who confess to be Christians, claim this text to mean that at the time of our physical death, we simply exist no more. In a sphere of nothingness, we are in a state of a non-coherent and non-existence. I am amazed that these beliefs are based on the miss- interpretation of a Scripture that is clearly speaking about the death of the physical body only. Moreover, at the end on the book, Solomon writes:

Ecc. 12: 7

Then the dust (our physical bodies), *will return to the earth as it was, and the spirit will return to God who gave it.*

Throughout the Scriptures God clearly teaches us that we are made with a two-part nature, Body and spirit and even Solomon confess to this truth.

Ecc. 3: 20
All (every physical body that lives on the face of the earth), *go to one place; all are from the dust and all return to the dust.*
Who knows the spirit of the sons of men, which goes upward...?
If we move on to the teachings on the Master Himself, Jesus Christ, we will find that Jesus repeated taught that we are made of dust, and of spirit.

John 3: 6
"That which born of the flesh is flesh, and that which is born of the Spirit is spirit."
Jesus clearly divides the physical body, the flesh, and the spirit. He goes on to say that, *"It is the Spirit that gives life, the flesh profit nothing."* It is the spirit that contains life and the flesh of these physical bodies are a shell, a vessel to house our spirits.

James 2: 26
For as the body without the spirit is dead....
Again, there is a distinction between the spirit and the body. The body without the spirit is a dead body like a car without an engine.

Now the Scripture tells us that we are *a new creation in Christ.* So, what does that exactly mean? It does not matter what we are, but it is all about who God is. We were made in the *image and likeness* of God, which means the first couple, was in complete union with God. There was no wall of separation (sin), in Adam or Eve. Therefore, they were fully alive naturally and spiritually, no death existed in them. However, they fell and brought death upon themselves, and us, being their offspring. In this hopeless place of death, separated from God, who is the Creator, the Author of all life, God had a plan. Although the offence of sin was great, much greater than anything man could ever offer to redeem himself from the chains of death, greater is the mercy of God.

John 3: 16
"For God so loved the world that He gave His only begotten Son, that whoever believes in Him should not perish, but have everlasting life."
This new creation is spoken of and promised to all that believe. In the acceptance of the sacrifice of Jesus Christ through repentance, who paid for our every offence, we are forgiven.

Without God's forgiveness, we are trapped in the manure of sin, awaiting judgment. Moreover, we are unable to forgive others and even ourselves, when we are entangled in the thorns of resentment, bitterness and then separated from the truth, forgetting the promise in Christ.

Jesus gives us a great example of how forgiveness is given through repentance, which brings us to faith and to life with a heart full of gratefulness, as *a new creation in Christ.*

"There was a certain creditor who had two debtors. One owed five hundred denaril, and the other fifty. And when they had nothing with which to repay, he feely forgave them both. Tell Me, therefore, which of them will love him more?"

To set the scene of this statement, we see Jesus invited to a Pharisee's house to eat. Jesus accepts the offer and sits at the table. A known woman, who had a bad reputation as an ungodly soul, cries at the feet of Jesus, wiping her tears with her hair, and then anoints His feet with oil. The Pharisee thinks to himself that if Jesus were truly a prophet, He would know what manner of person the woman was. It is a funny thing about God, He is always teaching us something. We can learn from the Pharisee's experience as he thought in his heart that because this woman was drowning in her sin, that there was no hope for her, and she should have been thrown out of the house, no less touching Jesus with sin filled hands. As usual, we have a big lesson to learn from this small passage. The Master begins His story to show the error in the heart of the Pharisee and in our hearts also. The text tells us that the debtors owed the creditor. Some of us might be caught in the trap of thinking that God owes us something. Even some prosperity preachers, who exploit God's giving nature as owing us according to His word, preach that if you give to their ministry, God will give you back more. *God owes no man!* Don't let anyone deceive you in thinking that if you give to God with only the intention of receiving back more than you gave, that God will honor your giving, He will not! God weighs the motives and intentions of the heart. However, the lesson here is not how we give to God's work for ministry through the avenue of money, but how we yield our hearts to God's perspective of repentance and forgiving as we are forgiven which is by far a more important aspect of ministry. Forgiving is one of the most powerful acts of giving that we can display to the world of people that surround our lives. In the example that Jesus taught, the creditor forgave both debtors with equal forgiveness, although one debtor owned much more than the other did. It is easy to be caught up in the trap of thinking that because some of us might not have committed the obvious sins like murder, fornication, or grand theft: but gossip, slander and most of all complaining are all sin. Moreover, sin is a separator, a divider that sets us apart from God. Now we are not speaking about the occasional stumbling over life's consistent pressures that can certainly drive anyone to scream. Rather, when we speak about the sin that separates us from God, we are speaking about the living in that sin, and some people I know practice the sin of complaining every day. Remember that the Israelites wandered in endless circles in the desert because of their consistent complaining, among other things. Thank God for the mercy of God through repentance in Jesus Christ. If it were not for the sinless blood of Christ that allows our repentance to reach the throne of God, we also would be stuck in an endless desert of despair, sorrow, and shame. Therefore, if God can forgive us by the sacrifice of Christ, we can certainly forgive others by the knowledge of the redeeming salvation of God that is revealed to us.

Matthew 6: 14 & 15

"For if you forgive men their trespasses, your heavenly Father will also forgive you. But if you do not forgive men their trespasses, neither will your Father forgive your trespasses."
Sounds pretty simply, until resentment, bitterness and hatred come knocking on our door, and then it is not so simple. However, it can be, if we are willing to obey to the words that Jesus spoke.

If we do, then we are a *new creation,* we are back in union with God, spiritually, but not naturally, since these bodies are still destined to die. For it is in our spirits, what the Scriptures call the *inner man, the new creation in Christ* that we now have eternal life. The *new creation* is the spiritual reuniting in Christ that makes us alive to God, and dead to sin. We were separated by Adam's sin, which is death, but we are reconnected through the sacrifice of Christ, if we believe. Repentance through faith in Christ is the only womb were eternal salvation can be birth. If we remain separated from God, we are separated from life. Many, who might have a pulse and breath, are still spiritually dead, separated from God. However, if we are in Christ we are a *new creation.* It is a transformation by the power of God as His seed of His holy nature in planted in the heart of faith. Without His seed, the only seed that remains in us is the seed of Adam, which is contaminated by sin, like a spiritual cancer that brings forth death. Now Jesus taught that the only way to escape this fate of death that dominates our spirits, that separates us from the life of God, is to be *born from above.* Without this birth, which is a forgiving, re-birth of our spirits by God, we remain in our sin, and the nature of sin is death. However, if we come to repentance, asking God to forgive us as the debtors, who had nothing of value to offer the creditor, God is faithful to forgive our every sin, and plants His Holy Spirit, which is His seed of righteousness, faith, and life into our hearts. Moreover, the Holy Spirit will guide us into all truth, and that truth will make us free. However, the seed of God that is planted in our hearts needs to be watered by the pure water of the word of God so we can grow in the knowledge of Jesus Christ by the Spirit. Once the seed grows, it matures into a deeply rooted tree that will produce the fruits of the Spirit, which are truth, love, purity, and righteousness within a humble heart. Therefore, the *new creation,* the new person in Christ Jesus is no longer a slave, chained and bound to the command of sin, but is truly free by the power of God that resides in his or her heart, to choose good over evil, life over death by the power of God's seed that now abides in them. This is the power of God, and not the power of any person. For if any born-again, Spirit filled believer sins, He or she sins by choice and not by the slavery to sin. However, the unbeliever is dominated by the darkness of deception, blinded by the sin nature of Adam, and easily yields to the call of sin, as Samson was powerless against the whispers of Delilah.

2nd Timothy 1: 7, Romans 8: 15
For God has not given us a spirit of fear, but of power and of love and of a sound mind.

For you did not receive the spirit of bondage again to fear, but you (the new creation in Christ, born again, born from above), *received the Spirit of adoption* (The Holy Spirit), *by whom we cry out "Abba, Father."*

If we have the Holy Spirit of God, which is a seed of purity and power, then sin no longer has dominion over us because it is not stronger than the Spirit that is in us.

1st John 4: 4

He who is in you is greater than he who is in the world.

This is the evidence of God's power in the believer's life. It is not that that Spirit-filled person does not sin, but rather he or she does not abide in that sin. Moreover, if we do sin, we quickly repent, as if we spilled something of the floor, we would quickly clean it, by asking God through Jesus Christ to forgive us, and a make a decision to follow Christ in that area, so to prevent it from happening again, no matter what the sin might be, even complaining. This is by no means saying that believers are not accountable for sin. Forgiveness does not cancel out the consequences of sin in the natural, but it certainly does in the spiritual. By faith, we are saved. Once we enter into an eternal union with God, we are His, and He will even save us from ourselves if we begin to stray from the path of His holiness, because His nature abides in us, unless we make a choice to walk away. Moreover, within His nature is wisdom, love and power, His power that enables us to *overcome evil with good* and to become *more than conquers.* God promises us that if we trust Him with our very lives, if we submit to the direction of His loving guidance in the cry of repentance, He makes us His *new creation.*

1st Peter 1: 3 & 4

Blessed be the God and Father of our Lord Jesus, who according to His abundant mercy has begotten us again to a living hope through the resurrection of Jesus Christ from the dead, to an inheritance incorruptible and undefiled and that does not fade away, reserved in heaven for you, who are kept by the power of God through salvation ready to be revealed in the last days.

What I attempted to express in many words, Peter, through the power of the Holy Spirit says in one sentence. *According to His abundant mercy,* not according to anything that we might think worthy enough to contribute, we are made a new. We are *begotten to a living hope,* a hope with no death, that will have no end, an eternal hope filled with the life of God *through the resurrection of Jesus Christ from the dead.* Jesus tasted death for us all and nailed the power of death to the cross, making it powerless against the *new creation,* born in Christ, born from above child of God. God tells us that we have an *inheritance,* because it is something that we did not earn or work for; the work of redemption was already completed in Jesus Christ when He died on the cross. It is an *inheritance* that is *undefiled* by the works of sins made in ignorance. Therefore, it is *incorruptible* and will not perish or *fade away.* And the best part is that it is *reserved in heaven for* us. Our reservation in the kingdom of God is not reserved for us as a guest, but as a family member, as sons and daughters of the living God. We that believe are family with each other, *begotten* by the same Father in heaven, and sanctified by the same Savior, Jesus Christ. We will be with Christ forever!

." *John 14: 1 & 2*

"*In My Father's house are many mansions; if it were not so, I would have told you, I go to prepare a place for you. And if I go and prepare a place for you, I will come again and receive you to myself, that where I am, there you may be also*

What a promise! For all that place their faith in the Lord Jesus Christ that have been *born again* to a *living hope,* are homeward bound, and registered in heaven in the *Lambs Book of Life.* This is the reality for everyone that receives the sacrifice of Christ of the remission of sin and believes until the end. It is an eternal invitation by God to live with Him forever. Can any earthly pleasure, any material possession, or any earthly status be compared to the promise of eternal life with the One who loves us so much that He was willing to take our place on the cross of judgment? He is the King who was willing to die for the servant so the servant might live.

So then, how do we keep on the path of God's love? How do we resist the consistent barrage of allurements from the call of sin? How can we make it to the finish line of faith where Christ is waiting?

Psalm 119: 11
Your word I have hidden in my heart, that I might not sin
against You.
If we are struggling with some sin in our lives, or some
temptation has us against the ropes of our faith, God tells us to
hide His word in our hearts, because the power of God is in His
word. No evil can stand before the word of God without
bending its ugly knees to the ground in defeat, Sin has already
been defeated, but it our responsibility to walk in that victory,
to know the word of God and the power that it holds. Every
child of God who has the hope of the Spirit within is no longer
a victim of deceit, drowning in the quicksand of the enemies
lies, stumbling in the darkness of spiritual ignorance. For it is
the light of Christ, the flame of faith in God that leads us into
the pathway of His presence. The light of God brings victory
over the darkness of sin. This promise of God has no barriers
of race, age, or education. God does not love us because of how
great we think we are. God did not ask our permission to love
us, he loves us because of who He is, and He is love. And the
reality of that love came as a Man to this world.
John 1: 12 - 14
But as many as received Him, to them He gave the right to
become children of God, to those who believe in His name, who
were born not of blood, nor of the will for man, but of God.
And the Word became flesh and dwelt among us...

The Law of Liberty

James 2: 12
So speak and so do as those who will be judged by the law of liberty.
The founders of this country understood the price of liberty and the great responsibility that comes along with it. One had said it for all, "Give me liberty, or give me death." We could re-phrase it as, without liberty, we are as good as dead. The price for freedom was high, and once obtained, the responsibility was no less. For within the law of liberty, there is a responsibility to make sound righteous decisions according to God's judgment and not by our distorted opinions. God gives us a stern warning in that freedom does not abolish responsibility, but rather makes us more accountable since liberty gives us a choice to do good over evil. It is a hard road and a narrow path to obtain liberation from any dictatorship of evil, in the natural, or in the spiritual. The fathers of this country underwent the same process, since this great nation was birth through the canal of spiritual liberty. However, to maintain this liberty and even spread it is a high cost. Leading others to liberation is part of the responsibility that comes along with the privilege of freedom, naturally and spiritually. As history shows, and even in our current times, dictators that make themselves a god and rule by terror are natural manifestations of spiritual evil forces.
Liberty, whether it is spread through the church, spiritually, or through a nation, naturally, has a great cost. However, we should be aware that the true liberty that God speaks of is the freedom of the spirit. This liberty is not just establishing a governing body with free rights, but rather it is the liberation from the bondage of evil within the heart. This is the true liberty of the spirit, as Jesus Himself promised to all those that place their trust in Him. True freedom overcomes evil with good, as light that overpowers darkness. Moreover, without the light of Christ, only the darkness of bondage remains.
John 8: 36
"Therefore, if the Son makes you free, you shall be free indeed."

Freedom is not the thought pattern of, we can do anything we want without accountability to anyone, and no responsibility to help others. God tells us clearly that the law of liberty is accountability as to what we do with the precious gift of freedom and an opportunity to help others with it.

It is interesting to discover how many people, as I was one of them, thinks that they are free because they live in a free society, but are unable to see the chains of darkness that holds them captive to the will of sin.

Galatians 5: 13, 14

For you, brethren, have been called to liberty; only do not use liberty as an opportunity for the flesh (selfishness), *but through love serve one other. For the law is fulfilled in one word, even in this: "You shall love your neighbor as yourself."*

The *brethren*, to whom Paul addresses, is the body of believers in Christ, which many of the founding fathers of this country were openly confessed to be. Who then are our neighbors that we should love as ourselves?

Jesus was asked this very question from a lawyer that was testing Him and attempted to justify himself. Jesus tells the story of a man that was robbed, and then left for dead on the roadside. Three men came across the beaten man lying in the street. The first man was a priest, a religious official who saw the man and passed him by with no compassion on his misfortune. The second man was a Levite, another religious man who had no mercy on the hurting man and passed without stopping. The third man had no religious position in the church; he had no religious title. However, this man stopped, had compassion on the victim, helped him in his time of need and then went about his business.

Luke 10: 36

"So, which of these three do you think was a neighbor to him who fell among thieves?"

In the Scriptures, we often see God answer a question with a question. It is obvious that a neighbor is anyone that needs a hand of help from another person, and this is not limited to the people that live on our street, or in the same state, or even in the same country.

The will of God is that we do good and not evil with the natural liberty that was paid for by the blood of brave men with good conscience. As with the spiritual liberty that we have received in Christ Jesus that was also paid for by the cost of blood; His sinless blood on the cross. Freedom always has a high cost of sacrifice, and Jesus supplied the offering for our freedom from sin.

1st Peter 2:16

For this is the will of God, that by doing good you may put to silence the ignorance of foolish men- as free, yet not using liberty as a clock for vice, but as bondservants of God.

The apostle received and understood the accountability and responsibility of liberty. Unless we understand the will of God, which is to do what is right with our freedom, then we are simply imprisoned to the selfish ambitions of our egos, which God defines as the *ignorance of foolish men.* Therefore, the will of God is clear, use our freedom to uphold justice and help liberate those that are in the spiritual bondage of evil. The price was high, and the sacrifice was painful, but Christ suffered, died and rose again to break the chains of our spiritual slavery to sin.

Once liberated, freedom can be as dangerous as a loaded gun in the hands of a minor, if not used with divine wisdom. Liberty, without the knowledge of the responsibility on how to live in freedom, will result in the imprisonment to evil and blindness to the call of righteousness. This word righteousness is not defined as a holier than thou attitude. Rather it is the consistent desire to do the right thing in good conscience. To accomplish the task of defining the right thing, (righteousness), we need a point of reference. Not a point of reference that is based on opinion, especially the opinions of those that choose to live in unrighteousness, choosing to do the wrong or evil things.

Proverbs 12:15

The way of a fool is right in his own eyes, but he who heeds counsel is wise.

The only point of reference, the *counsel*, which is the word of God, must be a divine mandate that can penetrate the callous nature of those that desire to do evil. If a nation no longer has a desire to do what is good, the result will be a fallen society, as history has shown us repeatedly. This is clearly not the will of God, since no man is free, unless he is free from sin. Moreover, this is why Christ came, and nailed our sins to the cross, so we may live again in the freedom and victory over evil as Adam and Eve first experienced before their error.

Most of all, God clearly warns us that we are not to use freedom as a cloak, a cover for selfishness, deceitfulness and perverting the truth of God. This is the law of liberty, in that we are accountable for the freedom that has been entrusted to us. Unfortunately, more then ever before, we see the choice of evil preferred over that which is good, therefore, losing true freedom over the very darkness that can hold us captive. The reason why? Because the measuring stick, which is the point of reference to define what is good, which is the divine word of God, is currently substituted for the opinions of conscience numb leaders. Internet pornography, homosexual pornography and even child pornography have now developed into the big revenues. The HIV virus circles the globes as hundreds are infected daily, mostly the young, and the worst part of it is they do not even know that they now carry the deadly cells. Honest business practices have been eliminated by high-powered executives, not content with their six digit incomes; with the quest for more, they steal from their own investors and workers. To make things worse, they jest about the grandmother that now has loss her entire life savings to the deceitfulness of their lies. Her lost in now their gain, and so they celebrate with no remorse. Still think we do not need a point of reference to recognize evil, and prevail over it with good? The daily news reports say that we do, more than ever. Then we come to the all time new low of evil and cowardliness, terrorism! Men that hide their faces behind masks, and kill non-military civilians in the name of their god. This new threat of evil brings the depravity of man beneath the killing instincts of wild animals. At least animals kill to eat. The bible tells us that there is a time for war, but even war has boundaries, laws between injustice and righteousness.

God is an advocate of liberty, since from the very beginning; He gave Adam and Eve freedom of choice. What we do with our liberty is still our choice. God is not a dictatorship; since He even lets those that reject His counsel enjoy the gift of life, but only for a short time.

Galatians 6: 7

Do not be deceived, God is not mocked; for whatever a man sows, that will he reap.

We might think that the world goes on just as it has from the beginning, while God seems like a distant myth that has somehow allowed the world to run its own course. Well, the world does carry on, day by day, year by year, just as it has from the beginning. However, we will not be here for much longer. Even if we live in these bodies for one hundred years, it is a very short span of time compared to eternity. The big picture, eternity, is where our accountability will surface.

Matthew 25: 19

"After a long time the lord of those servants came and settled accounts with them."

Jesus told a parable of three men that were given goods from their master for his purpose, *each one according to his own ability.* Jesus tells us that a day came when the master held each man accountable for the goods that were entrusted to their care. We also have been entrusted with freedom to use for the glory of God and not for selfish ambitions, and some day the Lord of all lords will settle every account.

Those that have sown the seeds of murder, deception and hatred without remorse will not reap the fruits of peace in God's love. Ask any farmer, if you plant tomato seeds, what vegetable do you think will grow from that seed? If someone deliberately plants poison, do not think that something edible will grow from those seeds. It is the law of liberty, the accountability of freedom that will reap a harvest of blessings in this life and in the life after.

James 1: 26

But he who looks into the perfect law of liberty and continues in it, and not a forgetful hearer but a doer of work, this one will be blessed in what he does.

The Apostle Paul had many things to say about freedom to the churches in Corinth and Galatia, since it does appear that they were losing their understanding of the liberty that is in Christ. Although they were losing their liberty in Christ to legalism, we as a nation are losing our liberty to greed. Both separate us from God and leave us in the bondage of darkness. Paul told the Galatians that some have turned, *"to a different gospel, and want to pervert the gospel of Christ."* Anything else that we place our faith in besides the life, death and resurrection of Jesus Christ is a *different gospel.* It could be the gospel of fame, the gospel of greed, the gospel of pleasure, even the gospel of self-righteousness, or the gospel of legalism. There is no liberty in any other gospel, unless it is the liberty from God, which is the freedom from sin through Jesus Christ. Anyone can claim freedom in their country and in their lives, but if they are still chained by sin, a slave to sin, then there is no freedom, only a shallow imitation of false liberty, defined as independence. For Christians do not seek independence from God, but freedom from evil, that is the dependence on God to deliver us from all evil. The true believer is dependent on God, trusting in His wisdom, power, love and strength. God is all knowing, all powerful, and able to intervene in any struggle of our lives. Independence in our own strength is nothing more than a delusion of false security. It is an attempt to be our own god, that can never provide true inner peace and rest, since God alone is the Creator and healer of our souls. It is only where *the Spirit of the Lord is,* where we can find true liberty from evil and true security in this life and into eternity. Moreover, as a nation that proclaims freedom to the world, should seek the full dependence on God and not in the limited knowledge and strength of man. For one day there will be only one government, one King that will rule that government, and one nation that will glorify that King in every word and deed for eternity. In that day, sin will be abolished, and the holiness and righteousness of God, through Jesus Christ will reign on the earth as in does in heaven. Until that day comes, every Christian American should stand, vote and support all amendments that represent God's word of true justice, and live in His righteousness by the power of His truth, dependent on

His word of grace. For whatever nation is apart from God will fall, since *if God is not the builder of the house, the house will not stand.*

What did Jesus teach about freedom? Many of His followers were looking for Jesus to take Israel out of the bondage of the Roman rule in a time when Rome was the world power. According to Jesus, the only real freedom is in the truth.
John 8: 31 & 32
Then Jesus said to those that believed Him, "If you abide in My word, you are My disciples indeed. And you shall know the truth and the truth shall make you free."
This is not to say that those that say they believe can just live their lives with no accountability or responsibility for their words and actions in the name of freedom. Jesus told those that believed in Him that to be truly free in God, they needed to obey God's word. This is the only way to be free from the grips of evil in a generation that is looking to worship themselves, instead of worshipping the one and only God.
John 8: 14 & 36
"I am the way, the truth and the life."
"Therefore if the Son makes you free, you shall be free indeed."
The freedom that Jesus taught was the liberty from spiritual ignorance and blindness that are the results from the slavery to sin. If the Hebrews obtained the spiritual freedom, which Jesus taught, by trusting in the Son of God, then we might assume that God could have intervened in the natural to release Israel from the dictatorship of Rome. However, they did not only reject this freedom from God, but put to death the only way to enter God's liberty. This is the liberty the releases us from the payment of sin, that unlocks the chains of evil that bounds us with guilt and shame. There is no other way to live in the true freedom of God, besides in the liberty that is in Christ Jesus. For He paid for that liberty Himself, with His own blood.
Galatians 5: 1
Stand fast therefore in the liberty by which Christ has made us free...
True liberty, as true peace, is in the heart and spirit of a person. Without the liberty from God, there is no real peace, no

true freedom, no hope and no justice. For it is only in Christ that we can find the freedom in grace that has broken the slavery of sin in everyone who is willing to receive the gift of liberation that is in Jesus.

2nd Corinthians 3: 17
Now the Lord is the Spirit; and where the Spirit of the Lord is, there is liberty.

Faint Hearted

Isaiah 7: 4

"Take heed, be quiet; do not fear or be faint hearted..."

When first looking at the words *faint hearted*, we think of a person with a lack of courage, integrity and character, a coward. We think of a soul who would sell out for mere pennies, just to save his or her own skin. When looking up the word coward in Webster's dictionary, oddly enough, the meaning of the word is as follows: *One given to fear, faint hearted.*

When looking into God's view of a *faint hearted* person, which is really the only view there is, because He is all truth, it becomes a most sobering awakening about our weak, frail natures. We all have experienced cowardliness some time in our lives. Where does cowardliness really come from? It comes from fear. Where does fear come from? Fear can only be present in our lives when we have doubt and unbelief; the very opposite of faith. Faith gives us the light of the knowledge of God; fear is the results of faith being absent, out of our vision. Fear is when the darkness of uncertainty overshadows our hearts instead of the true light of confidence in God, which is the light that gives us reassurance. If we really want to see a real coward, I am sorry to say that we do not have very far to look, even in the closest mirror. However, some of the great men of faith proved to us that they also became *fainted hearted* due to unbelief, doubt and the inability to recognize God's light in that situation where fear overcame their faith. Fear comes from doubt, and then when something goes terribly wrong, we face it with the darkness of the unknown. This is the time when doubt and unbelief are given an open door into our spirits. It is just like when light is absent, there is nothing left but darkness. It is the same with faith. When faith is absent in our spirits, the only thing left is the darkness of doubt and unbelief, which is the real root of all fear. However, fear will flee from our spirits and minds with the life changing word of God, if we study it like the dedicated soldier that prepares for the day of battle. The believer's spiritual and mental preparations should be in focus when the day comes that they will have to use their weapons of spiritual warfare to conquer the enemy of evil. With no preparation, no weapon and no understanding how to fight the enemy, the soldier is reduced to a victim of the enemy's brutality. It is in the light of God's word; the true weapon that overcomes the darkness of ignorance, due to the blindness of sin, which causes us to stumble in fear and doubt. Unlike any other book, God's word has the power to change and build our spiritual beings. When realizing this doubt in myself, I began to be sorrowful of my own stupidity. However, out of God's abundant mercy, He reveals in His word that I have a lot of company, and some of them were great men of faith. I guess it is God's way of telling us that although we missed it, there is a great opportunity to learn and grow from our errors and the errors of others. Unfortunately, learning through our own errors, instead of through the errors of others hurts a lot more and will always have some consequences to follow.

Paul said of himself, *"That Jesus Christ came to save sinners, of whom I am the chief."* I could easily say that I am the chief sinner or coward, since no other one, besides God, knows our errors more than us. The apostle through the Holy Spirit understood our frail nature when faced with the problems of this world, and most important of all, God understands our individual weaknesses.

Psalm 103: 14

For He knows our frame, He remembers that we are dust.

These words should be very comforting to us, since we all fall short of perfection by a rather large margin compared to God, who is perfect. We forget who God really is, since most of us view Him from a distance, therefore we have seen a very small image of His power. However, if we have ever taken the time, and time is needed to get close to God, we would see the overpowering strength in His presence. We would see how big God really is, and that knowledge will free us of every speck of fear and doubt that attaches itself to our minds.

John 8: 36

"Therefore, when the Son makes you free, you shall be free indeed."

We can all remember in the early school years, where there was always a bully, a kid that would enjoy intimating other kids much smaller or weaker then himself. As a terrorist, he would use fear as a tool to rule over the kids that did not know their rights as students. These students, blinded by fear, did not realize that if there were enough complaints made against the bully, the bully would have to behave, or be removed from school. This also teaches us that there is strength in unity. Today, we also have terrorists, world bullies that impose a threat to God's justice and righteousness with fear using physical weapons. We need to realize that the terrorist behind it all, Satan, has no real weapons, only empty threats, unless he can deceive some to use physical weapons of hate, which he has accomplished already. Satan also often points at us with several guns labeled sickness, poverty, rejection and shame. However, we must remember that Satan can do nothing without the surrender to fear, therefore, the believer must surrender to God in faith. Satan has one agenda for believers and unbelievers alike.

John 10:10

The thief (Satan), *does not come unless to steal, and to kill and to destroy.*

We have all faced this enemy in our lives at one time or another. Sometimes it may appear as if this enemy has set camp in our house, on our jobs and even among our relatives. Satan, the inventor of terrorism, can rule the thinking of man through the means of fear and doubt, attempting to make us cowards in the battle against evil. The word coward might be too strong of a word to use to describe our heart failure, but even man himself defines faint heartedness as a coward. The coward could easily be defined as one who runs from the fight against injustice, against unrighteousness and against all that is contrary to the truth of God. This might be visible in even the smallest decisions of our everyday lives. However, if God's word is the final authority of our lives, then each decision is a choice between courage and cowardliness. Acting on God's word in our everyday life does not mean to simply agree with an 'Amen', but it does mean to live as God has instructed, based on the direction of His word.

I wonder how many of us would spend hundreds of dollars for private instructions on any given hobby or sport that we were interested in and not do anything that the instructor taught. Would we spend our time and money hiring a financial consultant and then ignore his or her advice? That would be foolish and a waste of money. We have all been guilty of turning away from God and pursuing the lust of selfishness and the thirst of our own gain, instead of pursuing God's purpose.

Luke 6: 46

'But why do you call Me "Lord, Lord," and not do the things which I say?"

When we read the Gospels, we repeatedly hear Jesus command His disciples, *"Fear not."* We also hear the Master ask this question many times of His disciples, *"Where is your faith?"* It is interesting to see that every time there is an absence of faith, there is an abundance of fear. The two, fear and faith, cannot exist in the same place at the same time. God has taught this lesson throughout the New and Old Testaments.

Faith and courageous, or fear and cowardliness all come from the heart. This raises some questions within us and can reveal the true condition of our hearts. Is there true faith in God in my heart, in every decision that I make? Do I trust God's promises in every area of my life no matter what the gain or loss could be? Who really controls and leads my heart?

Proverbs 21: 2

Every way of a man is right in his own eyes, but the Lord weighs the heart.

Now, it is in the heart of a man or woman that either faith or fear will influence our actions of courage or cowardliness. Coming to this place in Scripture, we become faced with another question; do we really have a choice between faith and fear?

There is no doubt that God gives us the ability to make choices, even if those choices are against His commands. Many times in the Scriptures, we see many people walk away from God, or are simply disobedient to what God commands, which prove that we have a free will. On the other hand, we might think that if we can only do what God commands us to do, then what kind of free will is that? If we really have free will, we should be able to do anything we want without any judgment from God. This way of thinking is exactly the same lie that Satan told Eve in the garden when he convinced Eve to exercise her free will right against the command of God. Eve's heart failed her from the seed of doubt, planted by Satan.

Genesis 3: 4

"For God knows that in the day you eat of it your eyes will be opened and you will know good and evil."

Satan played on the free will of Eve, challenging her curiosity to know evil. She had already known all that is good, since she was in complete union with God. Was it good for her to know evil? Would you want your young child to know first hand through their own experiences the evils that are present in the world? Would you tell your young daughter that you give her permission to become a prostitute so she can experience the evil, the torture, the misery, the guilt and the shame of being a prostitute? No loving, caring parent would give permission to their child to experience something that would hurt them, strip them of their dignity and integrity and possibly end their life. What has happened to the world is the exact same thing that happened to Eve in the garden. It is the lie of all lies, as the enemy sows the seed of deception in the hearts of those who do not know the power and love of God. God tells us that even the angels, who do know the power and love of God, have free will. However, there is no grace in their decisions of rebellion against God, since there is no faith required for them to make choices. Nevertheless, we do have free choice to do wrong, but God does limit even our choices according to His plan. I say limits our free will, because God does allow us to make our own mistakes, but He will only allow us to go so far according to His will and purpose. It is interesting how God did not intervene when Eve decided to eat the forbidden fruit. He did not rush in the garden to stop Eve from taking that first bite, but allowed her to partake of it. We have seen this privilege of free will exercised many times in the Scriptures. However, there are times where God will intervene, according to His purpose, to put things in the hearts of people. God is certainly the King of hearts, He rules, He is the final authority and all are subject to His counsel. God is also always righteous! What that means is that God is always doing the right thing according to true justice.

The insecurities of not knowing that God's judgments are true can give birth to greed, lies, deception and even murder if left uncorrected. This type of heart failure is like a self-inflected wound.

Now, since God knows every heart, and every thought of every person, He is the final authority of the future according to His purpose.

Romans 9: 18
Therefore, He has mercy on whom He wills, and whom He wills He hardens.

God does use people for vessels of judgment and for vessels of mercy for His purpose. However, God has already shown mercy on the world by sending His Son to pay the price for the sins of all people that are willing to receive this gift of redemption. God has extended His hand of grace to a world that is worse than the world was in the days of Noah and the days of Sodom and Gomorrah. What more can God do to save us? Nevertheless, we see a world today that rebels against the grace of God in the darkness of their hearts. The hard heart is a coward heart, a dark heart that has an inability to see and understand God's love because of the absences of God's light. In this darkness of doubt, there is no or little hope. This is why the doubting, coward heart spreads a message of negativity, since without the expectation of God's intervention; the faithless heart is living in a place of hopeless depression. Although most people will never admit this, but it becomes evident when their speech is full of negativity. This negative outlook is the doubt and the lack of hope that is within them. This consistent dark perception is a direct result of the guilt and shame of sin; the heart that is unable to forgive, because he or she has not received God's forgiveness. Moreover, in the doubting and unforgiving heart, there is a fearful expectation of judgment. Of course, no one in the state of unbelief would ever be able to recognize this terminal, spiritual heart condition unless God reveals it, in which I believe, is in the power of praying for the lost.

The current media of news and entertainment thrives on the heart failures of man; often showing in graphic details the results of sin. The headlines of corruption, greed and murder are a clear testimony, relevant evidence that man has indeed failed without the power of God's love in his heart. This negativity grows worse as man drifts farther away from the only life jacket that is able to rescue him from the violent, raging sea of sin. Although God's invitation of forgiveness is always offered with open arms, the unbelieving, blind heart is like a pilot that has lost his navigation system and flies further into the night of the unknown. Without the spiritual visibility, which is the navigational tool of God's word for our journey, it is only a matter of time before a crash will take place. Even the believing heart can be side tracked from God's righteousness, resulting in poor decisions, which can conceive sin and gives birth to shame and guilt.

From the beginning of man's journey, we see the fall of Adam and Eve, right through the denial of Christ by Peter. Many great men and women of God have become victim to the faint heart and then attempted to cover their shame with lies, corruption and even murder.

Romans 5: 12

Therefore, just as through one man sin entered the world, and death through sin, and thus death spread through to all men, because all sinned.

We have all attempted to cover our errors, not knowing that unrighteousness cannot be covered, but needs to be washed away, removed. There are many examples of this in the Scriptures, in the lives of those around us and certainly in our own lives. God does give us choices and a limited freedom to make those choices. We also have seen so many times in Scripture, when God allowed even His chosen to make mistakes. However, we must realize that God has the final word in all creation.

One of the examples of a man's heart failure in the Scriptures is the story of David and Bathsheba. This is not to say that there are degrees of heart failure. Sin is sin, no matter how it

manifests in our lives. However, in this story, we can clearly
see that sin brings shame, and shame brings every type of
deceitfulness in attempting to cover the guilt.

2nd Samuel 11: 2 & 3

And from the roof he (David), *saw a woman bathing, and the
woman was very beautiful to behold. So David sent and inquired
about the woman.*

King David, who had witnessed the power of God at so many
times in his life, who knew the principles of God's
righteousness through His word, becomes blinded by lust for a
beautiful woman that belonged to another man. David's heart
fails him and the sin in his heart is shamed when things get
worse, as we see the coward heart begin to work. As with Eve,
again God allowed David to make a choice. God did not come
running down to the palace to tell David not to sleep with this
married woman.

2nd Samuel 11: 5

And the woman (Bathsheba) *conceived; so she sent and told
David, and said, "I am with child."*

David is now in a spot, and as in all sin, it will eventually come
back to haunt us. Nevertheless, David begins to cover his sin
by arranging for Bathsheba to sleep with her husband, who
was a soldier in the army of Israel. Unfortunately for everyone,
the husband refuses to sleep with her, being dedicated to the
service of David as a soldier and requested to join his follow
comrades in battle. Truly this honorable man, with a
courageous heart shows integrity and willingness to partake in
the battle for the good of the country. David's heart was now in
a panic and desperate people do desperate things. So, when all
else fails, David turns to murder! It is hard to believe how this
man who received so many Psalms of poetic words of praise
and worship to God, is now reduced to deceitfulness that is
now leading to the murder of an innocent, honorable man.
This is a powerful example of how the cancer of sin can even
blind the heart of a man that was in a very close relationship
with God.

2nd Samuel 11: 15

And he (David), *wrote a letter, saying, "Set Uriah* (the woman's husband), *in the forefront of the hottest battle, and retreat from him, that he may be struck down and die."*

We clearly see the results of sin, which in this case, turned to premeditated murder. As in the garden with Adam and Eve, God allowed David to make his own choices, not interfering until the day when the guilt of his sin pierced his heart like a knife. David repented, but the puncture of that sin left a scare in his heart and in his life. God was faithful to forgive David for what he had done. However, as we all know, there are consequences for our actions!

2nd Samuel 12: 13 & 14

So David said to Nathan, "I have sinned against the Lord." And Nathan said to David, "The Lord also has put away your sin; you shall not die. However, because of this great occasion to the enemies of the Lord to blaspheme, the child also that is born to you shall surely die."

God did not create the sin in David's heart, but we see that God will allow us to make our own decisions. The Pharaoh of Egypt did not repent as David. Therefore, he drifted deeper into the darkness of sin, his heart becoming harder. For even with the repentance of David came the consequences of his sin, image how much worse it is with the one who does not repent!

Romans 1: 21 & 24

...But became futile in their thoughts, and their foolish hearts were darkened.

Therefore, God also gave them up to uncleanness, in the lust of their hearts...

God did not create the rebellion in the heart of Lucifer, or in the hearts of the billions of people that turn against Him. God simply allowed Lucifer and everyone else that has chosen to rebel against Him to continue for a certain time.

At times, God's judgment will make the rebellious heart more rebellious and angry, because the rebellious heart wants to justify their sin instead of repenting of it. Therefore, God simply allows the rebellious heart to sail its own course. Unbelief and doubt, which is sin, will always cause a heart to grow cold, hard, faint and resistant to the love of God. It is from the heart that faith or doubt is conceived, and the birth of our actions will follow what comes out of our hearts.

Romans 10: 10

For with the heart one believes unto righteousness...

It is in our hearts where God will reside or will be absent, pending on His grace and our choices to live in faith or in doubt. It is in our own hearts that we will either believe the word of God as truth, or doubt it in the darkness of error and establish our own so-called truth, which is no truth at all, just opinions. What did Jesus teach about our heart conditions? Jesus said plenty about our hearts and a good place to start is in the Gospel of Matthew. As usual, Jesus reveals the light of truth in direct and truthful words.

Matthew 6: 21, Mark 7:20 & 21

"For where your treasure is, there your heart will be also."
And He (Jesus), said, "What comes out of a man, that defiles a man. For from within, out of the heart of men, proceed evil thoughts, adulteries, fornication, murders, thefts, covetousness, wickedness, deceit, lewdness, an evil eye, blasphemy, pride, foolishness."

As we read the headlines and turn on the news, we see all of the things that Jesus spoke about, coming out of the hearts of men and women. It is nothing more that a heart condition, a faint heart, a defect in the heart of man called sin that has infected our spirits. The science world of man's logic and theory will justify these behaviors from poor upbringing, birth defects, body chemistries and childhood traumas. However, God tells us the real reason why man's system is failing as we witness a world in turmoil, is sin.

Genesis 6: 5

Then the Lord saw that the wickedness of man was great in the earth, and that every intent of the thoughts of his heart was only evil continually.

This is why King David cried out to God, *"Create in me a new heart."* David knew that his heart was the real problem. Currently, as we face a world with the evil of terrorism, plagues and every corruption known to man, we see a world with a heart failure from the malfunction of sin. God did not create this condition, but does allow it to continue until that day when He will return in judgment.

Romans 1:21 & 28

...Although they knew God, they did not glorify Him as God, nor were thankful, but became futile in their thoughts, and their foolish hearts were darkened.

And even as they did not like to retain God in their knowledge, God gave them over to a debased mind...

In simple terms, God will give us what we want, up to a certain point. If we want to walk away from His love and allow the chains of sin to hold us bondage in exchange for a few years of temporary pleasure, God will let us go, according to His purpose. However, if we make a choice by His light of mercy, to place God in our hearts as the final authority in all we say and do, then God's grace is unlimited. Once His light of grace penetrates our hearts, we can then receive a heart transplant, a heart that now is connected, grafted into the love of God. It is only then that our hearts can be receptive to the purpose in which we were created, that is to love God with a pure heart. The very thing that prevents this to happen is sin, because sin separates us from God, because God is holy! However, it is God alone that can bring us to the decision of repentance, since we all at one time or another were drowning in a sea of error. Anyone who is drowning is unable to save him or herself!

Isaiah 59: 2

But your sin has separated you from your God; and your sins have hidden His face from you.

This is why without the sacrifice of Jesus Christ as the eternal blood offering for the sin of man; our sin remains with us. There is nothing else in heaven or on earth that is powerful enough to remove, forgive our sin except the pure holy blood of Jesus Christ.

Romans 5: 9

Much more then, having now been justified by His blood, we shall be saved from the wrath through Him.

God alone knows the condition and position of our hearts. There is nothing hid from His eyes, He knows every truth and every lie in our lives. For there are times that we even deceive ourselves.

However, what God continually tells us through the truth of His word is, *"Believe in Me."* God is faithful and can be trusted in every aspect of our lives, if we are willing to have a believing heart in Him. There are many in this short earthly life that might obtain what the world defines as success, but have missed the kingdom of God. Pharaoh had all that this world could offer, but became an enemy of God and found out the hard way that God always wins. The Pharaoh was dead spiritually long before the waters of the Red Sea came upon him and his army.

The conclusion is this; God's will is that none should perish, not even one, to the deceitful lies of the enemy that blinds the heart of those that have lost their way. God does not like the things that we do; however, He loves us, and even those that have chosen to walk away from His endless mercy. On the other hand, God is God, all knowing, all truth and all righteous. Therefore, if God decides to use a vessel to show His mercy or judgment, so be it, for He is God. This is not to say that God takes away our free will. The resentful heart still has a choice to drown with bitterness, or to repent, and God is willing to forgive all because He loves us and wants us to be with Him for eternity. However, without God's intervening power to shine His light of understanding in the heart, no one comes to repentance. This is why the Holy Spirit was sent.

Isaiah 59: 1

Behold, the Lord's hand is not shortened, that He cannot save.
Man's quest for answers to the questions of why the world has sickness, sorrow, pain and death is in one simple answer. The answer is heat failure due to sin. This heart failure is due to the spiritual hardening of the arteries. This spiritual infection became manifest in an angel who became a lover of self, instead of a lover of God. It was passed through Adam and Eve by an act of disobedience, infecting every offspring thereafter. There is no mystery, no hidden secret to the fallen state of heart failure. God gives us a clear description of the condition of every heart that has been contaminated by the spiritual life-threatening virus called sin.

Jeremiah 17: 9 & 10

The heart is deceitful above all things, and desperately wicked; who can know it?

I, the Lord, search the heart; I test the mind, even to every man according to his ways, according to the fruit of his doings.

God knows all things, especially the heart of man. God can see right through us like a powerful x-ray and sees our inner motives behind every action. Moreover, one of the most amazing aspects of God's nature is that though He sees our selfish, immature behavior of always wanting our own way, He sees something else in us. God never gave up on humanity, but humanity gave up on God, because we want God to do things our way. Think about how ridiculous that is, in that the Creator should follow the creation. Even in our limited understanding, we should be able to reason that God's ways are higher than ours, since we cannot even fully comprehend the things that He has made.

Isaiah 55: 8 &9

"For My thoughts are not your thoughts, nor are your ways My ways," says the Lord. "For as the heavens are higher than the earth, so are My ways higher than yours, and My thoughts than your thoughts."

God sees us in our selfishness, He sees all the imperfections that sin has caused in our lives, but He also sees the life given to the dust from the earth, made in His *image and likeness.* God looked beyond our sin and saw what man could be if only our sin were removed, washed away from our hearts.

Mark 6: 52

For they had not understood about the loaves, because of their hardness of heart.

The small group of followers that walked with Jesus through His earthly ministry was still lacking understanding because of their heart condition. The Holy Spirit makes it a point to tell us that although these men were casting out demons and healing the sick by the power of the name of Jesus, their hearts were still faint because of their unbelief. Jesus asked His disciples again a question that He had asked them many times before.

Mark 7: 18

So He said to them, "Are you still without understanding also?"

Jesus was revealing the condition of their hearts, because a hardened heart has no understanding of the things of God. The heart produces actions as a tree produces fruit. The hardened heart cannot produce the fruit of God's word because the word has not entered the heart, like a seed that falls on a stone. Since sin had stripped us of our spiritual understanding and wealth, resulting in a poisoned heart, we could never have paid a price for the eternal redemption for our errors. Therefore, man's ability to be reconciled to God was beyond his reach, because of the contamination of his heart. We can look at humanity as a man who was shipwrecked far out in the sea. The man is unable to save himself, but now must depend on someone who has the resources to rescue him, a savior. Once the man's boat is destroyed beneath him, he no longer has any means of rescuing himself, but is now subject to the conditions of the sea, alone with only one hope. If we take away that one hope of someone coming in a vessel and rescuing the man, since he is too far out to ever swim to shore, the drowning man is going to die. Any so-called religion that denies the truth that man needs a Savior to rescue him from the drowning sea of sin will die in a false hope. There is only one hope, one truth and one Savior, that has the spiritual wealth of holiness, able to save man from the powerful waves of sin. That only hope is Jesus Christ.

Mark 14:24

And He (Jesus), *said to them, "This is My blood of the new covenant, which is shed for many."*

We have the free will to make a choice, whether or not to accept this truth or to deny the truth. If we did not have a choice between the truth and a lie, between good and evil, then we could never be held responsible for our actions. God tells us repeatedly that man is accountable for his actions; moreover, there will be a day of judgment, a day of accountability.

Revelation 21: 12

And the dead were judged according to their works, by the things which were written in the books.

Jesus asked His disciples two questions that I believe He asks us everyday.

Mark 8: 17
"Do you not yet perceive nor understand?"
"Is your heart still hardened?"
Sometimes, before we are willing to trust God at His promises, He will let us do things our own way, and then deliver us from ourselves. The parable of the prodigal son is one of the best illustrations of God's patience, forgiveness and His love for His creation that often runs from Him instead of into His arms. While we will experience dark times in our journeys that will test our faith to the limits, we need to remember that God is stronger than all darkest. Just when things get the darkest, we will discover that He has been working through the dark times of our lives. However, we have a responsibility; we have to believe God by giving attention to His word, and acting on it, which will give birth to the prayer in faith.

Think about it, the Israelites had to walk through two walls of water that were defying gravity. That would be like someone asking you to walk on the water, it simply is against all logic, just ask the Apostle Peter as Jesus told him to step out of the boat in faith. When we face the dark trials of our lives, we need to look through the eyes of faith, by the word of God, because God alone can renew our hearts to victory

Psalm 119: 166
Lord, I hope in your salvation, and I do Your commandments.
Jesus marveled at strong faith and questioned weak faith; both come from within the heart.

Luke 12: 28
"O you of little faith?"
Revelation 21: 8
"But the cowardly, unbelieving, abominable, murderers, sexually immoral, sorcerers, idolaters, and all liars shall have their part in the lake which burns with fire and brimstone, which is the second death."

This is God's judgment, and He alone can know all the motives and intentions of the heart. God tells us the ones who remains a coward, a fainthearted unbeliever, will all share in the same judgment, because they have rejected the mercy of God. However, through our repentance and the power of God's love toward us in the sacrifice of Christ Jesus, we can live in the courage of faith in Him, who died for us and rose again.

2nd Corinthians 5: 15

And He (Jesus) died for all, that those who live should live no longer for themselves, but for Him who died for them and rose again.

All of our actions begin with the things in our hearts, whether they are things of love, or things of hate and resentment. God, out of the abundant love in His heart has chosen to rescue us from our own fate of error. Moreover, He does not only rescue us from the drowning sea of sin, but brings us into His family as sons and daughters.

The New Heart

John 3: 3
Jesus answered and said to him, "Most assuredly, I say to you,
unless one is born again, he cannot see the kingdom of God."
A high-ranking religious ruler came to Jesus by night to ask
Him some questions. I am sure that this prominent man with a
title had many questions for this Carpenter who had no formal
religious training. We need to take a step back behind the
scene and understand that God does not show up to please or
satisfy the likes of men. In any case, here we see the men of the
ruling religious class of Israel, highly educated in the law given
to Moses, and then we see Jesus. Jesus had no titles, no degree
from the Moses University. He was a Carpenter by trade, which
means that He looked like a man from the working class of the
age. We always see these paintings of Jesus as skinny, almost
looking like He was suffering from malnutrition. This could not
have been the physical stature of Jesus during His earthly
ministry. A carpenter in those days was extremely dependant
on his physical strength. One of the demands of the job was
very heavy lifting, and anyone who has worked like that from
his youth would be physically strong, with calloused hands. On
the other hand, the rulers never lifted anything heavier than a
scroll. So here comes this fine dressed, well educated, well
versed in the law, religious ruler to Jesus the Carpenter. Now
to show how powerful the teachings and the presence of Jesus
was in the mist of these religious leaders, this leader comes to
Jesus and calls Him *"Rabbi."* What a twist, what a reversal in
roles that the educated man would call the uneducated Man a
teacher! This goes to show us that God does not play the title
game. He is not impressed by the fact that anyone might
achieve academic growth, unless it is in the knowledge of Him.
Could Jesus have known more than the teachers of the law
who were trained from their youth?
Jesus stops this religious leader right in his tracks, totally
shakes up his theology, all his years of training, all the
questions that he was ready to ask with one sentence. What
Jesus was saying to this ruler was, 'before you even get started

with all your questions, unless you are born from the birth
canal of the Spirit of God, unless you have been given spiritual
eyes and spiritual ears, you are spiritually dead, and unable to
see, nor understand the things of the Spirit.' The religious ruler
tries to reason out the words that he just heard.
John 3: 4 & 9
"How can a man be born when he is old? Can he enter a second
time in his mother's womb? "How can these things be?"
I am sure that none of these questions was on the agenda
when the ruler was planning the meeting with Jesus. With one
sentence, Jesus turns this man's theology in a nosedive crash
right into the hypocrisy of all his years of training. To this man,
this statement by Jesus about being born again was insane, out
of control, totally absent from logical reasoning. It is no
wonder why Jesus said that unless you are born from the
living seed of God, you cannot enter the kingdom of God, you
could not even see it, because you never received it by faith,
resulting in spiritual blindness.
So what is the secret, the missing piece that prevents the
ability to see the Kingdom of God? We cannot come to God
unless we come to Him by faith, and faith is not in our logical
reasoning, because God is much higher than out thoughts. Just
imagine trying to take a monkey and teach him calculus. Even
that comparison is an understatement when it comes to our
limited knowledge and God's infinite knowledge. One of the
things that bother me so much about the theory of evolution is
that the missing link, the connection between a human and an
animal is not the size of a pothole, but more like the size on the
universe.
As the religious leader who was questioning Jesus, so are the
evolutionist of today, who are limited by the blindness of
doubt and unbelief, they search in vain for an answer.
1st Corinthians 2: 14
However, the natural man does not receive the things of the
Spirit of God, for they are foolishness to him; nor can he know
them, because they are spiritually discerned.
If the natural man does not receive the things of God, then the
only way for man to receive the things of God is through the
Spirit. Moreover, if the Spirit of God has not entered your

heart, then all that is left is the natural, which is but an empty shell of flesh, bone, and marrow. For life is in the Spirit.

In the next chapter of the Gospel of John, Jesus meets a woman at a well, and though He is speaking in the Spirit, she is listening in the natural, no different from the well-educated ruler.

Jesus comes to Jacob's well, tired from the journey, He stops for a rest and something to drink. A woman comes to the well. It is interesting to see that the religious ruler who visited Jesus at night was no better off than this woman at the well who was living in sin. Spiritual blindness is not prejudice; it does not escape the educated, or the non-educated.

Jesus said to her, "Give Me a drink." John 4: 7

Jesus might have been asking for a physical drink of water, but His intentions were to shift into the spiritual. It is also interesting to note here that there was obviously nothing different about the appearance of Jesus compared to any other working person of that day. The woman at the well did not look at Jesus and think that He was somebody important. Jesus revealed His true nature by the words He spoke. Even when Jesus stood in front of these people, they could not see the King in His kingdom. There is no doubt that sin is a blindfold, a darkening of the things of God that leaves a person in a fog of doubt and confusion. The religious ruler was confused because his understanding was darkened. Jesus tells the women at the well the same message He told the ruler that came to Him by night. Without the living water of the Spirit of God, we are in the desert of despair; we thirst for the true meaning of life. Jesus tells the woman that the true living water of life is given through the Spirit of God into our spirits, and not through religious obligations. The Spirit gives life, the flesh accounts for nothing. In addition, unless we are born into the Spirit we are spiritually dead, unable to see the kingdom of God.

In the Scriptures, the spirit of a person is often referred to as the heart. God is not talking about the heart in our bodies that pumps blood, but the spirit that is the spark of life, which gives life to these bodies made from dust. Jesus tells us that the mouth is the window of the heart.

Matthew 12: 34
"For out of the abundance of the heart the mouth speaks."
How else can we know a person except by the things that he or she might say, and eventually act out those words? However, not all hearts are clearly seen by the words of the mouth. Deception is present throughout the world. Many live with the shades of lies over their hearts, but sin cannot be hidden for long. Sin always surfaces, with all of its shame and regret; it mocks all those that fall to the prey of evil, in which we all have suffered from a contaminated heart.

Matthew 5: 8
"Blessed be the pure in heart, for they shall see God."
So, if we all have been deceived by the likes of sin, and have repeatedly confessed the words of doubt and fear, even in our consistent complaining, how can anyone be pure in heart. The heart that Jesus speaks of is our spirits, the inner part that dwells in a shell of flesh and blood. Jesus has already said that the heart speaks though the vessel of our bodies, the mouth. But now, He says that the heart can also see, and *the pure in heart will see God.* However, does God use the physical eyes of the body to reveal Himself? In addition, if our hearts are contaminated with the evidence by the words of doubt that we speak, how can our hearts ever be pure and see God?

John 3: 3
"...Unless one is born again (given a new heart a new spirit) *he cannot see the kingdom of God."*
The heart is new through salvation. For us to see God, who is in His kingdom, a change has to take place, and it is a change of heart. It is not a change of mind, but a change in our hearts that no longer beats for itself, but for God. This change is referred to as a rebirth, *born from above, born anew.* It is a heart transplant that changes direction from our will to God's will. Moreover, Jesus clearly taught that without that change, we could not see God, even through *the eyes of our understanding*, the understanding of the heart. A repented heart that has been cleansed by the water of faith can see God, not physically, but through the understanding of the spirit. So, how does this transition, this change, this transformation of the heart take place? Jesus is very clear on this and it is not

subject to opinions. It all starts with a submission in obedience, through an open confession that Jesus Christ is your personal Savior. For who else can make such a claim, that through the sinless blood in His body, He paid the price for our sins on the wood, bearing the reproach of God, and suffered and died that we might have eternal life? Who else can claim to be sinless? Moreover, the testimony of eyewitnesses has been handed down to us by the forefathers of the faith, to reassure us without doubts, that not only did Jesus suffer and die for the punishment of our sin, but proved every promise to be true by the resurrection from the dead. He suffered, bore the pain of our exile from God due to sin, but was raised on the third day and was seen by many, even 500 people at one time!
John: 20: 29
Jesus said to him, "Thomas, because you have seen me, you believe. Blessed are those who have not seen and yet believed."
We might not be able to see Jesus in the natural, but all those that accepted His sacrifice for the redemption of sin, and place Him as the Lord of their lives, can see Him through a *pure heart*, a heart that has been born by faith. It all starts in the heart, and pending what is in the heart, which will be either a confession of faith in Christ, or a denial of doubt that will certainly send those souls into an eternal fire of regret. Clearly, there is no middle road, no compromising state of liking the left, but leaning to the right. There is certainly a line drawn in the sand that divides faith from doubt and without a new heart, a new spirit, we are on the wrong side.
Ezekiel 18: 30, Ezekiel 18: 31
" I will put a new heart within them, and take out the stony heart out of their flesh, and give them a heart of flesh.
Ezekiel 11: 19
"Repent, and turn from all you transgression..."
"...And get yourselves a new heart and a new spirit."
It is a failed heart that has come darkened because of sin. A cold stony heart that is unforgiving, unthankful, and unfaithful that needs to be removed, so a pure heart of God can be created.
2nd Corinthians 5: 17
Therefore, if anyone is in Christ, he is a new creation...

God changes hearts; He purifies those that place their trust in the sacrifice of Christ, and injects the heart with hope and faith. However, without Christ, without the atonement of His sacrifice, our hearts remain as stone, and unable to receive the seed of faith, which is the treasure of eternal life with God. Now with a new, pure heart comes the clarity of direction by the Holy Spirit to live in the instruction of God instead by the slavery of sin. The Scriptures clearly teach that God gives a new, pure heart through the confession of sin in repentance, opening the door of forgiveness through the acceptance of the sacrifice of Jesus Christ on the cross, which brings forth a new heart for God. However, although the heart, the spirit is new, reborn from above, it can still be easily tarnished again through the deceitfulness of sin if not directed by God. Only God can give us clarity of heart and mind through the avenue of a pure heart.

Though there are many examples of this in the Scriptures, the transformation of Moses is one of the most evident. Moses was a man who was given all the pleasures of the world on a silver platter. Raised in the King's house, all things were available for the taking. However, God changed this man so much that all the earthly pleasures that this world offered where superficial, without value, and Moses was willing to throw them all away in search for a true purpose. And although Moses did not know the whole plan of God from the start, God led him into the desert, a dry place that was free from the temptations of the pleasures of the world and purified his heart, cleansed him from the contamination of a former lifestyle. He received a new heart. He experienced a re-birth of the spirit, which brought him in position to do the will of God. God can do it for us, if we are willing to receive Him by faith. God can make all things new.

A Boy in the Light

2nd Timothy 3:16, 17
All Scripture is given by inspiration of God, and profitable for doctrine, for reproof, for correction, for instruction in righteousness, that the man of God may be thoroughly equipped for every good work.

These are the final lessons given from a profound teacher of the New Covenant, and a farewell of wise instruction to a beloved student. The Apostle Paul gives Timothy, by the directive of the Holy Spirit, some very important Christian principles, in that we can also benefit greatly. The aged veteran teacher instructs his student and us, that for every step of this life, whether in the ministry, or in the home at the kitchen table, the Scriptures must be the point of reference for our every decision and even our every spoken word. Paul wasted no time in pointing to the absolute truth of the living word of God, which by its power will take us through this journey of opposition and trials. For Scripture is the power of God against every evil, the final authority that the Holy Spirit calls *the equipment for every good work*. Without the weapon of Scripture in our lives, we have no power to overcome the consistent waves of evil that beat against us through many different avenues. Sometimes these waves are so small that we think they have no effect on us, but they do.

God tells us that the Scriptures are the holy truth and there should be no waiver in our thoughts about this fact. Paul also points out to Timothy that the Scriptures had been sown into his heart since he was a young boy and the sources that had planted the seed of faith were credible.

2nd Timothy 3: 14, 15
But you must continue in the things which you have learned and been assured of knowing from whom you have learned them, and from childhood you have known the Holy Scriptures, which are able to make you wise for salvation though faith which is in Christ Jesus.

We see the great value in the teaching of the Scriptures to a child. Timothy is but one example of many children in the

Scriptures that were raised in the knowledge of the word of God.

Proverbs 22:6

Train up a child in the way he should go, and when he is old he will not depart from it.

There is another young man in the New Testament that obviously had some strong Holy Spirit influences in his life that led him directly into the purpose of God. The young man's name is John Mark, who is the vessel that God had chosen to write what is to be believed as the first Gospel of Jesus Christ. We know that the Apostles John and Matthew were with Jesus from the beginning of His earthly ministry. We would think that one of these apostles should have been the first to write the greatest story ever told. However, we see this young man John Mark boldly write the account of God's plan for salvation for all that are willing to come to the cross of grace. Why did God elect John Mark to write the first Gospel? Let us begin with John Mark's mother.

Mark 15: 40, 41

There were also women looking on from afar, among whom were Mary Magdalene, Mary the mother of James the less and of Joses, and Salome, who followed Him and ministered to Him when He was in Galilee, and many other women who came up with Him to Jerusalem.

Mark tells us that there were *many women* who had followed Jesus that *ministered to Him in Galilee, followed Him to Jerusalem* and were at the crucifixion, *looking on from afar.* The Apostle Matthew says the same truth, almost word for word in his Gospel. John Mark's mother was named Mary. Although she is not linked to the other two women named Mary that are mentioned, the text does tells us that *many women* followed Jesus throughout His earthly ministry, even witnessing the cross.

Matthew 27: 55, 56

And many women who followed Jesus from Galilee, ministering to Him, were looking on from afar...

It is very probable that one of these *many women* that followed Jesus through His earthly ministry, and witnessed the crucifixion was Mary the mother of John Mark. There are several reasons why we can think this. We can even assume that the young boy, who would later be used to write what is believed as the first Gospel, could have sat under the feet of Jesus as He taught, healed and poured Himself out as an offering for sin. Timothy's mother and grandmother as well could have been among the many women that had band together behind the ministry of Jesus and gave into His ministry. We can also safely assume that where a mother is, so are her children.

Mark 10: 13

Then they brought little children to Him that He might touch them...

Any mother that was in the presence of Jesus must have huddled their children around Jesus for a blessing, for a mother's heart is with their children. Where there are many women, we find many children. One of those children could have been the vessel that God was going to use to write the first account of His mercy. Jesus could have well touched John Mark with the anointing to write the first account of the events that would change the world forever.

Mark 10: 16

And He took them up in His arms, laid His hands on them, and blessed them.

I believe that every child that Jesus touched was changed forever. We must also understand that it is like walking on a tightrope when we begin filling in the missing spaces of Scripture by our own assumptions. We are by no means attempting to add opinion, or subtract any holy truth to Scripture. However, God does reveal to us through Scripture the importance of feeding the word of God to a child from an early age. We certainly do not want to stray from that truth. Nevertheless, it is important to show the strong influence that this young child had, as he watched devoted parents and relatives give themselves to the ministry of Jesus. Moreover, this child could have been a witness to more of the ministry of Jesus than we think.

Concerning the question of how close this mother and her son were to the ministry of Jesus, we see in the book of Acts that their house became a place of prayer. It was also the first place where the Apostle Peter went to when he was set free from prison by a supernatural act of God.

At times when an investigator is attempting to fill in the spaces of the facts in a case, he or she will often attempt to place themselves in that situation. If we look at the circumstances with Peter's arrest, we will see that his life was certainly in danger. King Herod, that drunk that was dressed up as a king, had just murdered the Apostle James. The Scriptures tell us that since this murder pleased the Jews, King Herod said to himself, 'the Jews finally like something I did,' and proceeded to go after Peter. Therefore, Peter must have assumed that this was his time to go and be with the Lord. What is also very interesting in this text is Peter's reaction to this threat. If again, we would place ourselves in Peter's position, knowing that the time is near for us to depart and stand before God, most of us would have acted differently. Peter leaves us an example of faith that should certainly help us through our restless nights of worry. Moreover, this is a position that all of us will be in one day. The apostle, who now could be facing the final time on this earth, reacts to the threats of the King with a good night's sleep. Yes, while most of us would have stayed up all night praying on our faces for God to rescue us out of the hands of a death trap that Peter was in, Peter decided to sleep. Peter was sleeping so deeply that an angel had to hit him to wake him up. Even when he was walking out of the prison, he was still half asleep, because he did not even know if his rescue was really happening or a dream. Someone taking his earthly life obviously did not threaten Peter. After experiencing such a powerful move of God, as a manifestation of an angel leading him out in prison, we would think that Peter would want to run to the ones closest to his heart to tell them what he had just witnessed. After all, when we receive great news in our lives, the first people we want to tell are those closest to our hearts, whether it might be our spouses, our parents or friends. The first place Peter runs is Mary's house in Jerusalem, were John Mark and others were there in constant prayer on Peter's behalf. Peter's spouse might have also been there. This again tells us that Mary, the mother of John Mark was close to the ministry of Peter, and John Mark heard these things firsthand. The relationship becomes so close between Peter and John Mark that Peter refers to him as his son.

1st Peter 5: 13

She in Babylon, elect together with you, greets you; and so does my son Mark.

The Holy Spirit makes it a point to show us the closeness between Mary, John Mark and Peter. Now Mary had a relative, his name was Barnabas. Yes, this same Barnabas was chosen by the Holy Spirit to team up with the Apostle Paul for the first missionary journey of the infant church.

Acts 13: 2

As they ministered to the Lord and fasted, the Holy Spirit said, "Now separate for Me Barnabas and Saul (Paul), *for the work to which I have called them."*

So now we see this young man John Mark with an active mother of faith, who had all night prayer meetings in her own home. We also see a relative that was hand chosen by God to team up with the Apostle Paul and bring the light of the Gospel into the total darkness of the Gentile world. This young boy was taught Christ from every direction. He was grounded on the foundation of Jesus Christ from a loving mother, nurtured by a respected, knowledgeable relative, thought of as a son by the Apostle Peter and sat under the teaching of the Apostle Paul. Moreover, John Mark is thought of with such high regards, that he is invited to go with the Apostles Paul and Barnabas on the first mission.

Acts 13: 5

They also had John Mark as their assistant.

We can easily see the results of feeding any child the true bread of Jesus Christ from an early age. The very fiber of the Holy Spirit is sown, cross-threaded in a child's spirit, which is like a blanket that has been knitted with two different types of yarn and when the blanket is completed, it is one.

We also see something happen on the first mission, in that the Holy Spirit makes it a point to record. For reasons unknown to us, John Mark decides to leave the missionary journey before it ended. Maybe he left to begin writing the Gospel, in any event, he went back home.

Acts 13: 13

John, departing from them, returned to Jerusalem.
What is so interesting about his decision is that it caused a
division between Barnabas and Paul later. We would think
that such knowledgeable teachers of Christ's eternal love
would be able to work their differences out. The division came
when the two men were planning their second missionary
journey and Barnabas desired to take John Mark along. Paul
refused, causing a split of the dynamic duo.
Acts 15: 37, 38, and 39
Now Barnabas was determined to take with them John Mark.
But Paul insisted that they should not take with them the one
who had departed from them in Pamphylia, and had not gone
with them to work. The contention became so sharp that they
parted from one another.
Barnabas was *determined* to take Mark, but Paul *insisted* not to
take him. We can see that when one is *determined*, and another
insisted with no compromise, the result was separation. This is
a lesson we all need to learn concerning friendship, family
matters and most of all marriage. Barnabas felt so strongly
about the desire to bring John Mark on the second mission,
that he was willing to sacrifice his relationship with Paul. It is
interesting how the Holy Spirit makes it a point to show us
that Paul and Barnabas were far from perfect, and certainly
made errors in this instance and in other situations as well.
This example teaches us that all men are imperfect because of
sin, except the one Man that has no sin, Jesus Christ. After all,
we would think that two teachers chosen by God would have
at the very least compromise their difference of opinions.
Instead, we see the two men that the Holy Spirit had
commanded to work together, depart from one another.
Therefore, because of their differences, they were not obedient
to the command of God, for the Holy Spirit sent them out
together as a team and not solo.
On the other hand, we see Paul miss the boat on this one, for
later in his ministry, Paul requested that John Mark come to
him, because he was an asset to his work.
2nd Timothy 4: 11
Only Luke is with me. Get Mark and bring him with you, for he is
useful to me for ministry.

I believe that John Mark was also very useful to Barnabas, later useful to Paul, and useful to God in writing what is to be believed as the first Gospel account. John Mark could have been an eyewitness to the earthly ministry of Jesus Christ as a young boy. He not only could have witnessed the death of Jesus, but also the resurrected Christ as well. Mark mentions a young man in his Gospel who *followed* Jesus and His disciples to the Mount of Olives and witnesses the arrest of the Lord. Many believe that Mark was writing of himself, which would indicate that he was an eyewitness to more of the ministry than just the arrest. Anyone who follows Jesus has a desire, and that is to get closer to Him.

Mark 14: 51 & 52

Now a certain young man followed Him (Jesus), *having a linen cloth thrown around his naked body. And the young men* (those who came to arrest Jesus), *laid hold of him, and he left the linen cloth and fled from them naked.*

For Paul also testifies that those who followed Jesus from Galilee to Jerusalem, the many that witnessed His death on the cross, also saw Him alive in the resurrection power of God. Again, he tells us that over *five hundred brethren* saw the Lord Jesus Christ alive after His death on the cross. The young John Mark could have been one of them.

Acts 13: 31

"He was seen for many days (After the resurrection), *by those who came up with Him from Galilee to Jerusalem who are His witnesses to the people."*

1st Corinthians 15: 6

After that (seen by the twelve after the resurrection), *He was seen by over five hundred brethren at once, of whom some remain to present, but some have fallen asleep.*

The infant church was a very tight, close group of believers. Those many women that had followed Jesus, by no means had lost their reward, they had witnessed the risen Christ. The Scriptures gives us some hints that Mary the mother of John Mark had indeed witnessed this miraculous promise of God. Moreover, this must have greatly influenced the life of a young boy named John Mark. It is true that we do not know the age of this boy, and the Scriptures do not directly state that his

account of the earthly ministry of Christ was an eyewitness testimony. However, we do know that John Mark, his mother Mary and his household were part of the first stones to be set in place in the building of the New Covenant church. Moreover, John Mark leads the stone setters with the written testimony of truth, the account of Jesus Christ that would be declared as Holy Scripture for generations to come, even till the end of the age. Even the Apostle Paul, who criticized the young man's actions for leaving the first mission, had requested that John Mark might come to him later in his ministry. John Mark, who obviously was held in high esteem by the apostle, did join Paul.
Philemon 1: 23 & 24
Ephaphars, my fellow prisoner in Christ Jesus greets you, as do Mark, Aristarchus, Demas and Luke, my fellow laborers.
Colossians 4: 10
Aristarchus my fellow prisoner greets you; with Mark the cousin of Barnabas...
The above text shows us that John Mark had spent some time with the Apostle Paul, but also with Luke. Paul and Luke must have learned about some great things concerning the earthly ministry of Christ from John Mark, since we know that Mark's family was on the ground floor of the building of the young church. I would also reach out to say that Luke must have received some of his information to write his Gospel according to John Mark's testimony. Luke tells us from the beginning that he was not an eyewitness, but received the Gospel through eyewitness accounts, and one of those accounts could have been John Mark. While John Mark makes no claim of being an eyewitness, or not being an eyewitness
Luke 1: 1 & 2
Inasmuch as many have taken in hand to set in order a narrative of those things which have been fulfilled among us, just as those who from the beginning were eyewitnesses and ministers of the word delivered them to us
Luke declares three truths through the Holy Spirit to set his Gospel apart from the others.
- He first states that there were many accounts given of the Gospel of Jesus Christ. That amount of many would define more than four. If it were only four Gospels, he would have

said a few accounts and not many. We do not know how many Gospels were written, and how many were accurate.

- The second truth is that he received these testimonies from eyewitnesses. One of them could have been John Mark, since we do know that Luke had spent time with him, both being in the company of Paul.
- The third truth is that Luke, like a reporter of news, reports the greatest news in all of history in an orderly account. I believe that John Mark was instrumental to Luke and Paul in setting forth the truth of the Gospel of Jesus Christ, since many others were giving an account, and some may have been grossly inaccurate.

Luke testifies that the reason his account is written is to also establish the certainty of the truth that was passed down by eyewitnesses.

Luke 1: 4

...That you may know the certainty of those things in which you were instructed.

From a Spirit filled believing mother, an evangelist relative, two role model apostles, and what he had witnessed with his own eyes, even in the ministries of Peter and Paul; we have a young man chosen to record the greatest story ever told. This shows us that if any child is exposed to the presence of God through family and friends with consistency, the result will be glory to God through Jesus Christ, by the power of the Holy Spirit in their lives. While John Mark could have been in the presence of the earthly ministry of Jesus, there is no doubt that he experienced the glorified presence of the risen Christ by faith.

Mark 16: 16

"He who believes and is baptized will be saved."

Mark records the ultimate truth. Our eternities depend on the truth. The truth of the Gospel is a simple message, but it is the most wonderful news given to all of creation. It is the redeeming power of God's mercy toward man, defined by God as a gift, something we could never afford to earn or buy, even with all our so-called righteousness, which God defines as nothing more than *filthy rags*. As we know that the Apostles

John and Matthew were eyewitnesses to the testimony of Jesus Christ, and while Luke was a reporter gathering the facts, John Mark could possibly have had the best view of them all; seeing Christ through the eyes of a child. Moreover, as John Mark grew into adulthood, so did the church, both raised in sound doctrine on the solid foundation of Christ. Jesus taught us how to build the house of a marriage, a church and certainly the house of a child. The Master Builder uses the same foundation that every house needs to be built on, which is Jesus Christ!

Matthew 7: 24

"Therefore, whoever hears these sayings of Mine, and does them, I will liken him to be a wise man who built his house on the rock."

There should be no doubt in our hearts that as John Mark, Timothy and many others in the Scriptures that were nurtured with the true bread of life from an early age, became floodlights for God. Moreover, the mission of this message will not end until Christ returns.

John Mark's mother Mary and his cousin Barnabas built this child's life on the sure foundation of Jesus Christ. Mark records these powerful words from the risen Christ.

Mark 16: 16 - 18

"He who believes and is baptized will be saved; but he who does not believe will be condemned. And these signs will follow those who believe; In My name they will cast out demons; they will speak with new tongues; they will take up serpents; and if they drink anything deadly, it will by no means hurt them; they will lay hands on the sick and they will recover."

Though we may not be able to prove that Mark was an eyewitness of the earthly ministry of Christ, we do know that through the people closest to him, Christ was revealed. The young boy of faith became a man of faith, because the light of truth was nurtured in him, so that Christ was not a mystery, but a reality. Moreover, we may not know why Mark decided to leave the first mission with Paul, but we do know that Mark was instrumental in laying down the foundation of the true gospel of Jesus Christ, and spreading the greatest news that has ever been preached on the earth, or in heaven with accuracy.

Mark 16:20
And they went out and preached everywhere, the Lord working
with them and confirmed the word through the accompanying
signs.

Turn From Sin

Mark 1: 4, Mark 1: 15
*John came baptizing in the wilderness and preaching a baptism
of repentance for the remission of sins."*
*Now after John was put in prison, Jesus came preaching the
gospel of the kingdom of God and saying, "The time is fulfilled,
and the kingdom of God is at hand, repent, and believe in the
gospel.*

The last Old Testament prophet, who was chosen to prepare
the way for the Savior of the world, delivers a message that I
am sure was not politically correct, or sympathetic to the sin
of the people in that day. John pulled no punches as he tells
the people you need to repent. So, what is repentance?
Repentance is not only confessing to God as a request for the
forgiveness of past committed sins. Repentance also means to
change one's mind and purpose from evil to good, from death
to life, from our way to God's way of thinking. Repentance is
the seat of moral reflection that has been enlighten by the
word of God.
John is then thrown into prison, and Jesus picks it up were
John left off. If this is the truth, then we must realize and fully
understand what sin is. Sin is simply rebellion against what
God has already spoken. If God said not to do something, and
we do it anyway, it is sin. So, what are some of the things God
tells us not to do?
Romans 1: 28 – 3, 2: 2, 1st Corinthians 6: 9 & 10
*Being filled with all unrighteousness, sexual immorality,
wickedness, covetousness, maliciousness, full of envy, murder,
strive, deceit, evil minded,; they are whisperers, backbiters,
haters of God, violent, boasters, inventors of evil things,
disobedient to parents, undiscerning, unforgiving, unmerciful...
But we know that the judgment of God is according to truth
against those who practice such things*
 *Neither fornicators, nor idolaters, nor adulterers, nor
homosexuals, nor sodomites, nor thieves, nor covetous, nor
drunkards, nor revilers, nor extortionist, will inherit the
kingdom of God.*

God could not have made it any clearer that those that practice such things, or have made some or all of these things a lifestyle, will not be allowed in the kingdom of God and will spend eternity in the place outside the kingdom of God, which is judgment. Now some people might be quick to argue that the Scriptures clearly state that we are saved by grace. So then, if we are saved by the mercy of God and not by our so-called good conduct, how can a confessed believer lose his or her eternal salvation by sin if we are saved by faith? To answer that question let's begin to look at what Jesus said about how someone can enter into the kingdom of God. Jesus said to *repent and believe.* Now we just stated that repentance means to ask for forgiveness from past sins, with the intent to change, so as to not repeat the same sins. He goes on to say that if we *believe* God by faith, that He will empower us with His grace to be victorious over our past, and then change will come. However, if someone says that they *repented*, and says that they *believe,* but remains in the same mud hole of sin, unable to break the chains of bondage from evil, then it is not a matter of someone losing his or her salvation, but the sincerity of their repentance and their faith is in question. The Scriptures tell us that *whatever is not done in faith is sin.* Repentance and faith in Jesus Christ will bring forth a renewing, cleansing of the spirit when confessing sin, and confessing hope in Christ. However, we still have a free will, we still have a mind that has been tainted by the darkness of sin, and we still have the continued outside influences of an evil world that will consistently try to derail our faith in God. Therefore, if our repentance is not sincere, then we will never be able to resist the storms of temptation that will crash against the shores of our minds. This is what Jesus taught when He gives the parable of the sower and the seed.

Matthew 13: 20 & 21

"But he who received the seed on a stony place, this is he who hears the word and immediately receives it with joy; yet he has no root in himself but endures only for a while."

A cold stony heart cannot deeply receive the word of God without repentance. A confession of repentance cleans and softens the heart so the seed, the word of God, is able to take root, melt, fuse into the heart, and become a cornerstone in a new building of life with God. Moreover, the only way to truly ask God to cleanse us, change us, and establish our hearts is to give Him our hearts. For it is God's will and not our own, that is able to defeat every enemy that stands in opposition in our lives to the word of God. When Jesus gave the example of the word of God falling on a stony heart, He was not teaching about someone losing his or her salvation, He was showing us someone who never had it to begin with. Sincere repentance will always bring forth change. However, with no repentance, then there can be no forgiveness. No forgiveness, no peace, with no peace, there is no power to change, and with no change, more sin knocks at the door. Jesus said, *"Unless a man be born again* (born from above), *he cannot see the kingdom of God."* And how is someone born from above? Jesus said, *"Repent and believe."*

The wages of sin is death. However, the wages for our sin has already been paid for on the cross of Christ, as He made Himself a one-time sacrifice for the remission of our sins. The price has been paid in full, but we must acknowledge that we have sinned, and by the righteous judgment of God, we should die. Therefore, in the acknowledgment that we are sinners by nature, and asking God to forgive our sins by the power of the sacrifice of Jesus Christ, we are forgiven, and excepted in the beloved, but now must walk in His love as a *new creature in Christ; old things are now done away.* However, if we confess Christ as our sacrifice, and do not walk in the *newness of life,* which Jesus Christ paid for with His own blood, then we must wonder how sincere our commitment to Christ is. After all, He gave His all for us, that we should not perish in the judgment of God, outside the kingdom of God, where *the worm die not, and the fire is not quenched.* Jesus used this phrase repeatedly to express the torment of those that are outside the kingdom of God. Yes, many will denounce this truth, but Jesus was very clear in teaching that there is suffering after death for all those that reject the mercy of God in the sacrifice of Jesus Christ. Yes, by a fallen nature that we inherited from Adam and Eve, we are sinners, and bound with chains of slavery to our every offense. However, God by His mercy does not want us to stay in this fallen state, so He parted the sea of sin, in that we were drowning and created a pathway of dry land that leads to the cross of Christ. God spared no expense, but *gave His only begotten Son, that whoever, would believe in Him should not perish* into the sea of God's judgment reserved for fallen angels and evil men, *but have eternal life* for His names sake. God did not make ten paths, or five paths that lead to the mercy and grace of His love. He made one path and the only place that path leads to is the cross of Jesus Christ, who is the only sacrifice powerful enough to pay the price for our sin, in that just by believing in His sacrifice we are saved from judgment. However, how can you *repent, believe* in the sacrifice of Jesus Christ on the cross, and not be a *new creature*? After being cleansed from the mud of unrighteousness, how can we return to the mud hole, to the very sin that blinded us from the truth of Christ, and kept us as slaves to the call of death? For those that *fall away* from the truth of God for the salvation of our souls, and return to the same lifestyle of sin, pollute the *new creature in Christ* and lives again to fulfill every want and desire of the flesh, but does not seek to please God.

2nd Peter 2: 20 & 21

For if after they have escaped the pollutions of the world through the knowledge of the Lord and Savior Jesus Christ, they are again entangled in them and overcome, the latter is worse than the beginning. For it would have been better for them not to have known the way of righteousness, then having known it, to turn from the holy commandment delivered to them.

Sin is a murderer; it steals our lives in a vacuum of darkness and death. It robs us of any eternal vision, so that all that is left is what we can see in the natural, which is quickly fading. Sin is the veil that separates us from a holy, faithful, truthful, and righteous God. Sin is the stench of human failure that is a consistent reminder that humanity has indeed failed, and will continue to fail without the intervention of God. The witness to this is in the headlines of every current newspaper, that almost seems to take pleasure in magnifying the corruption of man in a world that refuses to repent, much like in the days of Noah, but continually chases after the very sin that holds the promise of death.

Galatians 5: 19 – 21
Now the works of the flesh are evident, which are; adultery,
fornication, uncleanness, lewdness, idolatry, sorcery, hatred,
contentions, jealousies, outburst of wrath, selfish ambition,
dissensions, heresies, envy, murders, drunkenness, reveries, and
the like;, of which I tell you before hand, just as I also told you in
times past, that those who practice such things will not inherit
the kingdom of God.

All of the above are the works of the sinful nature, in which
will control our lives, unless we have been born from the Spirit
of God. Although we might not comment all the acts listed
above, our nature is drawn to some or all if we have not
entered into the kingdom of God. For God's kingdom is a place
of the heart for now, and where our hearts we will be when we
leave these earthly shells. Unless we repent, and believe, trust
in the Lord Jesus Christ to help us change from a selfish,
greedy, cold-hearted sin-centered nature, to a Christ-centered,
giving and compassionate nature, then we simply cannot enter
into His kingdom, but are left out in the coldness of judgment,
outside the warm embrace of God's tender mercies. For while
many put on a mask of a smile and a laugh, the inside is
drenched with tears of sorrow and discontent, because the
judgment of death is a constant reminder of an absence of
hope. For the only hope for eternal life is in Christ Jesus alone.

2nd Peter 3: 9
The Lord is not slacked concerning His promise, as some count
slackness, but is longsuffering, toward us, not willing that any
should perish, but that all should come to repentance.

 A great way to dig deeper in the importance of repentance,
and even gain some insight of God's loving forgiveness is to
read the Book of Jonah.

Jonah 1: 1 & 2
Now the word of the Lord came to Jonah the son of Amittai,
saying, "Arise, and go to Nineveh, that great city, and cry out
against it; for their wickedness has come before Me."

This might be a favorite bedtime story for little hearts, but it is
packed with rich insight into the heart of God. Many people
looked upon this event a just a parable, pure fiction and just an
example of how God deals with disobedience. However, Jesus

confirmed this story as an historical fact. He underlines the importance of the event to reinforce that repentance is essential. Jesus used the fish in the story of Jonah to compare with His death and resurrection.

Matthew 12: 40

"For as Jonah was three days and three nights in the belly of the great fish, so will the Son of Man be three days and three nights in the heat of the earth."

Jesus also uses the story to show the power of God's judgment.

Matthew 12: 38

But He (Jesus) *answered and said to them, "An evil and adulterous generation seeks after a sign, and no sign will be given to it except the sign of the prophet Jonah."*

Oddly enough in the same chapter in the Gospel of Matthew, Jesus was healing multitudes of people. Even a man that was *demon-possessed, blind, and mute* was healed. Therefore, what sign were the Pharisees looking for? They were witnessing super-natural healing by the power of God day after day. However, anyone that has not repented is a blind and hardened heart, unable see or hear the things of God. Jesus goes on to tell the ruling class of religious leaders that the sinful men of Nineveh, even in their *wickedness* repented and you have not in your costume of religion.

Matthew 12: 41

"The men of Nineveh will rise up in judgment with this generation and condemn it, because they repented at the preaching of Jonah and indeed a greater than Jonah is here.

Jesus used the story of Jonah as a clear example of His death, resurrection, the importance of repentance, and the outcome of those that do not repent and believe in the power of Jesus Christ to change and transform the sinner's life of death to a life that is full with the rich mercies of God. It is the abundant life, the eternal life that God freely offers that was paid for by the sacrificial blood of Christ, which is now rooted in the kingdom of God. Jesus used the experience of Jonah to bring clarity to God's judgment without repentance, so we might know that salvation can only happen in we truly repent, and allow God to change our thinking from the world's thoughts, to His thoughts.

Now in the very first verse in the Book of Jonah, we see that God was putting out His hand of mercy to a very corrupt city. God tells us that their *wickedness* was so great that it *came before* Him. Even though their wickedness was great, God wanted Jonah to give them a stern warning that they must repent, change from their evil ways, to the good ways of the Lord, that they might be saved from the judgment that was to come. Now one of the most interesting parts about this story is that Nineveh was a sinful city. Let us just take a better look at what God was commanding Jonah to do. This was a non-believing, anti-God, anti-Israelite and an actual enemy of the nation of Israel. They hated the Israelites and had already dominated much of the northern kingdom of Israel. That would be like sending a Christian-Jew in the heart of Iran today to tell them that they must repent and turn to Jesus Christ. Jonah has gotten a bad rap over the years in thinking that he did want to go to Nineveh because he simply was rebellious against God. After all, Moses did not want to go back to Egypt when God told him to go, he was in fear of his life, and I am sure Jonah felt no different. As the story goes on, Jonah, basically tells God that you have the wrong guy for the job, just as Moses did, and starts making tracks in the opposite direction. How many times have we all done that? God says to go right, and we are running a hard left. We should all know by now, God always wins! We can run from the truth as hard and as fast as we can, but we cannot out run God. Johan's faith in God was overcome by fear. I think we can safely say that we have all been there at sometime in our lives. Jonah is on the run, and he is running, and running, but he is getting nowhere, much like the Israelites that walked in circles in the desert of unbelief, doubt, and complaining. Well God boxes Jonah in a corner, Jonah jumps ship and finds himself in real deep water. A great fish meets up with him and has him for an appetizer. At the bottom of Jonah's life, stuck in the belly of a fish, swimming around in there with all the seaweed, and God knows what else, Jonah meets up with God through repentance. Yes, I know that this story might be a little hard to swallow, but it was not for Jonah. His prayer is much like a psalm of repentance, and ends with a voice and heart of thanksgiving.

Jonah 2: 9
"But I will sacrifice to You (God), *with the voice of thanksgiving."*
Jonah was hurting with regret in the belly of the fish, but he
did not hesitate to thank God, because he knew that God still
cared, Although Jonah ran from the presence of the Lord, and
understood his own lack of faith in God, he also knew that God
heard his prayer. The fish on the shoreline then vomits Jonah
out, who was a complete mess by now. There is a good
possibility that there were witnesses that had seen Jonah come
out of the fish, which certainly would have gave some
attention to his warnings.

As we read on in the book, we realize that Jonah did not want
God to have mercy on the people of Nineveh. Therefore,
without the experience of being in the belly of a fish for three
days, even if Jonah went to Nineveh, he would not have been
very convincing. He would have told the people of that city to
repent half-heartedly, probably hoping that they would not, so
God's judgment would come upon them. However, after that
experience, Jonah must have been so convincing with his
testimony, that the city was frightened. They must have seen
the God-fearing reverence in his eyes as he told them, *"Yet
forty days Nineveh shall be over thrown."* Jonah was so
convincing that the people themselves declared a fast. Even
the King began to preach repentance.

Jonah 3: 8 & 9
*"Let very one turn from his evil way and from the violence that is
in his hands. Who can tell if God will turn and relent and turn
away from us His fierce anger, so that we may not perish?"*
The king knew that if the people turned from evil, repented,
then just maybe God would turn from His anger. And that is
what God did. He heard their cries; saw their fasting and God
knew that they were serious about repentance. Repentance,
turning away from the very evil that would like to kill us all if it
could, is the best thing we could ever do. Remember the
opening statement from Jesus as He first began to travel from
city to city. Jesus said the same thing to the Israelites as Jonah
said to the people of Nineveh, 'repent before it is too late, for
the judgment of God, who *is angry with the wicked everyday* is
at the door. This should certainly be the same message to a

dying world that *cannot discern between their right hand and their left.*

Romans 6: 23
For the wages of sin is death, but the gift of God is eternal life in Christ Jesus our Lord.

Repentance is not only for unbelievers who need to be saved, but it is also for the church. In the Book of Revelation, the Lord strongly rebukes the church of the Laodicea's, and tells them to repent. It is obvious that the church was beginning to go through the motions of church, but lost their passion for God along the way.

Revelation 3: 15 & 16
"I know your works, that are neither cold nor hot. I could wish you were cold or hot. So then, because you are lukewarm, and neither cold or hot, I will vomit you out of My mouth."

Jonah was vomited out of the mouth of the big fish because he did repent, but here Jesus tells the church that unless they repent, change from a religious ritual organization, to a living church that offers thankfulness and praise to God from a true heart and not from obligation, then we will be vomited from His mouth.

I learned some time ago that a child might not listen to everything that you say, but he or she will certainly listen to what you do. Actions do speak louder than words. And the world in no different than the child as they might hear the promises of the freedom from sin in Christ, but unless they see it, the message is just an empty, well-rehearsed phrase with no power.

Revelation 3: 19
"As many as I love, I rebuke and chasten. Therefore be zealous and repent."

Jesus is not speaking to the world of unbelievers, but to the church, the ones who have openly confessed Christ. Jesus tells the church to be eager about repentance. Do not wait until the believing heart grows cold and begins to go through the religious exercises of a service.

135

Psalm 32: 5
I acknowledge my sin to you, and my iniquity I have not hidden. I said, "I will confess my transgression to the Lord. And you forgave the iniquity of my sin."
I can see why God called David *a man after My own heart.* Even though David really missed the mark on his journey, (David was far from perfect), he knew how to ask God for forgiveness. We all can certainly learn from the words of this Psalm. The first thing David did was to acknowledge his sin to the Lord. There was no tap dancing, no excuses, no telling God that the devil made me do it. David took the blame, and therefore, agreed with God that *all have sinned a fall short of the glory of God.* David does not try to hide his sin from God, but confesses it in a plea to change.

Psalm 32: 6
For this cause, everyone who is Godly shall pray to You.
David made his share of mistakes, but he always knew that if you are honest with God, no matter what kind of trouble you might be in, God is faithful to forgive. It does not matter how bad the sin might be, God is ready, willing and able to throw our sin in the *sea of forgetfulness, as far as the east is from the west.*

Fruits

Galatians 5: 19, 22
Now the works of the flesh are evident...
But the fruit of the Spirit is...
Paul, through the inspiration of the Spirit writes to the church
(we are the church), that there are two different behavior
patters, two different life styles, two different leaderships that
we follow, and are evident. They are easily recognizable and
cannot be mistaken if we see through the eyes of our
understanding. Paul speaks about this *understanding* in a more
than one of his letters to the church.
Ephesians 4: 17.18. 5: 17
...You should no longer walk as the rest of the Gentiles
(unbelievers), *in the futility of their mind, having their*
understanding darkened, being alienated from the life of God,
because of the ignorance that is in them, because of the
blindness of their heart,,,
Therefore, do not be unwise, understand what the will of the
Lord is.
The flesh, the carnal mind, the mind that is fixed on self has no
understanding of *what the will of the Lord is.* Sin is a darkness
that covers our *understanding* like a blindfold would cover our
physical eyes. It prevents us from *understanding* the loving
kindness and giving nature of God. Either we have
understanding, or we do not concerning the things pertaining
to life. The *understanding* that Paul wrote about can come only
through the Spirit of God. It is the *understanding* of the truth of
God, as the Spirit of God bears witness to that truth. God has
given us the Spirit of truth, and if we are in Christ, then we
abide in the truth and can discern the difference between what
is of the truth and what is not. We are either in Christ, or not.
And if we are not in Christ, then the truth escapes us and we
believe the lie. Jesus said; *"The truth will make you free."* Free
from what, you might ask. Free from the lie that contaminates
our spirits and our minds with doubt and unbelief, and this is
where sin is cultivated. When we begin to trust ourselves, or
even other beings above God, we are destined to fall, no

different than Adam and Eve. However, we have a choice to make.

Now there are many places in the Scriptures where God clearly identifies two choices, two ways, two paths, and two very different outcomes at the end. The domination of the flesh is contrary to the leading of the Spirit, just as truth is contrary to a lie, and light is contrary to darkness. At times, this can cause a war within ourselves as the Spirit leads us in all truth, but the flesh (the carnal nature), is resistant, and is willing to listen to the lie. The direction of the flesh is clear and easily identifiable. It is simply the works of sin, and the works of sin lead to death, there is no life in them. The works of the flesh are also very temporary. Yes, it might appear that some people are committing crimes and escaping the consequences, but God is the final Judge and no one escapes His final word.

Galatians 5" 19 - 21

Now the works of the flesh are evident, which are, adultery, fornication, uncleanness, lewdness, idolatry, sorcery, hatred, contentions, jealousies, outburst of wrath, selfish ambitions, dissensions, heresies, envy, murder, drunkenness, revelries, , and the like of which I tell you beforehand, just as I also told you in time past, that those who practice such things will not inherit the kingdom of God.

What is Paul saying here through the inspiration of the Holy Spirit? The works of the flesh are obvious and are clearly displayed by a lifestyle that is a result of a lack of *understanding* concerning the *will of the Lord*. Now some people will state that they are a believer, a disciple of Jesus Christ and claim that they are Spirit-filled. However, if the lifestyle does not coincide with the confession, then the fruit is evident. After all, an apple tree produces apples, not peaches. Can a fig tree produce oranges? A tree or a plant are identified by what fruit it produces, and we are no different. We are not speaking about judgment, that belongs to God, but indentifying, even in searching our own hearts. Can we say that we are believers in Christ, yet act as if we are not and still claim that we are? Jesus said; *"You will know a tree by its fruit."*

Now Paul wrote to the Galatians, the Ephesians, the Corinthians, and the Colossians teaching the same principles, the same doctrine, that those you walk according to the flesh, will inherit the corruption of the flesh, which is sin, which is death.

1st Corinthians 9: 9, 10,

Neither fornicators, nor idolaters, nor adulterers, nor homosexuals, nor sodomites, nor thieves, nor covetous, nor, drunkards, nor revilers, nor extortionist will inherit the kingdom of God.

There is no place for sin in the kingdom of God. Now this is not to say that anyone who is held in bondage to sin, cannot receive redemption in Christ Jesus from that sin. Forgiveness is always there in Christ, through repentance. However, the deeper and longer that sin abides in our lives, the further we drift away from God. As a lost sheep that drifts further away from the shepherd, it is isolated, unprotected, and easy prey. Sin is also as a vine that grows around a pole, and before you know it, that vine is completely attached to the pole and the only way to separate them is to cut the vine away. God can and will cut sin away from us by cleaning our sin stained spirits with His sacrificial blood that was shed for this very reason on the cross. Of course, we still have the freewill to go back to the vine garden and be tangled up in sin again. And without the true light of God that lightens our *understanding* concerning the dangers of sin, we will end up in a worst vine garden then before. Paul prays for the church, that we may receive the *knowledge of His will in all wisdom and understanding.* For it is in the *eyes of our understanding* that we may see the Lord in the light of His love for us.

Colossians 1: 9, 10

For this reason we also, since the day we heard it, do not cease to pray for you, and to ask that you may be filled with the knowledge of His will in all wisdom and understanding; that you may walk worthy of the Lord, fully pleasing Him.

Now Paul continues in his letters to expose the works of the flesh and warns the church not follow the world of unbelief. For that kingdom, which referred to as the *kingdom of darkness,* is a kingdom without the light of God in their understanding. Peter calls it *short sighted*, even to the point of *blindness* concerning the things of God. It is a place of stumbling in the darkness of sin, committing the same errors, and expecting different results. Jesus called it *the blind leading the blind and both will fall into a pit.* This is why we need *the eyes of our understanding enlightened* by the power of God. Paul wrote strongly to the Ephesians, reminding them that sin is dangerous and should be avoided at all cost.

Ephesians 5: 3 – 5, 4: 31, 4: 29, 4: 19

But fornication and all uncleanness or covetousness, let it not even be named among you, as is fitting for saints; neither filthiness, nor foolishness talking, nor coarse jesting, which are not fitting, but rather giving of thanks,

For you know that, that no fornicator, unclean person, nor covetous man, who is an idolater, has any inheritance in the kingdom of Christ and God.

Let all bitterness, wrath, anger, clamor, and evil speaking be put away from you, with all malice.

Let no corrupt word proceed from your mouth.

These are the fruits of the spirit of darkness, which blinds the eyes of those who are perishing, holding their souls in bondage with deception.

Now the Sprit of God is light, He gives us a clear understanding of truth, true joy, and peace in love. God gives us His Spirit *without measure* to those who seek Him. The fruit of the Spirit are also easily recognizable. For the fruit of the Spirit is unlike the sour fruit of darkness, which is saturated with selfishness and greed, which also leads to spiritual corrosion and death. For the fruit of the Spirit is life.

Galatians 6: 22, 23, Ephesians 5: 2

But the fruit of the Spirit is love, joy, peace, longsuffering, kindness, goodness, faithfulness, gentleness, self-control.

And be kind to one another, tenderhearted, forgiving one another, even as God in Christ forgave you.

And walk in love as Christ has loved us...

The fruit of the Spirit is a reflection of who God is, just as our fruit reflects who we are. And if the Sprit of God is in us, then His fruit is reflected in us. God wants to reveal His love to the lost and tormented people in the world, and He wants to use us to do it. What higher honor could we have then to be *co-workers with God, ambassadors for Christ*? What greater achievement could there be, to help save a soul from eternal destruction? Moreover, this can only be accomplished by the power of the love of God. Without that power, we are just *a sounding brass or a clanging cymbal.* Without the love of Christ in our hearts, we are just a bunch of noise, and an annoying noise at that.

Paul writes the same message to the church in Corinth concerning the fruit of the Spirit in a different presentation, focusing on the importance of God's love in us.

1ˢᵗ Corinthians 13: 4
Love suffers long and is kind; love does not envy; love does not parade itself, it is not puffed up.

The fruit of the Spirit is love, which, *suffers long and is kind.* It is obvious that the fruit of the Spirit is also humility in love, which is *tenderhearted,* with *self-control.* Such fruits are a witness, a neon sign that expresses God's love to a lost and unbelieving world. Moreover, without such fruits, our impact to testify as a living witness to the mercy and love of God is just a bunch of annoying noise. God has given us His Spirit that we may speak His word without fear, but also, so we may live His word without doubt. That takes power, and God has given that power to every believer. The evidence of that power is in the *fruit of the Spirit.*

Ephesians 5: 9,10
For the fruit of the Spirit is in all goodness, righteousness and truth, finding out what is acceptable to the Lord.

We cannot see the *Spirit of God* within us, but we can see the fruit, the evidence of the *Spirit,* just as *faith is the evidence of things not seen.* We cannot see faith no more than we can see gravity, but the evidence that gravity exist is in the working power of gravity, and faith in the Spirit is no different. The power of God, according to His will, produces fruit, and that fruit is the evidence that the Spirit of God is within us. Moreover, that fruit reflects the characteristics of God. However, if we confess God, but deny His power, then we will live a fruitless life that is full of contradiction, because it leaves us in a double-minded state. Paul writes many times about *knowing the will of the Lord.* Jesus taught that the will of God is that we *bear much fruit*, and that can only be accomplished by the power of the *Spirit of God* in our lives.

Colossians 3: 12 – 14

.Therefore, as the elect of God, holy and beloved, put on tender mercies, kindness, humility, meekness, longsuffering, bearing with one another, if anyone has a complaint against another; even as Christ forgave you, so you must do also. But above all these things, put on love, which is the bond of perfection.

The Spirit of God through the apostle gives us the recipe, the blueprint on how to live in the Spirit of God. He teaches us that *above all these things, put on love* and the fruit of the Spirit will be evident, clearly seen among those around you. Against love, there is no law, because love is the fulfillment of the law, it *is the bond of perfection.*

1st Thessalonians 3: 12, 4: 12

And may the Lord make you increase and abound in love to one another and to all...

...That you may walk properly toward those who are outside, and that you may lack nothing.

Without the life of Jesus Christ in our hearts and minds, we cannot walk *properly, godly* because the nature, which we inherited from Adam, is dominate in the hard drive of our beings, we are infected with sin even from Adam. However, with the life of Christ in our spirits, we are born into a new nature, the nature of God. We are a new creation in Christ. With Christ, we can walk the journey of this life in *kindness, humility, tender mercies, longsuffering, righteousness, truth, faithfulness, gentleness, peace, joy, self control, and above all love.* The true witness of the Spirit is the *fruit of the Spirit*

Two Faces

2nd Peter 2: 21
For it would have been better for them not to have known the
way of righteousness, than having known it, to turn from the
holy commandment delivered to them.
As we read the Scriptures, we see how God's mercy had
renewed the minds and spirits of many that had turned to Him
with a humble heart in the birth of the early church. We also
see some people that had turned away from God, and we then
see another side of God's nature, which is judgment in all
righteousness. God does provide a way from judgment to
mercy through one Man who is His *expressed image, His exact*
representation.
Before we go any further, let us establish the *expressed image*
of God, for the *expressed image* is the direct *representation,*
which differs from the word *image* alone.
Hebrews 1: 1 – 3
God, who at various times and in various ways spoke in time
past to the fathers by the prophets, has in these last days spoken
to us by His Son (Jesus), *whom He* (the Father), *has appointed*
heir of all things, through whom (Jesus), *also He* (the Father),
made the worlds; who (Jesus), *being the brightness of His* (the
Father's), *glory and the expressed image of His* (the Father's),
person...
Colossians 2: 9
For in Him (Jesus), *dwells all the fullness of the Godhead* (Deity),
bodily.
In the days of old, God spoke through prophets, and through
that word the people of God could understand something of
God's will and nature. However, the Holy Spirit reveals that it
is now through the life of Jesus Christ, through His word that
we cannot only understand the nature of God, but also
accurately come into a personal relationship with God.
Therefore, the fact was established by the word of the Holy
Spirit that Jesus is the full manifestation of God to the human
race. God the Father's very nature was always revealed
through God the Son, as it is written that even through Jesus,

He, the Father, *made the worlds*. In knowing that, we then need to examine the life of Jesus, for it is through His life that God speaks to man, even today, and redeemed man from the error of his sin. Laying down that foundation of truth, we can move on to the danger of knowing the truth of Christ and exchanging it for a lie. For if the mystery of Christ has been revealed to us as the true manifestation of God, then that leaves us with the enormous responsibility of devotion, surrender and obedience to the unquestionable teaching of Christ. Therefore, if we want to search for the divine person of God, we must look to Jesus. Many will be offended by this statement and walk away, as some did in the time of the earthly ministry of Jesus. When some that followed Him began to leave for their unbelief, Jesus turned to those that remained and asked:

John 6: 67

Then Jesus said to the twelve, "Do you also want to go away?"
Peter gives an answer in the form of a question that should bring us to the same answer.

John 6: 68

But Simon Peter answered Him, "Lord, to whom we shall go? You have the words of eternal life."

Every word and every action that Jesus said and did was the expressed will of God the Father, and God's will is for us to live with Him for eternity. I realize that this is hard to understand, but God truly loves us. However, there is an order of justice, righteousness and truth that abides in heaven, in the presence of the Almighty. This brings us to the issue of what God has patience and mercy with, and what ignites His anger and causes His swift judgment as displayed in the earthly ministry of Jesus. At the top of the list concerning the things that please God is the subject of *love*. When Jesus was asked, *"Which is the great commandment,"* He answered directly with the greatest gift given to every person that has ever walked on this earth.

Matthew 22: 36

"Teacher, which is the great commandment in the law?"
This would have been a relatively easy question for any teacher of the Jewish faith. However, the Pharisees at the time knew how to answer this question with words, but not in deed.

They knew what the Scriptures said, but did not follow them in their daily lives.

Matthew 22: 37 – 40

Jesus said to them, "You shall love the Lord with all your heart, with all your soul, and with all your mind.' This is the first and great commandment. 'And the second is like it; 'You shall love your neighbor as yourself.' "On these two commandments hang all the Law and the Prophets."

1st Corinthians 13: 13

And now abide in faith, hope, love, these three; but the greatest of these is love.

This would have been the answer from any teacher of Judaism at that time, and even today. However, it is easy to memorize the textbook answer when presented with the question. The real test is to answer this question in our everyday decisions. We can make a statement more with our actions than we do with our words, because anyone can say anything, but the true proof of love is in how we react to life's situations. This is where the true test in life is asked from us repeatedly. The religious leaders of that day knew the answer in their heads, but their hearts were far away from it. This leads us into the question that arises in our own hearts, that tells us if we have two faces, or one face that is seeking God in truth and love. It is in the boundaries of this question that we are to understand the very purpose of our existence and to fully comprehend the depth of our eternal security.

The following statements from Jesus, concerning the hypocrisy of the religious leaders of that day is a revelation for us in understanding how God views one of the greater sins of man. We need to keep in mind the compassion, mercy and grace that Jesus had for the prostitute, the cheating tax collector, the thief and even the women living in sin, out of wedlock. Jesus did not condemn these sinners, but condemned the sin that kept them in slavery. God showed mercy on the prostitute and told her to sin no more. God showed grace on the tax collector and said, *"Follow Me."* Jesus showed compassion on the thief that was hanging next to Him and said. *"Today you will be with Me in Paradise..."* He revealed with gentleness the error of the woman at the well that had five husbands and was currently living with another outside of marriage. However, when it came to the hypocrisy of men, we see anger, judgment and rebuke from God. Jesus tells these leaders about the *love* they should have toward God and for one another. Then Jesus begins to question these leaders concerning their hypocrisy, exposing their selfishness, hidden beneath a costume of religion. As we read through the remainder of this chapter and into the next, we see Jesus turn the table of the conversation and begin to question the religious leaders about the Christ and even about their own motives and actions. Jesus hurls a question at them that showed their obvious ignorance concerning the identity of the God, since Christ is the *brightness, glory and expressed image* of God.

Matthew 22:42

"What do you think about the Christ?"

With this question, Jesus begins to perform a spiritual autopsy to show them how spiritually dead they really are. When they come back with an answer that has no spiritual insight, Jesus begins to cut through the mask of religion using the sharp blade of the word of God. We begin to see here, as in other situations in the Gospel, another side of God that has very little patience for the hypocrisy of religious leaders that hide behind a costume of titles and man appointed positions. This is also a lesson that deals with the daily hypocrisy in our own lives. Anyone that claims that they have no struggle in this area is shortsighted. Jesus shines His truth on the men that were in leadership, the shepherds that should have been an example to the flock and true servants of God. This chapter is vital for anyone that is in full time ministry, and gives the members of the church a sharp, clear portrait of what a true shepherd for God's flock should represent. Jesus begins to peel off the costume of religion as He asked the simple question, which is the question of all questions concerning our eternity. The answer to this question can take us into the merciful presence of God, or condemn us to the everlasting judgment of the Almighty.

Matthew 22: 41 & 42

While the Pharisees were gathered together, Jesus asked them, saying, "What do you think about the Christ? Whose Son is He?"

Jesus wastes no time in beginning to cut through the phony outward appearance of religion and shines His light of truth, exposing their distant relationship with God. With this question, Jesus begins to reveal the selfish hearts of the religious leaders that should have been servants, but instead, desired to be served as kings. This gives us a discerning view of how false teachers and false prophets will use the members of the church to fulfill their own lust. As we see in the same verse, the Pharisees give the wrong answer to the most important question in all of creation.

Matthew 22: 42

They said, "The Son of David."

All the bells and whistles begin to go off, wrong, wrong answer! Here we see the experts of the Scriptures, or they confessed to be, and they did not even know the identity of the Christ who is the *expressed image of God*. Let us keep in mind, that they had been anticipating the arrival of Christ for hundreds of years. This promised Messiah, as all the prophets beginning with Moses and throughout the Old Testament had spoken of, is the Savoir of men. How could it be that they did not know the answer to this simple question? That would be like asking a trained accountant how to add, subtract, divide and multiply. The identity of the Christ should have been the cornerstone of their knowledge according to the Scriptures. Instead, something happened to these leaders that has happened to even some religious leaders today, they were blinded by the temporary riches and pleasures of this present life, and have forgotten the true riches of God. The religious leaders had fallen into the same trap that Samson had fell into, but were held captive by money, greed and pride instead of the lust of beautiful woman. We can see that lust is not defined to only the acts of fornication or adultery, but is present in many different forms. The religious leaders of that day were overtaken by it, even to the point that they turned the house of God into a marketplace. As we can see by the anger of Jesus as He drove the merchants and moneychangers out of the temple, that God was not pleased with their hypocrisy. This is where the hypocrisy of those religious leaders will be fully accountable to God. God tells us to keep our hearts pure, keep our motives clean and seek righteousness in all we do with one face.

Matthew 5: 8

Blessed are the pure in heart, for they will see God.

When Jesus taught that the pure in heart would see God, He was saying that those people whose hearts are aligned with God's would see God through the eyes of their understanding, and one day be in the full manifestation of His glory. Those that truly believe will not be blinded by the lust of greed, pride and selfish ambitions that in turn steal our knowledge of God causing spiritual blindness. The Pharisees, infected by the pride of a prominent position, the greed of money and the pleasures of a lavish life style, could no longer see God. After all, He was standing right in front of them in the flesh at the time. If anybody should have recognized Him, it should have been the custodians of the Old Testament, which pointed to the coming Christ. However, they could not see Him through the thick fog of sin and through the blackness of greed. Moreover, the worst part of it all was that the leaders that should have been the shepherds for God's flock were leading the sheep right into the same error that they practiced. Jesus warns every religious leader about the enormous responsibility of caring for the flock of God and leading them astray.

Matthew 23: 33

"Serpents, brood of vipers! How can you escape the condemnation of hell?"

We all face some sort of hypocrisy in our lives, as the flesh wages war against the spirit. At times, it is a struggle, like a wrestling match going on inside our minds. However, in this chapter, Jesus is revealing the two faces of the religious leaders of that day that put on a mask of holiness and righteousness, but inside were full of selfish ambition, deceit and corruption. As the New Testament was unfolding, through men filled with the Holy Spirit, we see a consistent warning about false teachers and false prophets. At the time of the birth of the church, even false teachers that confessed to be teaching Christianity were rapidly growing and leading people astray. Therefore, Jesus begins the lesson by teaching us how to live our lives in truth, righteousness and in the love of God. The lesson is one that the Pharisees were unable to see, because true love produces unselfish actions.

Matthew 5: 24, 42, 44

"...Love one another..."

"...Love your neighbor..."

"...Love your enemies..."

John 15: 9 & 10

"As the Father loved Me, I have always loved you: abide in My love. If you keep My commandments, you will abide in My love..."

Jesus gives us the formula to live the Christian life. However, without the very love of Christ in us, this is an impossible task. As the Pharisees did, anyone can put on a mask of religion, but our hearts are always naked, revealed before God. We might be able to fool every person on this earth, but we cannot fool the Almighty God of heaven and earth. Jesus tells us that justice, mercy and faith are the true foundations of the law, and love fulfills all three. We can see that when we are simply performing duties out of obligation, those tasks are self-centered, motivated by selfishness. Therefore, before God's eyes our efforts are in vain, since God weighs the motives and the intentions of the heart. The Pharisees obviously paid their tithes and prayed their prayers in the street, but they did it to be seen by men, to gain recognition from people instead of trying to serve God from a giving heart. This is where Jesus begins to cut into the very nerves of their hypocrisy. This is also where we must realize that it is the intentions of our hearts that are seen before God. Moreover, unless our motives are true, then we are not. Jesus goes on to cut away into the costumes of the religious leaders.

Matthew 23: 25

"For you cleanse the outside of the cup and dish, but the inside are full of extortion and self-indulgence."

Jesus used another two words to reveal the true intentions of the Jewish ruling class of His day. He uses the word *extortion*. This word is used to describe a person that gains material goods through the means of deceitfulness, force and threats, which is a thief. The other word He uses is *self-indulgence*, which defines one that saturates him or herself with pleasure at any cost. When we look around at the current world; we see these two words through the actions of people that are blinded by selfishness, and some in the name of God. Others are simply blinded by greed, thinking that somehow, the more they posses, the more fulfilling their life will be. What a pity, to live a life of always attempting to fill a bucket with a hole in the bottom. No matter how much you pour into the bucket, it remains empty. Therefore, the bucket loses its purpose, its reason for existence and it is good for nothing, except for a showpiece. The Pharisees and scribes were just that. On the outside, they were fully dressed, but their insides had a hole in it, they were empty.

Throughout this chapter in Matthew, we see the anger and judgment of God toward the hypocrisy of religious leaders that confess God with their mouth, but with their hearts, they denied Him. Jesus repeatedly gives us a stern warning not to follow the error of leaders that are only interested in glorifying themselves, and have forgotten the very God that gives breath to every lung, and a beat to every heart. For we clearly see, that Jesus had very little patience for the sin of hypocrisy.

Matthew 23: 23, 25, 27, 29 & 31

"Woe to you, scribes and Pharisees, hypocrites!"

"Woe to you scribes and Pharisees, hypocrites!"

"Woe to you scribes and Pharisees, hypocrites!"

"Woe to you scribes and Pharisees, hypocrites!"

"Therefore you are witnesses against yourselves..."

Forsaken

Judges 2: 2
Why have you done this?
We have all felt forsaken by someone at some point in our
lives. We have all had our share of heartbreaking tragedies,
disappointments, failures and setbacks that had taken the
wind out of our sails. We all have had people in our lives that
we thought we could count on, only to discover that when we
really needed them, they were gone. Moreover, what about
God? Did you ever ask God, 'how could You let this happen to
me?' We have all asked that question at some time in our lives.
However, the above Scripture from the book of Judges is not
from a person who is questioning God about a tragedy in their
life. It is not from a parent who had lost one of their children
or a middle-age mother or father who has just found out that
they have a life threatening health problem. It is not from the
successful executive who has just lost all his assets on business
deals that went bad. Anyone of us would ask God this question
in any one of the above situations. It is interesting how all the
above took place in the life of Job, yet his faith did not fail. Who
is the person that has been forsaken, that asked the only
question that can arise in our minds when our hearts have
been ripped in two? The question *"Why have you done this?"*
comes from God to us.

Judges 2: 12
And they forsook the Lord God of their fathers...
And followed other gods from among the gods of the people who
were all around them, and they bowed down to them...
What is that you say; you have never forsaken God? Does not
God tell us in the Epistle of Romans that *all have sinned and fall*
short of the glory of God? What is that you say; you have never
followed any other gods? Whatever or whoever occupies our
thoughts, actions and desires and we give first place in our
lives, is our god. We have all placed other things and other
people ahead of the true God. A bold statement you might say,
but let us face the fact that whatever or whoever holds our
passion also holds our devotion. God has watched us all chase
after the passion of our careers, hobbies and even our sin. He

has seen our hearts grow cold to His love as we chase after the dead material things of this life. Has God ever felt forsaken? The answer is yes!

Judges 2: 13

They forsook the Lord and served Ba'al and the Ashtoeths.

If this Scripture were written today, it would read; they forsook the Lord and served money and pleasures. This is not to say that God is asking anyone to make a vow of poverty. This has been a misconception of some religions for centuries and some of those religions that promote this concept are themselves very wealthy. The many giants of faith that are recorded in the Scriptures were prosperous people that owned land, livestock and even had many servants. Poverty is a curse and not a blessing from God. God is not asking us to be poor, but to be rich in Him. When we place our faith in material wealth, professional status or our own limited knowledge, we forsake God. When we place other things or other people before God, we are telling God that He is less important than our desires. We do not only do this with God, but we also do it to each other.

One of the greatest examples of a man forsaking his powerful gift and anointing from God is the story of Samson. We have heard this story many times of a man that was forsaken by a woman for a ransom of money. However, it was Samson that was careless with the power that God had given him. Samson took what was holy and used it for his own pleasure, instead of for the purpose and glory of God. It is not for us to judge the errors of Samson, or any other person's sin, since we all have made errors. However, there is much to learn from the life of Samson and many others in the Scriptures, so we might escape the same trap that so easily entangled them, and learn from their experience.

Matthew 7: 6

"Do not give what is holy to dogs: nor cast your pearls before swine, lest they trample them under their feet, and turn and tear you to pieces."

What Jesus said is exactly what happened to Samson. Samson used his God given holy gift of strength for his own purpose and pleasure, throwing it to a swine named Delilah. Many

times, we are also like Samson, as God has also given us many
pearls that we carelessly throw to dogs, and the results are the
reaping of what we have sown. Just one of the many holy
pearls that God has given to us is the joy of sharing each other
with that special someone in an intimate, lifetime commitment
of a covenant, namely marriage. However, once we carelessly
give that gift to another for the lust of the flesh, we will soon
discover that we have carelessly given something away that
God has looked upon as holy. Is not that pearl worth more than
just a temporary pleasure? God honors the covenant of
marriage, because it is a lifetime bond of commitment. It can
withstand the worst storms of this life when two are
committed to the covenant as one. However, when the pearl of
intimacy is traded for the mere pennies of a few moments of
pleasure outside the covenant of marriage, the results will be
ruin. Samson had also found this out the hard way as he gave
what was holy to a dog that used it to destroy him. Yes, Delilah
forsook Samson, but Samson also forsook God.

As Samson, we also at times chase the whispers of Delilah. Our
Delilah might not be another person, but it could be our
occupations, our hobbies, or our material possessions. It is
whatever holds our passion and dominates our decision-
making. We all should know that God should be our first love
and all else fall behind Him. Samson found this out and it left
him blind and enslaved to an evil enemy. Spiritual, we will find
ourselves in the same position if we cast our pearls before
swine. Although Samson had some problems with his pride
and his lack of patience, God used those character flaws to
accomplish His purpose and deliver the children of Israel from
the hands of their enemy.

Did Samson feel forsaken as he worked blind with his eyes
gouged out in a prison cell? He did indeed, but he knew that
God was not the one who had forsaken him, and was still able
to hear his cry. Let us face the fact that Samson had made
errors, the same as we all have made at one time or another.
His first error was that he was in a place where he had no
business being. After all, we must take responsibility for the
places we go. Would we ask God for His blessing if we spent
our time at a bar? Samson was obviously impulsive, and was

easily lured by the beauty of the flesh. However, we also can be impulsive and at times be lured by appearance, but this is where we need God's wisdom to discern right from wrong. It is sad that Samson stood in the position of a judge for Israel for twenty years, but could not make a good judgment concerning the circumstances in his own life. We also might be proficient in whatever occupation we are in, but when it comes to personal decisions, we fail to make the right choice; thank God for His mercy.

All of us could look at Samson's life and say that his life was a failure, he made unwise choices, and these led him to ruin. However, God says no. When the Holy Spirit revealed to the apostle the faith giants of the Old Testament, guess whose name appears with many others like Abraham? God tells us that Samson is in the same league as Noah, Abraham and Moses. That is impressive company to be compared with. This is a powerful lesson from God in teaching us that faith in Him can overcome even our failures. Moreover, the Holy Spirit revealed that God did not remember Samson's errors, but God did remember his faith and that faith was worthy to be mentioned in the New Testament.

Samson did forsake God, and therefore, was forsaken by a dog, when he carelessly gave away his pearl. We see that the circumstances turned for the worst, just as Jesus said would happen, *"lest they trample them under their feet, and turn and tear you to pieces."* Samson not only forsook God and his people, but also forsook himself since he bore the punishment of his error.

Judges 16:21

Then the Philistines took him and put out his eyes, and brought him down to Gaza. They bound him with bronze fetters, and he became a grinder in the prison.

I believe that when we do not make God the desire of our lives and allow Him to fill our hearts with His love; we will attempt to fill our hearts with everything else, leaving us empty and as blind as Samson. When we push God out of our lives, it is God that is forsaken and not us, but God remains faithful to His every promise.

Throughout the Old Testament we see the nation of Israel forsake God and then later cry out to Him for deliverance from the enemies that had overtaken them. Samson was no different as he prays one last prayer of faith, one last battle cry against his enemies.

Judges 16:23

Then Samson called out to the Lord, saying, "O Lord, remember me, I pray! Strengthen me, I pray, just this once, O God..."

God heard faith calling as He gave Samson the strength to bring down the house of the enemy. God is somewhat funny that way; He cannot resist the call of faith. He cannot ignore the one that calls out to Him with a true, humble, believing heart. We have seen this repeatedly throughout the Scriptures, in the Old and through the New Testament, God hears faith calling! Samson may have lost his physical eyes and eventually lost his body, but Samson went to God in a flame of faith, a light that testified to the power of God. Samson knew in his heart that he had forsaken God, since he cries out, *"O Lord, remember me."* but he also knew that it was not over yet. Samson knew in his spirit that as long as he had faith in his heart, God would hear his cry. We need to learn that lesson from Samson. Although he was blind and imprisoned, mocked and bound, Samson still had one thing the enemy could not touch. However, we must remember that it was Samson that turned his back on God. He chased after his own lust and thought nothing of the consequences that would follow.

If not anything else, the life of Samson reveals to us that with faith in God, there is always hope; even when we mess up so bad that we are blind and bound by the enemy's lies, which is the same state of an unbeliever.

Matthew 5: 13

"You are the salt of the earth; but if the salt loses its flavor, how shall it be seasoned? It is good for nothing but to be trampled under foot by men."

Again, we see Jesus teach that if we forsake God, we forsake ourselves. Once this takes place, the fire of our faith has become nothing more than smoldering smoke. Moreover, the faith which had once overcome the world in our lives will be used for a doormat by a darkened world. This is no doubt a warning from the Lord. The examples of Samson and many others in the Scripture that forsook the mercy of God is a validation of what Jesus is teaching in the Gospel. The realism of His words can be seen through the experiences of the people recorded in the Scriptures and in the experiences of the people today. Those who had forsaken God in the days of old went through this life with no hope and unseasoned, as empty shells of bones and flesh. It is no different today as we see many who are not only unseasoned without faith, but have become sour with perversion, murder and corruption. Has God forsaken the world? No, the world has forsaken God!

John 3:16

"For God so loved the world that He gave His only begotten Son." God has not forsaken the world, but the world has forsaken His mercy and grace, seduced by the pleasures of sin and blinded by the temporary riches of this life. Samson was blinded by the beauty of Delilah, by the desire of her pleasure, therefore, it cost him his eyes, his freedom and his future because he forsook the wisdom of God and trusted in the world of Delilah that took his salt and trampled it under her feet.

As Samson made his choices, so we have the option to live in faith or doubt, light or darkness, victory or defeat. Samson, who was the strongest man that ever lived by the anointing of God, traded his gift for the temporary pleasure of Delilah. The current world is following on the same path in darkness as we read the daily headlines of crime, deception and greed, even in the levels of government, as was Samson, since he was a judge of Israel. Instead of using this example as just a bedtime story, we need to look at the life of Samson as a witness, a testimony that what Jesus taught us will happen just as He has said. However, though Samson forsook the anointing of God at that time in his life, there is no doubt that he glorified God through his death with the same anointing that he cast to the swine of Delilah. We can see that it does not matter where we have been, but where we end up. Samson stumbled and fell under the deception of Satan, but he ended up a faith giant that believed God for the final victory in his earthly life and God responded to that cry of faith. As the Holy Spirit compares

Samson to Abel, Enoch, Abraham, Jacob, Moses, David and Samuel, God tells us that there is still hope in error and that faith can break through our wrong choices. Most of these men had forsaken God in some way in their lives, but by faith they where redeemed and returned to the only God that holds creation in His hands.

Hebrews 12: 1

Therefore we also, since we are surrounded by so great a cloud of witnesses...

As they did, so we also can experience the blessing of God in our lives by following their examples in steps of faith and learn from their errors, before we fall and forsake God, our loved ones and ourselves. The Lord Jesus Christ has already paid for our errors, therefore, He has not given up on us; we also need not to give up on Him, He is faithful. For every single word spoken out of the mouth of God will come to pass. Therefore, we can certainly place our faith in His faithfulness and not in our own works, knowing our many failures are forgiven in the blood of Christ, if we are willing to accept His payment. The sin issue has already been settled on the cross, we only need to walk in the victory of Christ by faith, since the charge against us has been taken out, erased and can no longer be used against us. We no longer need to live in shame, since He has wiped our record of trespasses clean by the blood of Christ, and has brought us into the light of His presence from the darkness of guilt and sin.

Beware of Darkness

Luke 11:35
"Therefore, take heed that the light which is in you is not darkness."

Jesus gives us a word warning concerning our spiritual condition. It is a word of caution, asking us to beware and know that the darkness of the soul is void of the love of God. We can never underestimate the small morsels of darkness (sin) that can easily contaminate our daily intake of God's light of truth and love.

We can view this word *darkness* from many different angles. In some cases, the word is defined as ignorance, and at other times viewed as rebellion. However, we can all agree that *darkness* is separation from light. Moreover, the two cannot exist in the same place at the same time. Therefore, if the light of God is absent in a spirit, the only thing that remains is darkness and how great that darkness is.

Psalm 107: 10, 11
Those who sat in darkness and in the shadow of death, bound in affliction and irons, because they rebelled against the words of God, and despised the counsel of the Most High.

The Scriptures gives us a clear picture of the two conditions in where the human soul lives, even while in these temporary suits of flesh and bone. The above text explains what happens to a person when they reject God, count Him off as nonsense, and live their lives as their own god. I have heard many people tell me that they can only trust themselves, that the God that I proclaim as my Savior is only a crutch, an aid for the weak, a comfort to a hurting heart. They are advocates of freewill, and believe that they are truly free. It does not matter how they might perceive their status, God gives us the truth concerning a human soul that is separated by choice from the directive of the only loving God.

Strangely enough, unbelievers will say to the believer that you are the ones who are enslaved to the commands of a man-made religion, as they *sit in darkness and in the shadow of death*. But God gives us a very clear statement throughout the

Scriptures that apart from Him we are dead, even if our hearts are beating and we have breath in our lungs. Without God, the darkness of death (separation from life), reigns in our spirits and holds us captive to fear. We have seen many people, some famous, some friends and family members vanish in the darkness of unbelief, *bound in affliction and irons* of not knowing what their final destination will be. The chains that they cannot see are the shackles of worry, fear and confusion, which leads into the deeper darkness of doubt. It is a state of hopelessness and torment, as they grasp for anything that might give a few moments of contentment and peace. But sin could never give us peace. They *sit in darkness,* unable to move out of their position because the weight of sin has paralyzed them. Yes, I know that anyone can put on the make-up of a laugh and proclaim that all is well, but the fruit of sin will soon come to a season when it cannot be hidden. However, there is another way, a lighted path in the warm glow of God's love. It is a path, which is far away from the cold, damp darkness of hopelessness and death. The light of God's forgiving mercy warms the heart, and ignites the spirit with a flame that melts away the chains of uncertainty and renews life. His forgiving power is life changing with a new understanding of what true love really is. It brings us out of the ignorance of the night and into the new day of knowledge and hope. For the knowledge of God is enlightening and everlasting.

Psalm 27: 1, John 8: 12, 1st Peter 2: 9

The Lord is my light...

Then Jesus spoke to them again, saying, "I am the light of the world, He who follows Me shall never walk in darkness, but have the light of life?

...That you may proclaim the praises of Him who called you out of darkness and into His marvelous light.

The darkness of unbelief and doubt is a place where fear is a terrorist that holds our minds as hostages. It is a place where we no longer can recognize the lies of evil, but are held prisoners to them. But the light of truth can and will free us from the lies that torment our minds. God's light of mercy brings us to a place of being forgiven and forgiving others, so we are no longer weighed down with the weight of past hurts and grudges. And most of all, God's Spirit will bring us to a place of trust, away from the unsettled sand of uncertainty. He builds us up on the solid rock of His promises, which cannot be moved. He cleanses us with His truth as a fresh water stream that washes away the daily corruption of lies that attempts to be attached to us. Peter calls it a *marvelous light,* and so it is. For God's light of redemption shines through the darkness of our sin, giving us eyes to see His salvation, and ears to hear His promises. But how can we enter this place of God's love. How can we leave the dark dungeons of doubt, which breeds confusion, fear, worry, and blindness? Can we really have a new beginning of life? Can we leave behind the shackles of shame that chain our minds in a prison cell of resentment? Jesus said, *"Come to Me..."* Come as you are, and He will make you a new person, a new creation who is no longer an orphan of creation stumbling in the dark. He brings us into His light of truth, love, and mercy, and we become children of light. He gives us His heart, He gives us His peace.

We simply need to give our hearts to God through Jesus Christ, who spared not Himself, but poured out His life on the altar of the cross so that we might live forever in His light. He took upon Himself our darkness and gave us His light. Jesus took the love that the Father gave Him, and gave it to us.

The Blackest of Darkness

Jude 1: 12 & 13
These are spots in your love feast, while they feast with you without fear, serving only themselves. They are clouds without water, carried away by the winds; late autumn trees without fruit, pulled up by the roots; raging waves of the sea, foaming up their shame, wandering stars, for whom the blackest of darkness has been reserved forever.

This is a chapter that most people will likely skip over; however, I believe that is by far the most important chapter in the book.

At the risk of repeating the same simple message of the Gospel of Jesus Christ, as the Apostle Paul did throughout the letters to the newborn church by the power of God, we also need to review such a great salvation.

Many people have looked at God's gift of salvation and turned away with comments like, 'that's not for me, or these Christians are weak people who need something to believe in because they don't believe in themselves; they have no self-esteem.' I've heard Christians called losers; 'they couldn't make it in the world so they turned to God.'

The one thing I can say to all those who do not believe in the Gospel of Jesus Christ, is that one day your body is going to give out. What then?

The man Job spoke of the grave as a place of no return, a place of darkness and without any order.

Job 10: 21 & 22
Before I go to the place which I shall not return, to the land of darkness and the shadow of death, a land as dark as darkness itself, as the shadow of death, without any order, where even the light is like darkness.

Job tells us about a place where even *the light is like darkness*, and Jude tells us about a place of *the blackness of darkness*.

Though many might argue that there is no place of eternal punishment, the place that is void of the light of the love of God is certainly a hell.

What do you think is going to happen to you, who confess unbelief? Well most people would answer, 'I am a good person, and I'm going to heaven.' When anyone begins to justify themselves as a good person, reasoning that by their own measuring, they will go to heaven; then what they are really saying is that they do not need a Savior, they can pay the debt of their sin on their own. Therefore, they judge themselves, making themselves their own god, instead of obeying the true God, who is the true Judge of all.

Moreover, If God is a distant stranger to you, what makes you think that you are going to live with Him for eternity in heaven? Would you just knock on a stranger's door and then walk into their house and live with them?

There is a way, another choice you can make, in that you can enter in a personal relationship with God and know Him as your personal Savior. Jesus Christ paid for that choice with His own blood. This way will erase any doubt and fear concerning leaving this life.

You see God is holy and by our acts of sin, we are not! Therefore, someone had to pay for our sins so we could enter in the holy presence of God.

The point is that if you have not accepted God's Son, Jesus Christ as your Savior, who died on the cross for your sins and was raised on the third day, you will not live with God for eternity. Without an eternal sacrifice for all your sins, then you are not going to heaven, because we cannot take our sins with us to heaven in the presence of a holy God.

Romans 6:23, 3:23

The wages of sin is death...

For all have sinned and fall short of the glory of God...

Therefore, the judgment for sin is death (separation from God's presence), and we all have sinned sometime in our lives. In the days of old, God instructed His people to sacrifice an innocent animal (as an animal has no sin), as a sin offering. The innocent blood was shed for the guilty and this was only a temporary atonement. Now, someone might say, 'that is an extreme action for the forgiveness of sin.' In an age of accepting sin in our society, we need to realize how serious sin is, how it affects our daily lives and our eternities. Is there any

other way for our sins to be forgiven? Remember that the wages, the consequences of sin is death (separation from God), and even one sin is enough to separate us from a holy God.
John 14:6
Jesus answered, "I am the way and the truth and the life, no one comes to the Father except through Me."
Now if Jesus is who He says He is, the Christ and Savior of the world, and if He did die for our sins and was raised on the third day, then we should listen to Him. If you are not sure where you are going to spend eternity and you still reject God's offer by confessing that you do not believe it or it's not for me, you are taking a very big chance. Moreover, if you are willing to take that risk for yourself and your loved ones, according to the opening Scriptures, this is where God says you will spend eternity.
It will be the darkest, blackest place, where even the light is darkness! Your spirit will be burning with regret, guilt and shame as if someone had thrown you into a fire that never ends. Unable to see the light, yet you will feel the pain of the blackness in that the light of the love of God is totally absent. No day or light, but only burning pains of grief in darkness! This is the judgment, the wages of sin.
2nd Peter 2: 17
These are wells without water; clouds carried by a tempest, for who is reserved the blackness of darkness forever.
The prophets of old spoke about the deep darkness of sin, the blackness of ignorance concerning the salvation of God.
Psalm 107:10, 11
Those who sat in darkness and in the shadow of death, bound in affliction and irons – Because they rebelled against the Lord, and despised the counsel of the Most High.
What is sin, but rebellion against God. God says not to do something and we do it, it is sin. Moreover, if sin results in separation from God and God is light, therefore, if we remain in sin, we remain in darkness. However, darkness must flee in the presence of light, but without light, there is only darkness.
John 1:5
God is light and in Him is no darkness at all.

Is this darkness only symbolic to a lack of understanding, or a refusal to walk away from sin? Not according to the Scriptures, the bible gives us a view of a place where there is only darkness and pain, void of God's holy light of love and peace. A place that God has reserved for the judgment of rebellious angels, with no presence of His mercy. Jesus warned us about this place more than He spoke about the glories of heaven. Hell is a real place, with real pain and torment.

Matthew 25: 30, 41, 46

And cast the unprofitable servant into outer darkness...

...Into everlasting fire prepared for the devil and his angels.

And these will go away into everlasting punishment...

What Jesus is describing does not sound symbolic for spiritual blindness, but a real place of judgment, composed of real darkness and real pain. This is not a figment of someone's imagination, or an illusion of what Jesus said, Hell is a real place!

However, some might ask, 'where is the proof to all these things, or who has gone to such a place and returned to validate these statements?' There have been countless testimonies of people who have had near death experiences, actually pronounced dead and have witnessed a dark tunnel with no bright light at the end. However, the real proof is not in the testimony of a man, but is in the testimony of God. The Scriptures, written by God through men, warns us that there is a place of judgment, a place void of God's mercy.

Matthew 6: 23

If the light that is in you is darkness, how great is that darkness.

God does tell us that there is an inner darkness as well. A place in the heart that is missing the love of God, a lost spirit, blinded from a lack of God's love in their hearts, as we witness evil acts of tormented souls that have allowed their minds to be perverted with sin. Jesus tells us that the love of God within us is a light that allows us to see and understand His mercy and compassion. However, if that light is out, there is nothing remaining but great darkness.

Isaiah 9 & 10

We look for light, but there is darkness! For brightness, but we walk in blackness! We grope for the wall like the blind, we grope as if we had no eyes.

The darkness of a person's spirit who has turned away from the love of God is in a state of rebellion that is also missing the peace of God. Therefore, it is a place of fear from condemnation and judgment. We see a current world in this condition, full of greed and hate, blinded by the darkness of hate and selfishness, stumbling deeper into the darkness of sin.

1st John 2: 11

But he who hates his brother is in darkness and walks in darkness, and does not know where he is going, because the darkness has blinded his eyes.

Yes, there is a place in the soul of a man where the darkness of sin can control his mind, void of God's peace, which is a living hell. However, there is also a place, a real place reserved for the rebellious angels of evil, a place of judgment where all those that reject the love of God will be sentenced for eternity. Therefore, I say to those who do not believe, enjoy these few years that you have here in this world, because someday, we don't know when, could be today, you will be required to leave here without knowing where you will spend eternity. Will it be the blackness of darkness in the judgment of hell, or in the light of God's mercy in paradise? Sound like some sort of Hollywood science fiction movie? Guess again, it is real! The price of sin is real as we can see in the lives of those that practice the more obvious evils, such as murder, corruption and hatred. Even some of the rich and famous that have bowed their knees to evil have paid the price of great loss in this world. Moreover, if they leave this world without a sacrifice for sin, the price gets higher. This is not just some sort of scare tactic to convince someone to join a certain religious group so that an organization will have more strength with more members. The Scripture repeatedly reminds us that hell is a real place according to real judgment. This is no joke, and the clock is ticking.

Matthew 23: 33
How can you escape the condemnation of hell?
Luke 1: 79
To give light to those who sit in darkness and the shadow of death, to guide our feet into the way of peace.
Jesus came to pay the price for our sins, to take on Himself the judgment for all our errors; this is the greatest eternal news that we can receive on this side of life.
All who believe in Jesus Christ have a guaranteed eternal ticket to heaven; there is only one way. Jesus also said:
John 14: 6
"I am the way!"
Should there be another way? There can be no other way since it was by the blood of a sinless Man (Jesus Christ), in that our sins have been paid for in full, leaving no balance due on our part. No other so-called prophet or religious leader can make that claim! Jesus proclaims to be the only way because He is the only Man that could have paid for our sins. If anyone receives the sacrifice of Jesus Christ, they are openly admitting that they are guilty of sin and that Jesus paid the price for the judgment of their sin, which is a confession of faith.
Sound too easy? God made it easy for us, for He sent His Son to bear the punishment of us all.
John 3:16
For God so loved the world that He gave His only begotten Son, that whoever believes in Him should not perish but have everlasting life.
The Scriptures tell us that we have an eternal choice. We can spend eternity in the judgment of our own sins and in the blackness of darkness in eternal regret, or we can spend it with God, forgiven, in the light of His everlasting love in paradise. Hard choice to make? Not for me, I'll take the eternity with God any day. Do not think that you or I can add to the cross of Christ with more of a sacrifice than what He has already given. None of our so-called good deeds would ever come close to the payment for our sins. The blood sacrifice of Jesus Christ was perfect and priceless, that by only believing in it by faith, we are forgiven, washed clean from all our sin. Still sound too easy? It is for us, but it was not for Jesus, who

carried the price of every sin that we committed against God and was nailed with it on a cross. No other so-called prophet can make this claim as Jesus clearly proclaimed that He is the Savior of man.

But there is more! God gives us eternal promises that will take us through this life and into His everlasting presence.

John 11: 25, 14: 3

Jesus said to her, "I am the resurrection and the life. He who believes in Me, though he may die, he shall live."

"And if I go and prepare a place for you, I will come again and receive you to Myself; that where I am, there you may be also."

Jesus clearly tells us that though these temporary bodies may fall apart and die, our spirits are eternal, and everyone who places their trust in the Lord Jesus Christ will be where He is for eternity, in the spirit at first and then later in glorified bodies.

As we live in a world that is falling deeper into the darkness of greed and selfishness, God reminds us that with faith in Him, we can rise above the darkness of this world and begin this very day to live in the marvelous light of His love. We do not need to wait until our bodies die to begin living our eternal life with God, it begins the moment we accept the sacrifice of Jesus Christ for all our sins and believe that He was raised from the dead, and lives forever more.

Jesus is the only Savior, the only lifeboat who has given us the greatest gift in the entire universe, eternal life in His love, and rescued us from a raging sea of judgment.

Acts 4: 12

"There is no other name under heaven given among men by which we must be saved."

Romans 3: 23, 5: 12

For all have sinned and fall short of the glory of God...

Therefore, just as through one man sin entered the world, and death through sin, and thus death spread to all men, because all sinned.

Jesus paid the price of sin and promised us that many will come into the Kingdom of God and enjoy all that He has prepared for those that love Him. Nevertheless, for those that rejected Him, there is only darkness.

Matthew 8: 11 & 12, 13: 42, & 50, Luke 13: 28 & 29
"And I say to you that many will come from the east and the west, and sit down with Abraham, Isaac and Jacob in the kingdom of heaven.
"...And those who practice lawlessness will be cast into a furnace of fire"
"There will be wailing and gnashing of teeth."
"There will be wailing and gnashing of teeth."
"There will be weeping and gnashing of teeth, when you see Abraham, Isaac and Jacob and all the prophets in the kingdom of God, and you yourself thrust out. They will come from the east and the west, from the north and the south, and sit down in the kingdom of God."

To be absent from the loving presence of God is a place of deep remorse and regret. It is places of darkness where the spirit would spend an eternity in a pain of sorrow. It is a place of deep grieving where the tears of error will flow endlessly. Jesus warned us, but also provided a way from this awful fate. *"I am the way, the truth and the life; no one comes to the Father except through Me."* Jesus provided the only way from the judgment of eternity with the sacrifice of His own blood, and experienced the outer darkness of judgment, so we would not have to experience it ourselves.

1st John 1: 5 - 7
"This is the message which we have heard from Him and declare to you, that God is light and in Him there is no darkness at all. If we say that we have fellowship with Him and walk in darkness, we lie and do not practice the truth. But if we walk in the light as He is in the light, we have fellowship with one another, and the blood of Jesus Christ His Son cleanses us from all sin."

The Rich Man who was Poor

"So is he who lays up treasure for himself, and is not rich toward God." Luke 12: 21

Jesus had much to say about the deceitfulness of riches and how a man or a woman can become lost in the sea of worldly wealth, being carried out to the deep waters of selfishness and losing sight of the main land of God's salvation. Luke, the Gentile physician, who by the inspiration of the Holy Spirit had recorded many healings that Jesus performed and understood the level of these great miracles, also gives us many insights to the true riches in Christ and the error in falling into the deception of placing our faith in temporary wealth. Luke was an educated professional, who must have had some degree of wealth and must have seen many wealthy people with ill health. Therefore, he gives us an insight of these things that amazed his mind as evidence of Jesus being the Christ. Throughout the book, Luke brings the subject of wealth into focus to show us that there is nothing wrong with earthly riches, but when we place our trust in them instead of trusting in God, we are doomed for disaster.

Jesus tells us a parable as recorded by Luke about a rich man who is called a *fool*, because money was all he had. Therefore, in most bibles the title of the story is The Rich Fool. Jesus explains that this man prospered in worldly wealth, but proceeded through this life to inhale all his wealth for himself. God calls him a *fool*, saying that now your soul is required, you leave the earth with no material possessions and with no wealth in God.

Jesus continues to give us many examples of this error throughout the Gospel of Luke. For besides Luke's amazement of the supernatural healings that he heard about and witnessed, the theme of the deceitfulness of earthly riches is a consistent reminder of how someone could *gain the whole world and lose their soul.* Luke also records the parables of Jesus and then gives us a real life example in the people who came to Jesus searching for the fulfillment of their souls.

Luke 18: 10
"Two men went up to the temple to pray, one a Pharisee (a religious ruler), *and the other a tax collector."*
Now at first glance we would say that this parable is simply about humility, but it goes deeper. Jesus brings to light the hearts of two very different people. One man was a wealthy religious leader and the other a financially well-off tax collector. Both of these men had money, but only one realized that the money was not worth anything without Jesus. The Lord explains that one of the men, a priest, goes in the church to pray, patting himself on the back, and condemning everyone else. I found out very early in my journey with God that those people who are the furthest from the mercy of God are indeed the most critical of everybody else. These people smile and shake your hand, or greet you with a kiss, but as soon as your back is turned, they are quick to criticize you or anyone else that does not agree with them. The priest in the parable was no different as he criticizes the tax collector and places himself on a pedestal of saintly status. Can you image telling God how good you are, justifying yourself before the only God who knows every thought and every secret throughout your entire life? Then the tax collector comes in, with his head down, beating his heart with remorse, asking God for mercy. What does Jesus say about the two different men?
'I tell you, this man (the tax collector), *went down to his house justified rather than the other* (the priest); *for everyone who exalts himself will be humbled and he who humbles himself will be exalted." Luke 18: 14*
We can see from this text that when someone trust in themselves, or trust in their money, they are poor, spiritually bankrupted, because without faith in God, which is the true riches in Christ Jesus, all the worldly possessions are worthless
Philippians 3: 8
Yet indeed, I also count all things loss for the excellence of the knowledge of Christ Jesus my Lord, for whom I have suffered the loss of all things and count them as rubbish that I may gain Christ.

To paraphrase this statement, the apostle testifies that all the things that he had in his possession, even whatever status he might had obtained, compared to knowing Jesus Christ as his personal Savior was nothing but rubbish, junk and had no lasting value. After all, what can be more valuable than the gift of eternal life with God? God calls the person who settles for the mere temporary pleasures and possessions of this life and ignores the riches of God's love in Jesus Christ *a fool.*

Now it just so happens, two men, one a wealthy ruler, and the other a tax collector seek to see Jesus on different occasions. Both of these men resemble the two men in the parable that went into the temple to pray.

Now a certain ruler asked Him, saying, "Good Teacher, what shall I do to inherit eternal life. Luke 18: 18

Now Jesus speaks to this man in a different tone and asked, *"Why do you call Me good? No one is good but One, that is God."* If Jesus excepted worship as God, then why would he rebuke this man for calling Him good? Some cults use this Scripture as a proof that Jesus is not divine, stating that in this text Jesus admits He is not God the Son. However, I have had many teachers who would question a statement that a student made for the reason of not denying the statement was true, but questioning the reasoning, asking the student to explain why he or she believes the statement to be true. This is exactly how Jesus questions this *ruler* and also used this type of questioning with the Pharisees and Scribes that did not believe He is the Christ.

Well, Jesus already told the story of a Pharisee, a ruler of the church and the people who attempted to justify himself before God and this *certain ruler* was also quick to justify himself. Jesus tells the man to keep the commandments, but we know that no one is able to keep all the commandments. However, the man still replied, *"All of these things I have kept from my youth."* This *ruler* could not have kept all the commandments, because no one, except for Jesus Christ, has walked on this earth in the flesh without sin. The Scriptures tells us that *all have sinned and fall short of the glory of God.* Like the Pharisee in the parable, the *ruler* might have been convinced that he had some kind of note worthy self-righteousness that would save him from the condemnation of sin, but he only fooled himself.

Jesus saw this *certain ruler* as not only a man that was ready to justify himself before God, but also a person who loved his wealth. It is obvious that the *ruler* did not believe that Jesus was the Christ. For if he did believe in Jesus, he would have certainly left all his so-called wealth behind and followed Christ to eternity at the invitation that Jesus extended to him. But he did not, because it is obvious that he had no faith in Jesus. He trusted more in his earthly wealth, which is here today and gone tomorrow.

And He (Jesus), *said, "You still lack one thing. Sell all that you have and distribute it to the poor; and you will have treasure in heaven; and come follow Me." Luke18: 22*

The *one thing* that the *ruler lacked* was the most important thing in all creation and that is faith, trust in Jesus Christ, because without it we are lost, doomed for eternal separation from God. Jesus gives this *ruler* the same invitation He gave Peter and the rest of the twelve, but he loved his riches and his independent lifestyle more than he loved God. Therefore, he weighed the two and decided to enjoy the brief pleasures of this life and suffer a remorseful eternity without God, which by far defines the true meaning of poverty in the spiritual sense. Without Christ, we are spiritually bankrupted and will spiritually starve to death from the poverty of sin. Jesus asked Peter and the other eleven to follow Him, never mentioning any demand to sell all they owned first. However, with this *certain ruler*, Jesus sees into his heart and knows that unless he is willing to let go of his earthly wealth he would not place his faith completely in God. In the case of this man, he did not posses his earthly riches as having control over them, but the earthly riches possessed him and controlled him. He was a slave to the very things that he claimed he owned. Sad, but true, the allurement from earthly pleasures are like the whispers of Delilah, that bound and blinded Samson and moved him out of the will of God. Samson believed the lies of Delilah rather than trusting in the truth of God. The story of Samson was a tragedy, yet we see countless people who believe the lie that money is the answer to all their problems, instead of trusting in the eternal promises of God. The *certain ruler* was one of those people who walked away from the invitation of Christ, who could not let go of the worthless possessions of this life, losing the abundant wealth of eternal life with the Creator.

Now a second man comes to Jesus, a tax collector, again like the man that Jesus mentioned in the parable. Jesus sees this man and says, *"Zacchaeus, make haste and come down, for I must stay at your house."* Jesus goes to the tax collector's house, which caused criticism from the religious rules that had the same type of attitude as the self-righteous ruler in the parable of the two men who went into the temple to pray.

Luke 19: 6

But when they (the religious rulers), *saw it, they complained, saying, "He has gone to be a quest with a man who is a sinner."* The leaders of the church were quick to condemn and unwilling to forgive. This is a consistent observation throughout the gospels. In their own self-justification, their hearts were hardened and their eyes were blind from the wealth that came from their position. Zacchaeus quickly receives the words of Christ and welcomes Him gladly into his house. He stands in the mist of his quest and says, *"Look Lord, I give half of my goods to the poor and if I have taken anything from anyone be false accusation, I restore fourfold."* Jesus did not ask Zacchaeus to give to the poor as He did with the *rich ruler*, but he gave anyway and the Lord was pleased. This was an act of repentance, a turning away from former sins, and turning to God. Unlike the *rich ruler, Zacchaeus* offered freely and did not need to be asked, but willingly gave. Although this tax collector may have had a greater sinful past than the *rich ruler*, because of his humility, he was more open to Christ and therefore, excepted His words without hesitation. The *rich young ruler* was too much in love with himself and his earthly wealth to be of any use in the kingdom of God. We do not know how many days Jesus stayed in the house of Zacchaeus, but we do know that Jesus was welcomed there and also felt comfortable as Jesus blesses him and says, *"Today salvation has come to this house..."* What wonderful words of praise from the Savior that on that day this tax collector received the free gift of God's love in placing his faith in Jesus Christ. And the *rich ruler* walked away with the mere pennies of earthly wealth that would fade and rust away. The *rich ruler* walked away empty in spite of all that was in his possession, while Zacchaeus became rich in God.

In the opening parable, Jesus tells us that the tax collector went down to his house justified rather than the rich ruler. The only true justification is in the forgiveness of God according to the mercy of His will. This truth might not do much for our egos, since by our earthly natures we are driven by self-justification, desiring to be excepted by our own merit, so that we might have something to boast about, but not before God. God knows our sin; He knows our nature, the natural intent of our hearts. He knows what or who is in our hearts, and if any person fills their hearts with the love of money instead of a love for God, they are the poorest souls in all creation.

Luke 16:13

"No servant can serve two masters. Either he will hate the one and love the other, or he will be devotes to the one and despise the other. You cannot serve both God and money."

Asleep in Christ

1st Thessalonians 4: 13
But I do not want you to be ignorant, brethren, concerning those who have fallen asleep lest you have sorrow as others who have no hope.

The Holy Spirit gave many great revelations to the Apostle Paul concerning a wide range of God's truth. When the apostle addressed the church of the Thessalonians, he brings to light a truth that either was questioned by the church, or because the church was grieving the passing of loved ones. For whatever the reason, the Holy Spirit revealed to that church and to us the reality of our eternal hope. He begins by making a bold statement that should certainly wake us up if we have fallen into a slumber of faith concerning the Lord's promise of life. *"But I do not want you to be ignorant, brethren."* Some people might take this statement as an insult. Some might question, 'who are you calling ignorant?' God is simply saying that He does not want us to be uninformed in the matters of life. Whether it is our temporary stay here or our life after, He wants us to know His promises. However, if we remain alienated from God, then we are in the darkness of ignorance.

Ephesians 4: 18
...Having their understanding darkened, being alienated from the life of God, because of the ignorance that is in them, because of the blindness of their heart.

This opening text is addressed to the *brethren*, the church of believers because the church should understand and be comforted by the mighty promises of God, where as the world of unbelief is ignorant, blinded by the darkness of sin, as we all were at one time. Thank God that His mercy prevailed. Therefore, the church, the body of believers should certainly spread this hope to a dying world that has fallen under the deception of a hopeless future, as a light that shines in a dark place. This is the reason why people without hope fall into great depression, become bitter and resentful and finally have little regard for human life, even their own. God tells us to have understanding in these truths, because understanding will fill our spirits with faith and destroy the seeds of doubt that can easily grow into weeds of confusion, sorrow and hopelessness. I often see dedicated joggers that run faithfully every morning or evening in an effort to maintain good physical heath. However, as I watch them, I often wonder about their spiritual health, and the weeds of doubt that may reside within them. For while they diligently run to maintain a level of physical health, there may be no eternal hope within their hearts and minds. Therefore, they are running to maintain a temporary state of existence, which will pass in time no matter how much exercise they perform.

1st Timothy 4: 8

Bodily exercise profits a little, but godliness is profitable for all things, having promise of the life that now is and of that which is to come.

Physical exercise *profits a little* because it only benefits us in the rather short stay here in these temporary bodies, verses *godliness,* which *is profitable* for eternity, never ending life. Now some people physically run in fear of death, thinking that jogging will prolong the unavoidable. However, God tells us to run the race of faith with the same dedication, even more so, than those that run for the temporal.

As the Apostle Paul writes his farewell to Timothy, he says:

2nd Timothy 4: 7

I have fought the good fight, I have finished the race, I have kept the faith.

How many of us will be able to claim that statement when we are ready to depart? I think exercise is great and should be promoted at an early age to prevent some common known aliments that plague an age of high sugar and fatty foods. However, like the current buzz phrase that states, 'think out of the box,' we need also to think out of these bodies, and think in the book.

There is a balance that needs to be maintained for the physical body of exercise and diet, however, maintaining spiritual heath, which is godliness, far exceeds physical maintenance, knowing that on any given day our spirits will leave these bodies and enter eternity. Therefore, God tells us, *I do not want*

you to be ignorant, know the hope that is within you, the hope that the world does not have, but desperately needs to hear.
1st Thessalonians 4: 16
And the dead in Christ will rise first.
We need to take a second look at this great illustration in the Gospel of Luke as Jesus tells the parable of the rich man and a beggar named Lazarus. The story is about two men, one rich, successful and a worldly man, the other a beggar who lived in the gutter with the dogs.
Luke 16: 22
"So it was that the beggar died, and was carried by the angels to Abraham's bosom. The rich man also died and was buried."
Jesus tells us that the angels of God carried the beggar (named Lazarus), to Abraham; that is the beggars spirit was carried, not his physical body. Jesus does tell us that the rich man's spirit went to another place, but for now, He simply says that his physical body was buried. Jesus explains to us many other truths in this parable concerning eternal life. Jesus also told this parable because there were some around Him that were assuming that by their own righteous, by putting on religious clothes, they would stand before the judgment seat of God without their sin.
The rich man requested to send Lazarus to his father's house to warn his family of the error of not following God and seeking only the temporary pleasures of this life.
Luke 16: 27
Then he (the rich man), *said, 'I beg you therefore, father* (Abraham), *that you sent him* (Lazarus), *to my father's house* (on earth), *for I have five brothers, that he may testify to them, lest they come to this place of torment.'*
It is here that Jesus tells us that the rich man was in *a place of torment,* which in many others Scriptures God calls Hell. The request was denied and the former rich man was told that his family had Moses and the prophets to hear. Moreover, if the prophets did not persuade this man's family, then they will not listen to a man who had returned from the dead. Therefore, no one should expect to receive insight of the life after from loved ones who have passed over. God tells us that we need to listen to the people sent by God to minister to us. Of course, there are

many that come in the name of Christ, claiming to be true ministers, true witnesses of the Gospel, but preach for self-glory instead of for the glory of God.

Again, it is important to realize that both of the men's spirits, though they were in two different places, were both very aware of their surroundings. The rich man even felt thirst and heat as he attempted to bargain for one drop of water. Therefore, our spirits are very much alive without these bodies and have senses. We also see that the spirit of Lazarus was instantly carried to Abraham, as soon as his spirit left his body. Although the body of Lazarus was dead, or what the Scriptures refer to as *fallen asleep,* the spirit was alive and carried by angels. What will happen to those who fall asleep in Christ?

1st Thessalonians 4: 13, 14, 16

...Those who have fallen asleep... Those who sleep in Jesus... And the dead in Christ...

All of the above Scriptures are referring to the death of the body; the absence of the spirit from the body. For without the spirit, the physical body is lifeless, dormant, void of the spark of energy that causes physical life.

As the rich man painfully found out, he might have enjoyed the few temporary years he had on this earth, but eternity is an awful long time to suffer in judgment. On the other hand, Lazarus suffered for a short time compared to the endlessness of eternity.

Now the term, *dead in Christ* does not refer to a non-existent state, or non-conscience state of the spirit, since the spirits of the rich man and Lazarus are very much alive outside their physical bodies. The *dead in Christ* are those, whose bodies have fallen asleep, stopped functioning, but their spirits are with Christ, just as Lazarus was with Abraham.

Philippians 1: 23 & 24

...Having a desire to depart and be with Christ, which is far better. Nevertheless, to remain in the flesh is more needful for you.

The apostle again touches on something that we do not see very often, even in the higher levels of knowledge in the church. Paul knew by the Spirit of God that testified within him that leaving this temporary body and entering the full manifestation of the presence of God was the best thing that could happen to him. Therefore, any thought of his body ceasing to function, and his spirit leaving to be with Christ was something to be earnestly anticipated. This is not to think that Paul was suicidal or had a death wish. On the contrary, the apostle had a life wish, an understanding that the real person, his inner man, his spirit is the true container of life. Moreover, he knew that his true home was with Jesus Christ, and he eagerly looked forward to the day when he would see his Savoir, face to face.

Philippians 1: 21
For to me, to live is Christ, and to die is gain.
There are Christians that I knew, who have died what some might consider before their time. Some left so suddenly and so young while we see others that consistently rebels against God stay here for a long earthly time. We might begin to question God when these untimely departures take place. However, if we look through the eyes of the apostle and see what he saw as he looked in the face of death many times, we will see the big picture. This man was beaten many times to the point of death, shipwrecked with the threat of drowning, bitten by poisonous snakes, thrown into prisons, and even stoned to actual death, all for the sake of the Gospel. And in the face of all these life-threatening dangers, Paul says, *"To die is gain."* Paul simply knew who was waiting to receive him home on the other side. Therefore, there was no room for fear of the unknown, since Paul had known the unknown. Confusing? It should not be, if we know and understand the power of God's love toward us, and the promises the He made to all that give their lives in His hands through faith in Jesus Christ. Paul goes on to shine his light of faith, as he knows the certainty of his death is at hand.

2nd Timothy 4: 6
"...And the time of my departure is at hand."
Paul looked at the death of his body as a departure, not the end, but simply departing to another place, leaving his scared, deteriorating body behind. Paul viewed this as *gain,* since he knew what was waiting for all of us that place their hope in

Jesus Christ. His departure was *gain*, a promotion, and a rest from the battle of the flesh that wages war against the spirit. The Apostle Peter had the same perspective, but in different words

2nd Peter 1: 14

"Knowing that shortly I must put off my tent, just as our Lord Jesus Christ showed me."

Peter also refers to his physical body as a tent. Now a tent is a temporary place to live. If we viewed everything that God has allowed us to use as a temporary tent, in that we are only using them for a short period of time, it will help us see the big picture of eternity, where there is no time and no end. Peter, Paul and the rest of the apostles viewed the death of the body as simply moving into another residence, from a tent into a mansion. After all, Jesus said:

John 14:1

"In My Father's house are many mansions; if it were not so, I would have told you, I go and prepare a place for you."

No wonder Paul calls the death of a Christian *"gain."* Where would you rather live, in a tent, or in a mansion? Paul also mentioned that his earthly body was only a tent for his spirit and there was something far better on the other side.

2nd Corinthians 5: 1

For we know that if our earthly house, this tent, is destroyed, we have a building from God, not made with hands, eternal in the heavens.

The Holy Spirit bear witness with our spirits also; that we are heaven bound, and will be with Christ the moment we leave these bodies. Not that we should take this wonderful gift of life here on this earth for granted, but we should know that our home is with our Savior.

2nd Corinthians 5: 8

We are confident, yes, well pleased rather to be absent from the body and present with the Lord.

We also read how a man named Stephen, who was called to help in the daily distributing to the needs of widows, who was raised up by God to testify before the High Priest in that day. Now this man was not apostle, nor a pastor in the church, yet God used him with *great signs and wonders* as a testimony of the gospel of Jesus Christ. Stephen addresses the Jewish counsel and causes an uproar with the religious leaders, which leads to his death, the death of his body, but certainly not of his spirit. In his last physical breath, he cries out to the Lord Jesus!

Acts 7: 59

And they stoned Stephen as he was calling on God and saying, "Lord Jesus, receive my spirit."

The man Stephen knew where his spirit was going once separated from his mortal body. The Scripture says that he was calling out to God as they stoned him. Moreover, with what name did he call out to God with and to whom did he say, *"Receive my spirit?"* Stephen called out to the name that is above every name, *"Lord Jesus, receive my spirit."* Stephen knew that it was faith in the name of Jesus that had given him new hope for an eternal future with God. Therefore, it was by the name of Jesus, to Jesus, that Stephen cries out to God and says, *"Receive my spirit."*

Acts 7: 60

And when He (Stephen), *had said this, he fell asleep.*

The sleep that Stephen fell into was physical and not spiritual, since he asked God to receive his spirit. Again, Stephen had no doubt where his spirit was going; therefore, there was no fear of death.

The witnesses of the Lord's crucifixion, also testifies that Jesus gave up His spirit when His work was completed.

John 19: 29

He (Jesus) *said, "It is finished!" And bowing His head, He gave up His spirit.*

The Spirit of Jesus was separated from His natural body. The Scriptures tell us that His Spirit went into the pits of hell and preached God's offer of redemption to the spirits that had turned away from God in past days.

1st Peter 3: 18, 19

...Being put to death in the flesh, but made alive in the Spirit, by whom also He preached to the spirits in prison who formerly were disobedient...

Notice how the Scripture says that Jesus preached to the spirits that were in prison. It is then obvious that there were spirits in a place of judgment, and Jesus, in His Spirit, preached the word of salvation to them. Peter writes that Jesus went to the prison of spirits. Some groups do not believe that Jesus went to the place that He described as a place of torture, prison, or Hades. However, according to the Scriptures, Jesus went there, overcame Satan, and took away from him the keys of death, but He certainly did not remain there.

Psalm 16: 10

For You will not leave My soul in Sheol, (the abode of the spiritually dead).

You cannot be left somewhere unless you are already there. Jesus was not left in the place of the spiritually dead, but His Spirit was there, stepped on Satan's head and preached the gospel to those that were bound by the penalty of sin.

The death of these bodies and the continuing life of our spirits are issues that we all must settle in our hearts in order to move out of fear and into the confidence of God's love.

There will come a day when these mortal bodies will put on immortality. A physical resurrection will again take place as Jesus Christ returns to rule His kingdom here on earth. I say again, because it is recorded, that when Jesus gave up His spirit, the ground shook and the graves of those who believed and died, where resurrected from the dead.

Matthew 27: 52 & 53

And the graves were opened and many bodies of the saints who had fallen asleep were raised; after His resurrection, they went into the holy city and appeared to many.

There is no doubt that a resurrection of the dead took place when Jesus had fulfilled all prophecy that was written about Him. Jesus died on the cross and was the first to be raised up from the dead. The chains of sin were then broken from the spirit of man, and Jesus was raised first with many others to follow, but not until His return. Jesus taught that through His death, many would come to live in the faith of His resurrection. Now, during His earthly ministry, Jesus raised many from the dead, but later they physically died again like everyone else. Those that were raised after the Lord's resurrection were also raised temporarily and sent on a mission to witness to those in the Holy City. The Scriptures does not state that this was a permanent resurrection with glorified bodies, so it was a temporary resurrection, like Lazarus and many others that later died physically. There will take place in the future a permanent resurrection, as God has foretold in the Scriptures. As Christ lives, those that believe in Him will live also. Some churches had strayed from this truth, so Paul was quick to repair their foundation of faith in the resurrection of Christ, because it is in the resurrection of Christ that we are established in the faith.

1st Corinthians 15: 17, 18
And if Christ is not risen, then our preaching is empty and your faith is futile; you are still in your sins! Then also those who have fallen asleep in Christ have perished.

The Christian faith is centered on the power of the resurrection, the understanding that Christ was raised physically from the dead and so will we be with glorified bodies. Jesus gives us a great insight when He explains this truth to His disciples and to Martha, the sister of Lazarus.

John 11: 11
"Lazarus has fallen asleep."

Jesus first told His disciples that Lazarus was sleeping, referring to his death, but using the term *asleep,* as a temporary condition. This is also why we continue to see the word *asleep* in the Scriptures, because it is only a temporary state in that our physical bodies will be in.

Martha's brother Lazarus was dead for four days, and she was in deep sorrow when Jesus shows up. Martha's first reaction is if Jesus could have only been there while her brother was still alive, but now it is too late, he is dead. Then Jesus tells her:

John 11: 23
"Your brother will rise again."

Martha still accepting her brother's death as final, reassures Jesus that she understands that on the last day all will rise before the throne of God. These chapters are worth reviewing because the more we dig into them, the more we will find.

John 11: 24
Martha said to Him, "I know that he will rise again in the resurrection at the last day."

Martha did believe in the resurrecting power of God, however, was still thinking that her brother's death was final. She was confident that she would see her brother again. It is then that Jesus gives her and us a clear view of the Christian hope, established on His promises.

John 11: 25, 26

Jesus said to her, "I am the resurrection and the life, he who believes in Me, though he may die, he will live. And whoever lives and believes in Me shall never die. Do you believe this?"

Jesus was not talking about the temporary resurrection of Lazarus from the dead, but was teaching that though the physical body dies, eternal life is of the spirit. This is a powerful, revealing statement. Jesus pulls no punches when He clearly testifies that He is the resurrection of all life, in Him all life exists. Jesus takes it further as He assures Martha and us that although our bodies will die; our spirits will be alive with Him, never to be apart from Him again. Martha's response was the right one, as she quickly identifies the deity of Jesus as the Savior and says, *"Yes!"*

John 11: 24

Martha said to Him, "Yes, Lord I believe that You are the Christ, the Son of God, who is to come into the world."

Unless we can answer that question from God with the same response in faith, *"Yes, Lord, I believe"* then our eternities are hanging in the uncertainty of doubt. Although some might judge themselves righteous, because many have more faith in themselves than in God, Jesus tells us up front that without faith in Him, we are dead. He is the resurrection of the dead, the resurrection of our spirits, and some day of our bodies. Without Jesus Christ, we are simply without resurrection power. Jesus also told Martha something that we also need to learn and allow it to take root in our spirits. Martha was a realist; she accepted the physical reality of her brother's death. Martha was also the one who complained to Jesus about her sister Mary.

One day while Jesus was teaching in their house, Martha was running around trying to prepare something for the guest, while her sister Mary just sat at the feet of Jesus and listened to Him. Martha was serving the people and the Lord, when at one point she must have felt overwhelmed. Martha was a realist, she complained to Jesus that there were things that needed to be done, and her sister Mary was not helping her to do any of them. In Martha's perspective, there was a time to listen, but there was also a time to serve. Martha's realistic view was that if everybody just sat around and listened to Jesus, then who would serve? What Martha did not realize was that the food that she served would be gone, the guest that she served would eventually leave, and all her work was only for a fleeing moment. However, the words that Jesus spoke were for eternity, His words are more important than all the preparation, serving and labor that we could ever do in this short life, because His words are eternal life. Jesus said that He is *the resurrection and the life.* He is the very life source that sustains all living matter. There is no other name in heaven or on the earth that can give life.

When Jesus was teaching throughout the towns of Israel, He called a man into the ministry and said to him:

Luke 9: 30, 31

"Follow me." But he (the man) *said, "Lord let me first go and bury my father."*
Jesus said to him, "Let the dead bury their own dead, but you go and preach the kingdom of God."

Jesus was not unsympathetic to the man's loss of his father, but makes a distinction between the living and the dead. All those who believe in Jesus Christ are alive in Him and those apart from Him are spiritually dead. This is why Jesus taught that though the physical body of a believer dies, their spirits are very much alive in Him and with Him. On the other hand, those who do not believe in the salvation of God through Jesus Christ are considered already dead. Although their physical bodies are still functioning, their spirits are separated from God due to sin, resulting in spiritual death.

Psalm 115: 17

The dead do not praise the Lord, nor any who go down in silence.
The spiritually dead do not give honor, praise and worship to God. How can someone give praise to God if their spirits are dead, separated from the one and only Life Source, as we once were. Therefore, the dead in spirit cannot give life-filled worship to the one and only Creator. However, those who are born of the Spirit of God will not cease to give God glory from

now to eternity. For the Spirit of God tells us that where there is praise, honor and worship to the living God, there is life that has no end. This is why the Psalmist could boldly say, *'forever.'*
Psalm 115: 18
But we will bless the Lord from this time forth and forever.
Some religions teach that as long as you are a good person, and obey the law, you will go to heaven. However, God does not tell us that we will be granted a place in heaven or the earth by the merit of good works. We have all broken the law sometime in our lives; therefore, the only atonement that is strong enough to fulfill the required judgment of a transgressor of the law is the blood of Christ. This is a legal, spiritual justification that can only occur through faith in the death and resurrection of Jesus Christ.
Hebrews 2: 9
But we see Jesus, who was made a little lower than the angels, for the suffering of death crowned with glory and honor, that He, by the grace of God, might taste death for everyone.
Jesus told us very clearly that without Him, we are dead. However, with Him, by the power of His atonement, we are alive in the spirit as a new creature, born into a new hope of eternal salvation by the love, mercy and grace of God. We cannot earn His mercy, we cannot buy His grace, but because of His love for us, we have been granted a pardon from the judgment of sin by the eternal sacrifice of His blood. This is our eternal hope!
John 14: 3
"And if I (Jesus), *go and prepare a place for you, I will come again and receive you to Myself; that where I am, there you may be also."*
In this promise, we can be confident that whether Jesus receives our spirits, as He did Stephen's, or He returns while we remain in these physical bodies, He will come to us and bring us with Him. We can also rest assured that either way there will come a day of a physical resurrection for all people. Some to be resurrected for eternal life with God and others to be judged, since they did not receive the sacrifice of God, so their sin remains with them. Jesus Christ gives us a promise

that we can hold on to, even through the many storms of this life.

John 14: 18

"I (Jesus) will not leave you alone; I will come to you."

No matter what, once we belong to Christ, we will never be without Him. The day is coming when Jesus Christ will return in a full manifestation, in that every eye will see Him. On that day, there will be a first resurrection of those that sleep in Christ. Some may still ask, 'Is the physical resurrection from the dead a truth, or a misguided teaching that has found its way into Christianity?' God has much to say about this subject and if we confess to be Christians, then we need to know what God promises concerning resurrection.

Romans 8: 11:

But if the Spirit of Him who raised Jesus from the dead dwells in you, He who raised Christ from the dead will also
give life to your mortal bodies through His Spirit who dwells in you.

There are many places that we could easily start from in the Old and New Testaments, but why not start with the earthly ministry of Jesus Christ.

Luke 14: 14

"And you will be blessed, because they cannot repay you; for you shall be repaid at the resurrection of the just."

The two permanent resurrections that God clearly teaches will take place at different times, one for believers, and the other for unbelievers. The believer has been declared not guilty by accepting the eternal sacrifice of Jesus Christ on the cross as the payment for his or her sins. There is no self-justification in God's plan for salvation, but it is the gift from God. We are saved by God's mercy! This cannot be repeated enough, since some religious groups teach justification through works, which will never save our spirits from the righteous judgment of God, who is all knowing, all truth and all power.

Ephesians 2: 8 & 9

For by grace are you saved by faith; and that not of yourselves: it is the gift of God: Not of works, lest any man should boast.

Therefore, the just that God is talking about are all those that believe on Him, justified by faith for the atonement of their sins. All true believers in Christ are declared just, pardoned of all their errors and will rise first, physically from the dead. The debates among the scholars concerning the details, times and places of the Lord's return and the rising of the dead are proof that God is limiting our knowledge in this area. The Lord will return *as a thief in the night,* however, this we know, that when He does return, those in Christ will rise from the dead first.

1st Thessalonians 4: 16

For the Lord Himself will descend from heaven with a shout, with the voice of an archangel, and with the trumpet of God. And the dead in Christ will rise first.

This is the first permanent resurrection from the dead as the spirits of all those that believe will be reunited with their bodies, which *were sown in mortality, but raised in immortality.* This is the final state of every believer, since we are told that *we will see Him as He is.* Therefore, we will be like Jesus in a resurrected, eternal, glorified body.

1st John 3: 2

Beloved, now we are children of God; and it has not yet been revealed what we shall be, but we know that when He is revealed, we shall be like Him, for we shall see Him as He is.

This first resurrection will take place when the Lord Jesus returns to the earth for His church. Until that time, all of creation awaits for the returning of the true King and Lord of all life who will restore the order of all creation the way it was intended to be from the beginning, without sin.

Revelation 20: 6

Blessed and holy is he who has part in the first resurrection. Over such the second death has no power, but they shall be priest of God and Christ, and shall reign with Him a thousand years.

The second resurrection is a time of judgment when the dead that are not in Christ; that is all those that refused to believe in Jesus Christ, will be revealed.

Revelation 20: 13

The sea gave up their dead who were in it, and death and Hades delivered up the dead who were in them. And they were judged, each one according to his works.

This is the second resurrection, in that all those in the first resurrection will have nothing to do with. This will be the final resurrection for God's judgment. This will be the final word for them from God.

Revelation 20: 15

And anyone not found written in the Book of Life was cast into the lake of fire.

We know that all those that place their hope and trust in the Lord Jesus Christ have passed from judgment into life. There is a good reason for this. For Jesus Himself took the judgment of all our sins on the cross as He bore the pain and death for our transgressions. However, as far as those that have not accepted the sacrifice of Jesus Christ for the atonement of their sins, then payment is due. God alone is pure truth and justice. Although we might have our own opinions about what justice is, God wrote the book! We cannot even begin to compare our very limited so-called knowledge of truth, justice, or anything else for that matter, to the infinite, all-knowing wisdom and knowledge of God. There is no real comparison that can be used to illustrate this gap between the knowledge of the Creator, and the so-called knowledge of His creation. Even attempting to explain this fact would be like comparing our most brilliant scientist to the intelligence of a sheep, and even that would still fall far short in the measuring of the gap. Nevertheless, we can know the love of God through His word that reveals His eternal plan for His beloved creation.

1st Corinthians 15: 3 & 4, Isaiah 53: 12

That Christ died for our sins, according to the Scriptures, and that He was buried, and that He rose again the third day according to the Scriptures.

Because He poured out His soul unto death, and He was numbered with the transgressors, and He bore the sin of many, and made intercession for the transgressors.

This is the true gospel and in where our hope must remain. Forget about what good any of us thinks we might have done. They are all but filthy rags, soiled with sin in the presence of God. Forget about any sacrifice that any of us has made. They are soiled with the marks of error. The eternal salvation of our spirits and the future resurrection of our bodies are all by the grace of God, because Jesus satisfied the judgment against us as He was nailed to that cross and died in our place. There is no other sacrifice, no other plan of redemption, and no other way to reach the Father of all life. Moreover, the proof is not in the fact that Jesus died after a brutal beating and crucifixion from the Romans, but on the third day, He rose again.

The apostles were not witnesses to the Law of Moses, since the law needed no witness, it was judgment. The apostles were witnesses to the resurrection of Jesus Christ from the dead and in the resurrection was their hope.

Acts 4: 2

...They taught the people and preached in Jesus the resurrection from the dead.

This is what the apostles taught, preached and believed, because they were eyewitnesses to the resurrection.

Moreover, if we believe that Christ died for our sins on the cross and rose on the third day from the dead, then He will raise us up also.

The Apostle Paul was also an eyewitness to the risen Christ as he was struck down by the manifestation of Jesus on a Damascus road. Paul in time also received many revelations concerning the kingdom of God, as Peter also testifies in his epistle, *"As also our beloved brother Paul, according to the wisdom given to him, has written to you..."*

Romans 14: 9

For to this end Christ died and rose again, that He might be Lord. Therefore, whether we live or die, we are the Lords.

Whether our spirits depart from these earthly bodies, or they remain in them, it does not matter. For when we truly have surrendered to the lordship of Christ Jesus, then we are His in whatever state. Moreover, although our bodies might die, our spirits will not, since they are not bound by the same death as the flesh. Therefore, as the body sleeps, the spirit remains alive and in the care of the risen Savior.

Philippians 1: 21- 23

For to me, to live is Christ, and to die is gain. But if I live in the flesh, this will mean fruit from my labor; yet what shall I choose I cannot tell. For I am hard pressed between the two, having a desire to depart and be with Christ, which is far better.

There is no doubt in the heart and mind of the apostle that once his spirit departed from his body, he would be with Jesus.

This was not because the apostle was judged more righteous than any other believer, but because he understood the grace of God's love, and the promises that God has made to all that seek and love Him. Paul says, *"To die is gain."* This was by no means a statement from deranged man, wanting the easy way out of the trials of this life. On the contrary, Paul was willing to be used to fight any battle for the gospel's sake. Death to Paul was simply the putting off of the physical body; like the snake that sheds its skin, and the resurrection from the dead was simply the spirit returning to a new eternal body that will never die again. The understanding in the departure from the body, and returning to it is important to everyone, because both will happen to us all. God had granted great insight to the apostle, and in turn, that insight is given to us.

The church in Corinth was having some difficulties with this teaching, and is certainly our gain to learn from their questions. Since we have established that our spirits will leave these mortal bodies, let us continue to the returning to them.

1st Corinthians 15: 12

Now if Christ is preached that He has been raised from the dead then how do some of you say that there is no resurrection of the dead?

The apostle, by the teaching of the Holy Spirit, wasted no time in facing the issue head on. The issue was obvious, that the church was falling away from the sound doctrine of what the apostle had already preached to them. Therefore, Paul is ready to review the basics of the gospel, which is the confirmation of Jesus as Savior and Christ, by the proof of the resurrection from the dead. He begins to build the same foundation that somehow was beginning to crumble in the church. Paul starts at the beginning, stating that *Jesus Christ died for our sins, according to the Scriptures, and that He was buried, and that He rose again the third day.* This is the first stone of faith that must be set in place before attempting to go any further in Christianity. Paul sets it with the mortar of the Scriptures as his point of reference. Now if the faith is based on the resurrection of Christ from the dead, the apostle then asked, *"How do some among you say that there is no resurrection from the dead?"* I can see Paul shaking his head in wonder, thinking, what happened to the foundation that I laid in you? The entire Christian faith rest upon the fact of the resurrection of Jesus Christ from the dead. We say fact, because of the many documented eyewitnesses written in Scripture, and Paul was quick to remind them that Christ was seen by many people after His resurrection from the dead!

1st Corinthians 15: 5 – 8
He was seen by Peter, then the twelve.
After that He was seen by over five hundred brethren at once...
After that He was seen by James and all the Apostles.
Then last of all He was seen by me...

How many more eyewitnesses does God need? Paul, by the directive of the Holy Spirit, establishes the fact that Christ indeed was resurrected from the dead. With this proof, I can almost sense a lack of patience in Paul as he begins to systematically explain to them that without the resurrection of Christ, there is no Christianity! Therefore, we are false teachers, and what is worse is that we are all still in our sins with no hope for eternity. Paul goes so far as to say, *"In this life only we have hope in Christ, we are of all men most pitiable."* In other words, if Christ is not resurrected from the dead; we that believe are worse than all those who hope in the empty beliefs of the world.

1st Corinthians 15: 17
And if Christ is not risen, your faith is futile; you are still in your sins.

All the opposition against Christianity states that Christ did not rise from the dead; as the Jews, the Muslims, Hindus and the Eastern Mystics believe. However, for the Christian, the resurrection of Christ is the proof that Christ is who He said He is, He is the Savior of the world who came from God and not from man, but through the natural birth of a woman. No other religious leader can make this claim! This is why The Holy Spirit testifies repeatedly in the New Testament that Christ has indeed risen from the dead, which is the proof that His blood was shed for the offences of our sin. This is what Jesus taught, this is what the apostles taught, and this is what is now taught in true Christianity today.

1st Corinthians 15: 20

But now Christ is risen from the dead, and has become the first fruits of those who have fallen asleep.

It is here where we can rightly divide the word of truth. Paul explains that Christ is the first to be risen from the dead, and all those, whose bodies are now dead, will be resurrected, just as He was. Moreover, concerning the spirits of those whose bodies are dead, the Lord's physical body was also dead for three days. Did not Jesus give His spirit to God the Father?

Luke 23: 46

And when Jesus had cried out with a loud voice, He said, "Father, into Your hands I commit My Spirit."

Just like anyone else, the body of Jesus had died, but His Spirit was alive and committed into the Father's hands. As our bodies will fall victim to the decay of death, our spirits, being born into the family of God will continue to live in full conciseness, knowing all that is happening around us. The Holy Spirit brings a bright ray of light in the following Scripture, confirming that death was not God's original plan in creation, but was brought about by the sin of man.

1st Corinthians 15: 21

For since by man came death, by Man also came the resurrection of the dead.

This verse tells us two extremely important facts that every Christian should understand. The first: there was no spiritual death of man before the fall of Adam, for the word says that *by man came death* and not by God. For God is the Author of life, not of death. Man killed himself when Adam sinned. Sin is death, and before the act of sin by Adam, there was no death in his spirit.

Adam and Eve were most likely vegetarians, since I am sure that the fruits and vegetables in the Garden of Eden were nothing like the ones we have today. The results of sin caused a radical change in Adam and Eve, but also on the earth. God cursed even the soil of the earth. Sin brought forth death, and death continued, even until now. The first death for Adam was the spiritual, separation from God, and the second was the death of his body. However, as the spiritual death caused by one man resulted in separation from God, by one Man, Jesus Christ, we have reconciliation with God, resulting in spiritual re-birth, and will also result in physical resurrection from the dead.

1st Corinthians 15: 22

For as in Adam all die, even so in Christ all shall be made alive. The Holy Spirit is speaking about the resurrection of the physical bodies throughout this chapter, so it cannot be confused with the spiritual resurrection of our spirits that takes place through an open confession of faith in Christ. The resurrection of our physical bodies at the time of the Lord's return should be another hope of every believer. Until that time, Jesus promised us that He *is with us always, even until the end of time.* Paul was confident in this hope as he wrote; *"to live is Christ and to die is gain."* The shedding of these earthly vessels that have been stained with the curse of sin is the true liberty of our spirits, where sin can no longer touch us. The re-birth in Christ has made our spirits alive to God, but our physical bodies still live with the curse of sin and death, still in a state of corruption. *The outer man perishes, while the inner man is renewed daily.* However, one day the outer man will also be renewed with a resurrected body, free from sin and death. Then the inner and outer man will be truly one, even much more holy than Adam. For sin and death will have no place in the believer who was sown in faith and will be raised in God's glory. This is the sure promise of God for all those that place their trust in Christ.

1st Corinthians 15: 42 – 44

So also is the resurrection of the dead. The body is sown in corruption, and raised in incorruption. It is sown in dishonor, it is raised in glory. It is sown in weakness, it is raised in power. It is sown a natural body, it is raised a spiritual body.

As a seed that is planted in the ground does not resemble the plant life that will be raised from that seed, so our earthly, dead bodies will be raised as an incorruptible, glorified body, never to die again. Moreover, as we now resemble the first *man of the dust,* Adam, we that believe will also resemble the last Man, Jesus Christ; as Christ is, so we shall be.

1st Corinthians 15: 49, 50

And as we have borne the image of the man of the dust, we shall also bear the image of the heavenly Man. Now this I say,

brethren, that flesh and blood cannot inherit the kingdom of God; nor does corruption inherit incorruption.
In conclusion, as we place our hope in Christ Jesus as the eternal sacrifice for all our sins, and surrender our lives unto God through Him, then our spirits are now born unto God as family. This is the only true hope that God's plan for our salvation is built upon. For there is no other savior, no other mediator, no other sacrifice, no other way out of the judgment of God. Since Christ Jesus Himself bore our judgment on the cross, freely giving us a pardon for all our sins; past, present, or future. Moreover, though our spirits may be eternally sealed and approval of God, because Christ fulfilled the demands of the law on the cross, our physical bodies are not. The seed of death still reigns in our earthly tents; therefore, being corruptible, they presently cannot inherit eternal life. However, God will not leave our present bodies in this corruptible, mortal state.
1st Corinthians 15: 52
For the trumpet will sound, and the dead (those asleep in Christ), *will be raised incorruptible, and we shall be changed.*
There is a change that will take place when the Lord returns for every believer. Our spirits will return to an incorruptible, immortal body, resurrected and glorified, where death will have no place; a body that will have no place for sickness, pain or suffering, we will simply have no sin.
Romans 6: 5
For if we have been united together in the likeness of His death, certainly we also shall be in the likeness of His resurrection.
This was God's intent right from the beginning, as God's creation was brought forth to live and not die. For by one man, the curse of death brought forth sickness, sorrow, pain, mental distress and spiritual darkness. However, by one Man came life, which brings forth healing, joy, comfort, a sound mind, spiritual enlightenment and eternal life with God. Though the offense of one man was great, the grace of God through one Man is far greater; this is the *gift* of God.
Romans 5: 15, 16, 17, 18, 19
But the free gift... And the gift... But the free gift... ...And of the gift... The free gift came...

For if by one man's offense many died, much more the grace of God and the gift by the grace of the one Man, Jesus Christ, abound to many.

For as by one man's disobedience many were made sinners, so also by one Man's obedience many will be made righteous.

Though the physical body of the believer will die and be laid to rest by the offense of Adam, the spirit is alive to God, through Christ Jesus, who is the Author of all life! The Holy Spirit is the witness within us that has sealed our spirits in the family of God, testifying to our hearts that the promise of eternal life is ours in the spirit and later in the body.

Romans 8: 11, 24

But if the Spirit of Him who raised Jesus from the dead dwells in you, He who raised Christ from the dead will also give life to your mortal bodies through His Spirit who dwells in you.

For we are saved in this hope...

The believer in Jesus Christ will certainly experience the death of these temporary bodies as our spirits depart from them, but we will never experience the second death, which is the separation of the Spirit from God. This is the confident hope of every Christian, which is not a hope of not knowing, but knowing through the witness of the Holy Spirit, who dwells in the hearts of all who have placed their trust in Jesus Christ as Savior and Lord. For the unbelieving world might enjoy the pleasures of sin for now, but they are only for a brief moment in time. This life is like the sand in the hourglass that steadily pours through the opening of time, as it is certain that the sand will be gone before long. However, eternity is not bound by the limitations of time, nor is God, who was, who is, and will be forever. Our eternities are reserved with Jesus, by the power of His mercy and by the promise of His love, we are saved! Not by the power of our works or the determination of our own wills, but by His grace, which was spilled in the blood of Christ, for we are redeemed by faith.

Mark 16: 17, John 3: 18 & 19

"He who believes and is baptized will be saved..."

"He who believes in Him is not condemned; but he who does not believe is condemned already, because he has not believed in the

*name of the only begotten Son of God. And this is the
condemnation, that the light has come into the world, and men
love darkness rather than light, because their deeds are evil."*
There is no better place to rest than in the light of the glory of
God, which is in Christ Jesus our Lord. God gives us his word in
writing, so that we do not lose faith. This life is so short, and
the time seems to be speeding by our very eyes, therefore, we
need to be ready to depart at any given moment. The teaching
of eternal life is throughout the Scriptures, as Jesus repeatedly
promised that He waits for the believer with open arms, and is
not ashamed of the ones that place their trust in Him, even
before the throne of God.
The Apostle Paul writes some final words by the Spirit of God
within him, to encourage Timothy and the church, and should
encourage us, as he makes a bold statement in faith. Paul does
not change from his testimony, but continues in the hope of
faith in Christ, that where Christ is, we will be also.
2nd Timothy 4: 6 – 8,
*"For I am already being poured out as a drink offering, and the
time of my departure is at hand. I have fought the good fight, I
have finished the race, I have kept the faith. Finally, there is laid
up for me the crown of righteousness, which the Lord, the
righteous Judge, will give me on that day, and not to me only but
also to all who have loved His appearing."*
1st Thessalonians 4: 14, 5: 9, 10
*For if we believe that Jesus died and rose again, even so God will
bring with Him those who sleep in Jesus.*
*For God did not appoint us to wrath, but to obtain salvation
through our Lord Jesus Christ, who died for us, that whether we
wake or sleep, we should live together with Him.*

The Love Priority

1st John 4: 8
God is love...

Love is often a complicated word with a variety of meanings. Though many will interpret the word in many different ways, allow me to try with what little I know. Love is a devoted passion, in a faithful yielding surrender, which is willing to give all that is able to give for the heart's desire, by choice and not by force. Love is a commitment, a covenant within a promise. Love is a decision to care for, stand with and empty ourselves of ourselves for the good of another. Love is the common denominator between all people of every race, color and nationality. It is also the common ground between God and man. For we know that *His ways are higher than our ways, and His thoughts are higher than our thoughts.* However, when it comes to love, it is possible for us to connect on God's level, if we are willing to yield ourselves to His mercy.

For some, the real meaning of love is in material possessions, or for a favorite pastime, and then there is a love for someone else that is listed somewhere at the bottom of the page. The love for something that is not living is a one way shallow desire, which cannot reap any benefits of love being returned. This so-called love should be at a much lower level compared to loving someone else, another living being. People have a much higher value than any dead, material object and can reap the joy of returned love. This is one place where the current society has come to the point of confusion, holding the *love of money,* pleasures and material possessions far above the love for human life, and even the Author of all life, God Himself. On the other hand, how can any of us love the ones that are created when we do not love the one who created them? Complicated? Not really, if we are willing to listen to the heart of God. Only then can we see clearly how to prioritize God as the first love in our lives, with the proof of obedience to Him. Some of us make a bold attempt to keep the right priorities. Many will say that the most important ones in their lives are God and their families, but our actions can say something totally different. Even our occupations might become a love priority without us even realizing it. The true evidence of the love priority in our lives is in the motives of our actions and in our daily decisions based on our highest passions.

Deuteronomy 6: 5
"You shall love the Lord your God with all your heart, with all your soul, and with all your strength."

The first *commandment* given from God to Moses is to love, and not to love everything else before God, but rather love God before everything else. The word *commandment* is used, but we know that no one can force someone to love someone else, since love is a voluntary surrender. This is why we have a free choice, though it is limited to God's purpose. Moreover, we cannot love someone that we do not know.

Deuteronomy 30: 19 & 20
"I have set before you life and death, blessing and cursing; therefore choose life, that both you and your descendants may live; that you may love the Lord your God, that you may obey His voice, and that you may cling to Him, for He is your life..."

The Scripture says that if we choose life, only then are we able to love God and follow His words. God creates the choices, and then sets them before us to choose. God knows what choice we will make long before we ever make it, because God knows everything, past, present and future.

Due to the blindness of sin, we have all chosen at some time to fall in love with the temporary pleasures of this life, more than with God, or even each other. We know that there is nothing wrong or sinful with enjoying the blessings of material possessions in this short life, but possessions cannot be placed above the value of God and even above the value of human life. When the Creator is given first place in our hearts, which is honoring God with our lives, then can we truly enjoy the material blessings that God has given to each of us. We can only do this with God and not without Him. For it is only by the light of His grace that we can understand real love, since we are continually bombarded by influences in the world that are attempting to derail us from glorifying God. We are attacked with a barrage of advertising no matter where we go. It is in the mail, on the television, on the radio, on the Internet, and even on every bus and taxi that drives by us. It is a non-stop world of marketing, all through the clever schemes of advertisement.

Most of the marketing focuses are geared toward selfish wants, to get us to buy something that will make us feel good. All the advertisements will tell us that we are first and we have a right to feel good. It would be one thing if this feeling good over material possessions would last, but it doesn't. In time, a very short time, whatever it was that made us feel good becomes old, the feeling fades and we are now on the hunt for something else to help us feel good again. In my own life, once I confessed my sin before God, and understood that Jesus Christ died and rose again to remove my sin, I did not need anything new to help me feel good, I felt great! Once the burden of sin and shame are removed from our lives, then we can realize that material possessions can make us more comfortable and are pleasing to the eye, but by no means can supply us with true happiness. For these earthly possessions are not eternal, but temporal and soon rust, fade and simply wear out. However, the knowledge of God's love, and accepting that love into our hearts, can supply our spirits with a never ending peace and joy that can bring us through the barriers of time and into a timeless eternity with God.

Now some people might ask, 'are there not many people that we meet everyday who are happy without God?' Anyone can put on the costume of happiness. Many put on the mask of perfection, attempting to prove to all that their lives are perfect, and they have everything that they would ever want and need. However, we are not with that person all the time. We cannot see the guilt and fears in their hearts, or their worries in the middle of the night as they stare at the ceiling, which we all have done. Moreover, when their time comes to depart from this life, they will have no hope. There cannot be very much joy or happiness in that.

In the field of service, I have met many people who honestly try to do the right thing, but without God. They work hard and are good providers for their families, but without God, they are still incomplete, still filled with the fear of the unknown. They try to live a full and productive life, but the journey is uncertain and the end is frightening. They try to fulfill their dreams, hopes and desires, never really finding the true purpose for their very existence. Without God, no matter what dream we might obtain, no matter what goal we might accomplish, there will be a remaining hole in our hearts that only the love of God can fill.

Toward the end of King Solomon's life, after having everything that his eyes desired, his end conclusion was; *"It is all vanity."* It is a life with a void, a hole that is missing the love of God, which is by far the most unfulfilling, unrewarding life that can be found in all existence. It is a place of emptiness, darkness and uncertainty that lacks the understanding of God's faithfulness. There is no light, no love in dead material possessions, so how can we find more fulfillments in things that have no life? Real love is in life, and God is love, being the Author of all life. There is no joy in death, or happiness in hopelessness. Moreover, without love, we are dead.

1st Corinthians 13: 4 – 8

Love suffers long and is kind; love does not envy; love does not parade itself, it is not puffed up; does not behave rudely, does not seek its own, is not provoked, thinks no evil; does not rejoice in iniquity, but rejoices in truth; bears all things, believes all things, hopes all things, endures all things. Love never fails.

God not only explains to us how to love, but also reveals His very nature. God is patient, God is kind, God is not rude or self-seeking, God is not easily angered, and God never fails. God loves us because of who He is; He is love. However, God is also justice and truth; He cannot lie, or go back on His word. As in the case of our eternal salvation, God could not ignore our sin, so He paid for the penalty of our sins by sending His Son to bore the payment on a cross in our place. This is by far, the greatest act of love that has ever been witnessed on earth, or in heaven.

1st John 4: 9 & 10

In this the love of God was manifest toward us, that God has sent His only begotten Son into the world, that we might live through Him. In this love, not that we loved God, but that He loved us and sent His Son to be the propitiation for our sin.

God's love prevails over all our failures, over our blindness and certainly over our self-centeredness. For it was God the Father, who sent His Son from the Godhead, as a justified payment for our sins, with no balance due. There is no unfinished work for our salvation, in that we might attempt to complete with so-called good deeds, since all our good is stained with sin anyway. This is the real center of the love of God toward us in that the Father gave the request, and the Son obeyed, all out of love.

Philippians 2: 8
And being found in appearance as a man, He humbled Himself and became obedient to the point of death, even death on the cross.

The birth, life, death and resurrection of Jesus Christ, is the starting point in comprehending God's love for us. There is no other place that we can start, or for that matter end. We are empty vessels with a hopeless uncertainty unless we come to the understanding of the divine rescue mission of love.

God's love for us was not just a thought, or a good intention in the heart of God. God acted on that thought, and that action of love brought the greatest manifestation, in the form of a visitation of God into the natural realm.

1st John 4: 8
For he who does not love does not know God, for God is love.

After all the theories, the theological teaching and books from all the scholars, we can throw them out the window when it comes to love. Love is not always logical, but true love is always passionate. I have never met someone that had a real love for somebody else, which did not have a real passion for the person they love. In addition, passion will produce action, even sacrifice, because real love is willing to give all.

Can we truly know God and His eternal love for us? The greatest expression of love is the sacrifice of one's self for the good of another, which is exactly what God did for us. Just as we can know a person by their words that align with their actions, we can know God in the same way, as God gave His Son for us.

Moreover, all the beauty of creation is also a reflection of God's love for us. He created the earth and all that is in it for us to enjoy. Therefore, God alone deserves all the honor, glory and thanksgiving for all creation.

Romans 1: 20
For since the creation of the world His invisible attributes are clearly seen, being understood by the things that are made...
So why is the world in so much distress and turmoil? Could it be that we have lost the true definition of love, therefore, we are blinded by the darkness of selfish lust. Are we shortsighted in seeing the nature of God, which is love?
Love is not just words that are written on Hallmark cards, or poetic words to a melody. It is not a casual phrase used in daily small talk or in passing conversations. The world even defines love as sex, which could not be farthest from the ultimate truth. Love is not just sex, but it is a physical and spiritual encounter between a man and his wife, willing to come together as one and share the powerful gift of giving through their bodies and emotions with passion. The word love is a word that should be displayed by the actions of caring and giving, even in the bedroom. God tells us that the gift of physically making love should be kept, protected, guarded in the confines of marriage, since it is not just a passing feeling, but a gift, honoring a lasting commitment to one another. It is extremely important for the youth of today to understand that this gift of lovemaking between a husband and wife is a treasure from God that should not be given away carelessly, but cherished and saved for that special someone. Jesus taught on this very subject, that a relationship between a husband and wife is holy before God. Therefore, something that is holy and pure should be valued and not given away easily; it is like a priceless gem or a fine pearl.

Matthew 7: 6
"Do not give what is holy to dogs; nor cast your pearls before swine..."
We can only obey God if we love Him, because love has to be the motivation to be a disciple. If we attempt to obey God without love, we will fail, because it is in love that strength and perseverance will be nurtured. God gives us the power to overcome evil with His love.

John 14:21
Jesus said "Whoever has my commands and obeys them, he is the one who loves Me. He who loves Me will be loved by my Father, and I too will love him and show Myself to him."

The very meaning of love is the actions and motives that are shown toward the one that we claim to love. If we truly love a person we will be patient with them, we will care about their feelings, we will not just think about ourselves when we are dealing with the ones we love.

Love is the acts of consideration and kindness in truth. Love is a consistent self-denial action, that is willing to place the ones we love ahead of ourselves, testifying that their welfare is more important than our own. And if God is our love priority, then the fruits of His mercy should be evident in our actions. Apart from this, the word love is used as a careless phase, which is really referring to as what I like, not what I truly love. Like a shallow relationship, that is easily shaken by selfishness. However, real love is willing to give for the good of another. Jesus not only taught this, but also lived it as He gave Himself for us.

Galatians 2:20
I live by faith in the Son of God, who loved me and gave Himself for me.

God's love was clearly demonstrated at the cross. Make no mistake about it, God loves us, cares for us and wants to reveal Himself to us. God is not impressed with our education, our position of employment or our financial net worth. On the other hand, He is not discouraged with our selfishness, our lack of wisdom, and our sin. God is looking in our hearts; you know the part of us with the big hole in it. The part we keep trying to fill with money, careers, and other things that only make us numb. The only thing that will ever fill that hole is God's love. For all the other pleasures in this life will fade and that includes our physical bodies as well. However, God's love will never fade, wear out and will never die.

Throughout the Scriptures, God tells us repeatedly; *"I love you."* Therefore, God is patient, kind, faithful and gentle toward us, and has joy in sharing His love.

Jeremiah 31:3
The Lord appeared to us in the past saying: "I have loved you with an everlasting love; I have drawn you with loving kindness."
Romans 5: 8
But God demonstrates His own love for us in this; while we were still sinners Christ died for us.

The Scripture tells us that *while we were still sinners Christ died for us.* While we were drowning in a sea of sin, as the storms of judgment crashed against us, leaving us without hope, Jesus Christ became a lifeboat, a vessel of hope, carrying us safely to the secure ground of His mercy. If we are willing to believe, He will carry us to the mainland of His care. We can then stand on the solid rock of His eternal promise. There is a requirement that needs to be fulfilled before He can safely transport us to the shore of His salvation. The only requirement is faith: repentance in faith, a confession of faith and acting according to that confession will follow. The acting according to the confession does not save us. We can perform all the good deeds known to man, but all our works of goodwill are stained with sin. Therefore, whatever good we might perform can never be enough to achieve what Jesus has already accomplished for us on the cross. First comes the confession of faith in the sacrifice of Jesus Christ, then follows the good fruits from a thankful heart, that now surrenders to the will and love of God. If anyone believes in their heart that Jesus died for all their sins, and was raised from the dead on the third day, with an open confession of faith, they are received in His eternal kingdom by faith.

Romans 10: 9, 3:28, 5: 1
That if you confess with your mouth the Lord Jesus Christ and believe in your heart that God raised Him from the dead, you will be saved.
Therefore, we conclude that a man is justified by faith and apart from the deeds of the law.
Therefore, having been justified by faith, we have peace with God through our Lord Jesus Christ.

There are no other requirements for receiving the eternal love gift of everlasting life in the presence of God, except by faith! Now we know that God is love, which is gentle, kind, long suffering and merciful. However, God also tells us that He is jealous.

Exodus 20: 5 & 6

"For I, the Lord your God, am a jealous God, visiting the iniquity of the fathers upon the children to the third and fourth generations of those who hate Me, but showing mercy to thousands, to those who love Me and keep My commandments."

We would think that jealousy is defined as someone over possessive, insecure, and needs the devotion of another to make him or her feel wanted and needed. Jealousy is often provoked by an act of unfaithfulness, causing distrust in a relationship. Even the suspicion of one being unfaithful to another can give birth to jealously in a man or a woman, but not in God. God is referring to one fact that we can draw from this statement that is not based on a human emotion.

Exodus 20: 3

"You shall have no other gods before Me."

This is the real issue, since God is Almighty, Supreme and the only Creator of the galaxies and all that is in them, then God alone is worthy of our devout worship as God. There is no compromising on this point. The jealousy of God is not some mad emotion from an insecure mind that needs to possess another. Rather, it is God's anger toward those whom He has given the gift of life and opened His heart to, yet they refuse to give Him the thanks and honor for their very existence. Some even deny God's very existence, totally ignoring the Creator of all creation. This is not an insecure emotion, but the righteous judgment of God, as we all were under at one time, when we worshipped everything else rather than the only living Creator. So where is God's love in this? Although we have all turned our backs on God, God never turned His back on us, but provided a way.

John 3: 17

"For God did not send His Son into the world to condemn the world, but that the world through Him might be saved."

The life, death and resurrection of Jesus Christ, was and still is a rescue mission of love from God the Father to save us from our sin. Out of His love, came the sacrifice for every sin that we could ever commit against Him. It is an open invitation to a sin-free, pain-free, tear-free, death-free, never ending eternal life with Almighty God. I cannot speak for anyone else, but I myself cannot think of anything more wonderful than that! This is the love of God in Christ, which we as believers should use as an example to love one another, which is expressed so clearly in the words of our Lord Jesus.

Luke 6: 36, Matthew 5:45
"For He (God), *is kind to the ungrateful and evil."*
"For He makes His sun rise on the evil and the good, and sends rain on the just and the unjust."

This might be the hardest teaching to comprehend, but it gives us the most pure understanding of the long-suffering in the love of God. He is even *kind* to those that dishonor Him, or not even give Him a second thought of thanks. This is the ultimate understanding in the heart of God, because if we can understand this statement, we can see God's eternal love for His creation. Moreover, if God *is kind to the ungrateful,* how much more merciful will He be to those that are grateful and honor Him as God? For even when we were all in a state of rebellion, *Christ died for us.* Even in our drowning condition of darkness, He still loved us and paid the price for all our sins. When we really take a moment and realize the love that God has for us, it should startle our minds in amazement and wonder. For God does not need our love, He is God, self-contained, infinite, all-powerful, all knowing, yet the Scriptures tell us that *God is love.* Therefore, He loves us and desires a relationship with us, through His Son. This is the doctrine that Jesus taught His disciples.

John 16:27, 17: 23
"...For the Father Himself loves you, because you have loved Me, and have believed that I came forth from God."
"...And that the world may know that You (the Father), sent Me (the Son), and have loved them as you have loved Me."

Any attempt to replace God's love with earthly pleasures and possessions is like attempting to replace food with air. No matter how much air we consume, it will never fill our stomachs; it is the same with the love of God. No matter how many dead things we try to fill our hearts with, they simply amount to zero. God designed us with a natural and spiritual understanding of love, since we were made in His *image and likeness.* Without abiding in His love, we are incomplete. We therefore are missing the main ingredient of our very structure, which is the love. This is not to say that those without the knowledge of the love of God live a life without natural rewards, but they are incomplete, lacking the most important factor.

A great example of this is the story of Cain, who killed his brother Abel in pre-meditated murder. God cursed him as a *fugitive and a vagabond.* Moreover, we hear no repentance from Cain, but we still see that he lived what the world would classify as a productive, fulfilling life.

Genesis 4: 17

And Cain knew his wife, and she conceived and bore Enoch. And he built a city, and called the name of the city after his son – Enoch.

Although Cain was cursed and a fugitive of the land, from the world's perspective he was successful, but not to God. I am sure that Cain had no peace of mind, was empty hearted and his life was full of sleepless nights. So are many in the world today, as we often see many famous, wealthy people, seem to have everything the world has to offer, but are empty and many turn to drugs and alcohol. For without the love of God in our hearts, all the rest amounts to an empty space that we attempt to fill with everything from work to pleasures. We are then merely empty shells missing the true substance of life. Yes, this world of rebellion against God has many attractive offers, even the misconception of freedom, which declares that every person has individual rights. Oddly enough, the same ones that preach this message never consider the rights of an unborn baby. Whether we consider the embryo to be a developed human being or not, it is still a higher form of life and should be given the same chance to live as we all had. When Jesus looked into the hearts of the religious leaders of that day, though they kept all the rituals, He saw them as empty shells going through the motions of religion, hearts that were missing God's love.

John 5:42
"I know you, that you do not have the love of God in you."
This was the real problem then, and is the root of the problem
today. We can take all the errors of history, all the brutal wars
launched by history's coldest leaders, and the root will be the
absence of the love of God in their hearts, because true love is
not self-seeking. The love of God is the only force strong
enough to dissolve the hardness of selfishness in the heart of
humanity. There is no other solution. There is no other plan
that can cleanse the heart of a person or a nation from sin and
release them from the bondage of continuing error. God has
provided one way, and that way is in the ultimate, redeeming
sacrifice of love, in His Son, Jesus Christ. Jesus taught that if we
truly love God we would keep His word, because true love
brings forth the actions of caring, sharing and understanding
the hurts of one another.
John 15: 10
*"If you keep My commandments, then you will abide in My love,
just as I have kept My Father's commandments and abide in His
love."*
Keeping the word of God in our daily lives will result in us
abiding, living in the love of God. What better place could we
possibly live than in the protecting, caring love of the
Almighty? For in His love is the full assurance of our security; *a
peace that surpasses all understanding* and *He is our fortress,
our refuge* from all our foes. That is not all! In God's love is also
eternal life, never ending life with God, which death has no
longer any power over.
John 15: 9
"As the Father loved Me, I have also loved you; abide in My love."
As we will notice in many verses in the Gospel of John, Jesus
abides in the love of God the Father in obedience and gives
that love to us. Obedience and love coincide with one another.
Jesus promises that if we abide in His commandments because
we love Him, we abide in His love as He abides in the Father's
love.
There is no mystical, magical or hidden formula for abiding in
the love of God. If we love God as our first priority, and love
our brother and sister as ourselves, every other letter of the

commandments will be fulfilled. How can we say that we love God and are willing to place Him first place in our lives, but not follow His instructions? Can we say we love God, yet cheat, lie, gossip and complain toward one another? Of course, some will say that they do not commit the more obvious sins like murder, adultery or stealing. However, the less obvious sins are still sin, and bring forth the weeds of hypocrisy in our lives. Those weeds eventually grow into vines that choke the word of God and leave our hearts in a hardened, cold state.

Moreover, our words are either in faith or in doubt. If they are in faith and aligned with the power of the word of God, then they are in His love. If our words are in doubt, then we simply lend our voices to evil, which is expressing to God that we do not really trust Him. Where then is the love of God in doubt and unbelief? Doubt and unbelief will only bring about fear, resentment and confusion, and all of these will harden the heart, leaving us in a sea of uncertainty, despair and ignorance, which is spiritual darkness.

The Apostle John wrote about the results of hate, which is every word and action that is opposite of love that leads us deeper in error.

1st John 2: 11

But he who hates his brother is in darkness and walks in darkness, and does not know where he is going, because the darkness his blinded his eyes.

It is God, through His Son Jesus Christ, who shines His light of love into our darkened spirits, and brings us into the fellowship of the Godhead, since there is no longer any violation held against those who believe. Jesus Christ paid that cost in full, so the charge against us is no longer in the way. This was God's intent from the beginning, to re-establish a relationship between the Creator and His creation. This was accomplished through no other means, but by the power of His love toward us. Once we can understand the strength of His love, through the sacrifice of Christ, then we can walk in the light of His grace with that knowledge. However, without that understanding, we can never live in His love, which is an eternal love that brings us eternal life, through His eternal word.

Jesus made it clear that no man can have two masters. Our hearts cannot contain the love for riches and the love of God, since the two are in opposition with each other, as light and darkness cannot exist in the same place at the same time. Therefore, we serve whatever it is we love.

Matthew 6: 24, 1st John 2: 15

"No one can serve two masters; you cannot serve God and money."

Do not love the world or the things in the world. If any one loves the world, the love of the Father is not in him.

Anything that we value more than God is the very thing or person that we serve and worship. Whatever or whoever we serve is our heart's passion and our love priority. God simply says in the above Scriptures that we cannot serve and love the world; as money, pleasures, careers, houses, cars, hobbies, or whatever else that the world offers, above Him. For if we do love all else above God, it is that very thing that we will serve as our god. There is nothing wrong with any of these things, but they cannot be our first love.

Colossians 3: 16

But above all these things put on love, which is the bond of perfection, (lacking nothing).

It is this very reason why we were created, to love God first. This first love belongs to God, because God alone is worthy to receive it, since it is fact that God alone granted us life. For by Him we exist and can enjoy the creation that was created for us. Therefore, we can be grateful to God for all things, and love Him first, which is the true definition of worship.

1st John 2: 16

For all that is in the world – the lust of the flesh, the lust of the eyes, and the pride of life – is not of the Father but of the world.

It is not the material possessions, or the successful careers, or the enjoyment of recreation and sports that cause us to stumble in darkness, but it is the question of where is the love priority in our lives? Although we might enjoy all these things for now, they will all pass away.

1st John 2: 17

And the world is passing away, and the lust of it; but he who does the will of God abides forever.

Conditional love, which changes as the seasons, will never fulfill our hearts. We can always find conditions, reasons why we should not love the people around us, even family members, or even our spouses. Moreover, in the law given to Moses, in that it was law that an eye is given for an eye, and tooth for a tooth, yet to avoid this judgment Moses taught *to love your neighbor.* Therefore, true love is before the law, above the law and beyond conditions. For in love there is no need for the law, since the law cannot be broken in love. This is why in His final departing words; Jesus taught His disciples the most important lesson of all.

John 15: 3"

This is My commandment, that you love one another as I have loved you. Greater love has no one than this, then to lay down one's life for his friends."

The ultimate manifestation of true love toward God and one another is not in pleasing words. We can say, 'I love you' a thousand times a day to the ones we proclaim to love, only to say empty words if the actions of love are not behind our verbal expressions.

1st John 3: 18

My little children, let us not love in word or tongue, but in deed and truth.

The true evidence of love is not only spoken in words, but by the actions of kindness and devotion to God and each other. This love is giving, strong, dedicated and patient. This love is slow to anger, quick to forgive and ready to help others. This is the proof of anyone's love, which fulfills the commandment of the law. It is also the proof of our faith in God.

James 2: 17

Thus, also faith by itself, if it does not have works (action), *is dead.*

The apostles wrote through revelation by the Holy Spirit, that God's love is the most important spiritual garment that we can wear. Unselfish love brings us into a *bond of perfection* with God, as we come to the knowledge and understanding of how much God loves us. If we can comprehend the riches of God's love, expressed through His word, in that God desired to save us through His Son, then we are rich even beyond our farthest imagination. As man's sin made it impossible to attain a bond with God, since God is holy, God's love made it possible for us to be in union with Him for eternity. It was not, nor ever can be a reward for works, but rather our eternal salvation is given as a gift of love, no fine print, or strings attached. As any true gift that is given with a pure intent, it is to share what one has, so God shared His gift of life with us.

Romans 7: 23

...But the gift of God is eternal life in Christ Jesus our Lord.

The giving of ourselves to God and each other is certainly the fruit of love. Whether we give our time, our money, or anything else to the service of God and to the aid of humanity, it is the light of God's love shining through us into a hopeless world that desperately needs His saving grace. Moreover, just as this love is in the Godhead, so it should be in the church, a corporate love, ready to take in, aid, and give to the hurting, the blind and the lost. Through the love of God, which lives in the heart of every believer, we can come to a richer knowledge of *Him who called us out of darkness and into His marvelous light of love.*

Colossians 2: 2

...That their (the church's), *hearts may be encouraged, being knit together in love, and attaining to all the riches of the full understanding of the mystery of God, both of the Father and of Christ.*

God tells the church that if it is knitted, bonded together in love, then the church is rich in the revealing of the mystery of God, which is God the Father reconciling us to Himself through His Son, Christ Jesus. It is God's love, which is the eternal bonding agent of the church that inter-weaves our spirits together as one body, Christ being the head. We are fused together in the spirit, and the Holy Spirit being our down payment for the riches of eternal life. What treasure on earth could be more valuable than that?

2nd Corinthians 4: 7

But we have this treasure in earthen vessels, that the excellence of power may be of God and not of us.

The matchless treasure of God's eternal love lives in the spirit of every believer. For it is this treasure that will take all believers that trust in Him through the roadblocks and potholes of this life, and into the glorious presence of God. As anything else that holds such a high value, it is inspected and tested, proving whether it is real, for our own benefit. God tests our hearts, revealing every hidden corner of pride, resentment and selfishness, so as to purify our minds, rinsing away the very things that can choke His word that He has sown in our spirits. As the gold is passed through the fire for purification to remove all the impurities, so God will send us through the fiery trials of this life. In those trials, the impurities of our hearts and minds are burned away, leaving the love of God, which can then be molded and used for the Master's desire.

1st Corinthians 13: 8
Love never fails.

Though all else might fail, God cannot! This is why Jesus teaches us to abide in His love, because all else will fail, even these mortal, imperfect bodies will collapse and turn to dust, temporarily. However, as God lives, so we live in Him, as Jesus explains:

John 13: 34 & 14: 2, 23
And he who loves Me will be loved by My Father, and I will love him and manifest Myself to him.
If anyone loves Me, he will keep My word, and the Father will love him, and We will come to him and make Our home with him."

The Apostle Paul understood the worth of God's love, for it was by the power of God's love that delivered him through rejection, even from his own nation. This is why the apostle prays for the church, that above all, they may abound in love, knowing that God's love will overcome all. Moreover, anything that is given in love will be treasured in heaven.

Philippians 1: 9, Hebrews 6: 10
And this I pray, that your love may abound still more and more...
For God is not unjust to forget your work and labor of love which you have shown toward His name, in that you have ministered to the saints, and do minister.

Love is not always easy. The birds are not always singing on a beautiful spring day. At times, love is a sacrifice, and other times it is long suffering. Love is also truth, and sometimes truth is not easy to deliver, or receive. Love is foolish to the blind, but to the wise, it is the only theology that's needed. Love is choosing the right and rejecting the wrong in every circumstance in our lives. Where love abounds, so does God. There can be no greater gift than to have an abundance of God's love in our life, since He is the Creator and the Sustainer of all life, whether in this life or the life to come. Without God, there is no life, therefore, no true love. The so-called love that exists without God is nothing more than a surface moment that exists for a short season, but quickly blows away, unable to withstand even the smallest breeze of disagreements, since it is not rooted in the Spirit, but in the flesh. For any desire that is only skin deep, based of the exterior with no understanding of the inner part, is temporal, it is a fleeing wind of pleasure. However, real love is deeply rooted in the Spirit, which births faith, where the change of times makes no difference, but remains the same in faithfulness and truth. We are easily moved by stories concerning the experiences of others, whether it is a story of hardship, heroism, or love. However, although these reports of human experiences might change us for a moment, in time, even a few hours later, we forget what we heard and continue as if we never heard the story. The difference with the truth of God's eternal love is that it is not just a story that fades from our hearts. The truth of Jesus Christ, which is the full manifestation of God's love toward us, is indeed life changing, since it does not only enter our minds, which is quickly to forget, but our spirits, and gives birth to faith. Moreover, once faith in conceived, it is nurtured by God's word of hope, which is an eternal word that cannot fade, rust, or be worn out by the elements of time.

1st Corinthians 13: 13, Galatians 5:6
And now abide faith, hope and love, these three; but the greatest of these is love.
For in Christ Jesus neither circumcision nor uncircumcision avails anything, but faith working through love.

To The End

Hebrews 3: 6
But Christ as a Son over His house, whose house we are, if we hold fast the confidence and rejoicing of the hope firm to the end.

The word *If,* defines a condition, a clause, a pending on whether something can take place or not take place. The writer of the letter that was believed to be written to the Jewish believers in Christ takes the word and applies it as a pending factor concerning what? Before we move any further, let us establish the fact that the Holy Spirit is speaking about *confidence and rejoicing of the hope, partakers of Christ, and the promise remains of entering His rest.*

The Spirit in the writer is not speaking about natural houses and families, but the true family of God. Therefore, we can establish the fact that there is one house of faith, one family in hope. This house is under the lordship of Jesus Christ, *whose house we are,* and those who were also led by Moses, *if* they entered by faith. If they did not enter by faith, they were not of the house of God, and either are we.

Now concerning faith, the writer of Hebrews goes in to the definition of what faith is.

Hebrews 11: 1
Now faith is the substance (realization), *of things hope for, the evidence* (confidence), *of things not seen.*

The writer goes into much detail in this chapter explaining how this faith, which is trusting God in confidence effected the lives of the men and women mentioned in the text.

By faith Abel, by faith E 'noch, by faith Noah, by faith Abraham, by faith Moses and so on, by faith, (by confidence in what God said) they were partners with God in accomplishing His master plan. They were confident in God.

This word also states that there is an obligation, a commitment, and oath of the heart when referring to the words *hold fast.* This continuing action takes a submissive will to Him who owns all life, and the fruit of this steadfast is a *confidence* (faith), *and rejoicing of the hope* in eternal salvation by Christ, through Christ, and to be with Christ forever, *if we hold fast to the end.* However, what happens if we do not *hold fast to the end*?

Hebrews 3: 14

For we have become partakers of Christ, if we hold the beginning of our confidence steadfast to the end.

The writer goes on to state that we are *partakers of Christ. Partakers* of what? We are *partakers* of His death if we put to death the works of the sinful desires. This is certainly not to say that we will never sin again, we will, but we will not live in that sin, for no sin can hold us into bondage again unless we willingly choose to enter into the captivity of that sin, whatever that sin might be. We are also *partakers* of His resurrection, *if we hold the beginning of our confidence steadfast to the end.* Again, the word *if* implies a condition and the condition is *if we hold steadfast to the end.*

In the letter to the church in Rome, Paul explains how rich are those who *hold fast to the end.*

Romans 11: 17

...And you being a wild olive tree, were grafted in among them, and with them became a partaker of the root and richness of the olive tree.

We who believe in Christ and *hold fast* the *confession of faith* are *partakers* of the Root, who is Christ.

The Apostle Paul by the power of the Holy Spirit brings this truth to light in the letter to the believers in Rome that through faith (confidence in God, trusting Him); we have been grafted in, adopted into the promise of life through the sacrifice of Christ and His resurrection from the dead *if we hold fast to the end.* That is great news, but Paul adds a warning here, that we should think twice about turning away from God and living in sin.

Romans 11: 20

For God did not spare the natural branches, He may not spare you either.

The *if,* the condition, the clause, or the pending factor is faith (*confidence*), in Christ, and whether or not we remain in that faith until the *end.* Therefore, it is not a matter of someone losing his or her salvation through a sin, but losing faith, losing confidence in Christ, which is the condemnation of unbelief. As believers in Christ, we are still subject to some extent to the flesh, since we do live in a polluted body from sin. The evidence is the death of these natural bodies. It then becomes a question of what will dominate our minds, the flesh, or the spirit. However, even in our deepest battles with sin, if faith (*confidence* in God), is still there, we can and will recover, but if faith is lost then we reside in doubt and unbelief.

Romans 11: 20, Hebrews 3: 12
Because of unbelief, they were broken off and you stand by faith. Do not be haughty, but fear.
Beware brethren, lest there be in any of you an evil heart of unbelief in departing from the living God.

These are strong words written by men that were moved by the Holy Spirit. *Beware brethren,* is a warning to believers, not unbelievers that the trap of unbelief has happened to many of Christians, who have turned away from the truth of Christ and believed a lie. I have met some, who once believed, but now doubt because of hardship or loss, or even for earthy riches and fame. Nevertheless, their faith did not endure. Therefore, where is their salvation? Where is the hope of the promise in their hearts? Have they not *departed from the living God?* God does not take away His promise, but we have the freewill to walk away from it. As Paul writes, "*Because of unbelief they were broken off.*" I have heard all the debates that question whether a person was really saved if they decided to walk away from Christ. However, this warning is addressed to faith-filled believers, because they are addressed as *brethren.* How could they be *brethren* if they are not saved?

In the letter to the church in Colossi, Paul continues giving a warning that we are to remain committed to the faith and not to the flesh. This is a letter, which obviously deals with some false teaching that had found way into the church and was spreading to the point that Paul caught wind of it. Somehow, the church there had *moved away* and was no longer *grounded and steadfast* in Christ alone, but began to seek communication with angels and follow *the traditions of men according to the basic principles of the world*, instead of seeking Christ and His command.

Colossians 1: 22, 23

He (Jesus) has reconciled in the body of His flesh through death, to present you blameless, and above reproach in His sight- if indeed you continue in the faith, grounded and steadfast, and are not moved away from the hope of the gospel, which you heard...

The warning is the same as in Hebrews and Romans. If we do not continue, remain in the faith of Christ, then how can we believe in the mercy of His sacrifice? Moreover, how can He present us *blameless,* if we go back to our sin of unbelief? This is the same unbelief that caused the people whom Mosses led out of Egypt to perish in the desert of doubt. They could only enter the promise land by faith. Therefore, the word *if* again is used as a warning that unless we live in the faith, we will certainly die in doubt. So where then is our redemption for which Christ died? Have we not then taken the sacrifice of Christ as a used paper towel and considered the temporary pleasures of this life worth more? If we walk away from the faith in Christ, and God's gift of eternal life, which is given through faith, then how can we reach the promise of God's gift of eternal life without faith?

1st Corinthians 15: 1, 2

Moreover brethren, I declare to you the gospel which I preached to you, which you also received and in which you stand, by which also are saved, if you hold fast that word which I preached to you – unless you believe in vain.

The Apostle Paul now writes to the church in Corinth with a strong word of warning. The church in Corinth received and believed the gospel of Christ. He goes on to tell them that the outcome of receiving the gospel resulted in your salvation, but then he adds, *if you hold fast that word which I preached to you – unless you believe in vain.* Is Paul teaching that if anyone does not *hold fast that word,* that person can *believe in vain*?

Paul goes on to warn the church in his second letter.

2nd Corinthians 13: 5

Examine yourselves as to whether you are in the faith. Test yourselves. Do you not know yourselves, that Jesus Christ is in you– unless indeed you are disqualified?

These are very strong warnings using words like *disqualified* and *believe in vain.* Can a person *be disqualified*, or *believe in vain*, when they depart from the word of truth?

We now see Paul write to the churches of the Colossians, the Romans, and the Corinthians, and here again we see the word *if* used in a place of warning. I do not see how much clearer Paul could have wrote it, teaching the churches that there are landmines out there that can and will derail our faith. Without faith in Christ, are we then lost again in the darkness of doubt, unable to see the light of hope?

Colossians 1: 21 – 23

He (God) *has reconciled...*

...To present you holy, and blameless, and above reproach in His sight – if indeed you continue in the faith, grounded and steadfast, and are not moved away from the hope of the gospel which you heard...

Paul is saying here that if someone has *moved away from the hope of the gospel*, then Jesus Christ cannot *present you holy, blameless and above reproach.* Remember that these letters were written to the church, to believers and not to the world of unbelief. Why would the writers of the New Testament use such strong warnings? Why would they continually use the word *if* concerning our redemption if there were no conditions or factors involved?

The writer of the Book of Hebrews gives us a very strong warning concerning the dangers of falling away from the living God. He uses strong words as he writes to the church, wherever that church was, it does not matter, we are all the church of Jesus Christ, and addressing the church, he uses the word *brethren*, meaning spirit-filled believers. He would not call those in the world, outside the kingdom, *brethren.* He told them and is telling us by the inspiration of the Holy Spirit.

Hebrews 3: 12

Beware brethren, lest there in any of you an evil heart of unbelieving departing from the living God.

The writer then begins to show the importance of endurance and picks up where the rest of the epistles leave off concerning the condition, the clause in the word *if.*

Hebrews 3: 6
But Christ as a Son over His house whose house we are if we hold
fast the confidence and the rejoicing of hope firm to the end.
Therefore he states that *if we do not* hold *fast the* confidence
and the rejoicing of hope firm to the end, *beware, lest then*
there be in any of you an evil heart of unbelief departing from
the living God. One of the important points made here, is that
you cannot depart from somewhere, or someone unless you
had been there. You cannot *depart from the living God*, unless
you have already been with Him. How can you depart from the
living God if you were never with the living God? The Sprit of
God is speaking to and talking about the *brethren*, saved
people, not unsaved people, not the world. Then the writer
brings us the example of the Israelites that fell in the
wasteland of the desert because they did not obey the promise
of God in faith
Hebrews 3: 17, 18, Hebrews 4: 1
Now to whom was He angry forty years? Was it not with those
who sinned, whose corpses fell in the wilderness? And who did
He swear that they would not enter His rest, but those who did
not obey?
Therefore, since a promise remains of entering His rest, let us
fear lest any of you seem to have come short of it.
Obedience is a sweet fruit from faith. Faith is trust and in trust,
we are obedient. Where doubt and unbelief is, there is
disobedience. The writer of Hebrews makes this very clear,
using the Israelites as a point of reference that since faith was
absent, they fell to sin, disobedience, they fell to death.
Moreover, as a result, they did not enter into the promise of
God's rest because they did not obey.
Hebrews 4: 3, 4: 6
For we who have believed do enter that rest...
And those to whom it was first preached did not enter because of
disobedience.
Again, we see warning after warning, more in this letter than
the rest of the epistles that there is a danger in drifting away
from the faith and beginning to see God's precious gift of
salvation that was paid for by pure and holy blood as a
common, casual thing. A fall from faith in the living God could

certainly leave us in a spiritual desert, disconnected from the very life source of God, void of the living waters of His love and truth and tangled in the choking darkness of sin and death.

Hebrews 4: 11

Let us therefore be diligent to enter that rest, lest anyone fall according to the same example of disobedience.

This is a strong example given by the writer to look closely how the Israelites wandered in circles for forty years because of their lack of faith, which is disobedience to the truth of God. Their fall was great, because they failed to trust God at His word. Each one of us needs to look into the mirror of our hearts and ask ourselves if we really do trust God at His word in every area of our lives. That trust brings forth obedience.

Hebrews 12:15, 16

Looking carefully lest anyone (brethren, believers),*fall short of the grace of God; lest any root of bitterness springing up cause trouble, and many become defiled; lest there be any fornicator or profane person among you like Esau, who for one morsel of food sold his birthright.*

We that believe have a birthright through Jesus Christ, who paid for that right with His own blood. We are now in the family of God, His children without question. However, even in the nature (which the writer uses as an example), a person can forfeit, give up, sell his or her birthright for something or somebody else that they think is more valuable than the birthright they already posses.

Hebrews 12: 17

For you know that afterward when he wanted to inherit the blessing , he was rejected, for he found no place for repentance , though he sought it diligently.

This was a sad ending for Esau, who sought for the blessing of his family birthright, but was rejected, because of a heart that was drowned in unbelief, with no repentance in it. This was written as an example for us.

Hebrews 10: 29

Of how much worst punishment, do you suppose, will be thought worthy who has trampled the Son of God underfoot, counted the blood of the covenant by which he_(a believer), was sanctified_a common thing, and insulted the Spirit of grace?

Esau sold out to the temporary pleasure of a good meal, which is symbolic to the temporary pleasures of this life. He *counted* his birthright *a common thing.*

2nd Peter 3: 17
You therefore, beloved, since you know this beforehand, beware lest you also fall from your own steadfast, being led away with the error of the wicked...

Even Peter warns the church, the *beloved* to *beware* because the fall from grace is a hard fall, God will judge the world of unbelief. The writer of Hebrews gives us the same insight.

Hebrews 10: 30, 31
For we know Him who said, "Vengeance is Mine, I will repay," says the Lord. And again, "The Lord will judge His people."
It is a fearful thing to fall into the hands of the living God

We have heard from Paul, we have heard from the writer of the letter to the Hebrews, and Peter about the dangers of falling away from the faith, but what did Jesus say about remaining steadfast to the end?

Matthew 10: 22, Mark 13: 13
"But he who endures to the end will be saved."

Mark and Matthew record the above verse word for word What we leave behind is a testimony, like the star that is long gone, burnt out for many years, but the light, which it once shown is still traveling through space, reflecting the glory of God's creation. We also, leave behind a living testimony of light for the generations to come that God is true, holy and *a rewarder to those who seek Him,* if we endure to the end. The light of faith in God is eternal, but we need to protect it within our hearts, above all else, hold our *confidence* in God to *the end.*

Breakfast on the Beach

John 21: 12
Jesus said to them, "Come and eat breakfast."
I could not think of a better way to end the book, than to pull
up a beach chair, watch and listen as the resurrected, glorified
King of all kings, that now sits at the right hand of God the
Father, has a quiet, intimate little breakfast with a group of His
disciples. The Jesus that healed the sick; gave sight to the blind
and raised the dead out of His compassion for our sufferings, is
the same, even after His resurrection, as we see Him prepare
and invite His loved ones for a breakfast on the shore.
Although John is the only one that recorded this event, it gives
us a clear insight of the personal relationship Jesus wants to
have with each and everyone of us. Moreover, after they all ran
for their lives and left Him alone at the time of His arrest, and
some even denied Him to His face, we see Jesus serve them, as
a loving parent would make their children something to eat. I
am sure that as the sun was rising against the water and the
sound of the sea was drifting against the shore, the voice of
Jesus must have echoed in the hearts of these men. This was a
tender moment with the Lord of all the galaxies that John
could not forget. John's record tells us that all was prepared
for them as soon as they found their way to the shore.
John 21: 9
*Then, as soon as they had come to land, they saw a fire of coals
there, and fish laid on it and bread.*
Jesus had everything ready, waiting for them to come and
enjoy. I can remember as a child, we would come in from
playing, and the table would already be set with hot food,
waiting for us, it was home. Jesus at this very moment is
preparing a place, a home for us; a table set with all the
fullness of the love of God. Although we might think that the
temporary things in this life are great, they will seem like
nothing when we sit in the full manifestation of God and
clearly understand the passion in His heart for us. For many
years, I was always so puzzled about God's love for us. When I
see the rebellion against Him, even in my own life, I wondered

how God could love us so much. He sees our stubbornness, our selfishness, and our lack of love for each other. He hears our consistent words of doubt and unbelief as we complain about everything from weather to the government, and then worry about the rising prices of the economy. Where is the trust, the faith in the one and only God, who created all the galaxies with a word? Where is the confidence in His promises? However, we must come to the sobering realization that God does not love us because of how great we are. This might hurt our already fragile egos, but it is true. God loves us because of who He is. *God is love.*

As the disciples raced to the shore, Jesus tells them, *"Come and eat breakfast."* This was a quiet moment with Jesus that morning while He cooked the fish and warmed the bread. There was no great sermon recorded, no warnings, or no rebukes as the fish cooked over the fire. The crowds were still in their beds; the new day was just beginning as the seagulls circled over the sea. After all that happened, the trial, the crucifixion and the powerful resurrection from the dead, here we see the loving Jesus, still serving, the same as He was the night of the Last Supper.

However, Jesus does ask a question that gives us some insight into the heart of God as He asked Peter, *"Simon, son of Jonah, do you love Me more then these?"* Peter says yes, and Jesus replies, *"Feed My sheep."* Here we clearly see that Jesus is asking Peter to take on the task of a shepherd for one reason and one reason alone. Jesus is saying that if you truly love Me, you will care for the believers that I love. The motivation behind the task then is based on love. For this was the motivation from God the Father as He sent Jesus to be a final blood sacrifice for the remission of our sins. Jesus wants to set that first stone in place in the foundation of the church, clarifying that if we truly love Him, then we can be used for His purpose of love, the love mission. It is then that His love can reach a dying world through every believer. However, that takes leadership in love and Jesus was telling Peter, 'if you love Me, you will care for those that I love.' It is like watching after someone else's children while their parents are away.

This little breakfast on the shore in the early morning hours also shows us God's desire for us is to love Him. Not that God needs our love, but desires it. For we are His creation, made in His image and likeness, created to have fellowship with Him. As the angels are called messengers, servants and guardians, we are called sons and daughters of the Most High. There is certainly a higher calling for us than the angels in heaven as God gave His all to save us from eternal error, but never once considered saving the fallen angels who rebelled against Him. This alone should bring us to our knees in gratitude, knowing how much God cares for us.

Peter reminds us twice in Scripture about this early morning breakfast conversation with the risen Jesus. I believe that Peter was changed that day on the beach from returning to a sea of doubt as a fisher of fish, to a fisher of men. For in the three years that Christ tutored him, Peter never returned to his former occupation of fishing. However, here we see Peter back in the boat and catching no fish again, in the same state he was in three years ago when Jesus called him into the ministry. Jesus again steps into the bottoming out of Peter's life, where no fish were to be found, and tells Peter again to cast his net upon the waters of the living word of God in faith, and the fish came pouring into the net. Peter remembers that day on the beach where his doubts and fears were washed away by faith. There was no longer any doubt in Peter's mind that he was called to catch men for the risen Christ, to the glory of God. I believe that Peter never fished for flounder again after that day, but he certainly did fish for the hearts of men and women for Christ. Peter then testified with no doubt or confusion of the true mission of God as he leaves the boat behind for the final time, never looking back, but looking ahead for the gathering of lost souls for the Kingdom of God.

Acts 10: 40 & 41
"Him God raised up on the third day, and showed Him openly, not to all the people, but to witnesses chosen before by God, even to us who ate and drank with Him after He arose from the dead."
2nd Peter 1: 14
"Knowing that shortly I must but off my tent, just as the Lord Jesus Christ showed me."

Peter is quick to testify that not only did he see the risen Christ, but he also ate with Him as the sun was rising over the sea. This is an important statement since it gives us a clearer reality that Jesus is alive and remains the same. John and Peter both bear witness that after the brutal beatings, death on a cross and being buried in a tomb, Jesus is alive and decided to visit the boys for breakfast on the beach. Jesus did indeed rise from the dead! This is the cornerstone of the Christian faith and Peter and John make it a point to testify that He is alive and well!

As they talked with Jesus over breakfast, He asked Peter three times, *"Do you love Me?"*

Whether we realize it or not, we answer this question everyday with everything we say or do in this life. Should we love God with a pure heart, willing to give Him our all? That is a silly question! For without God there would be nothing, no earth, no sky, no oceans, and no us! Without God there is simply no life, only a dead void of nothing, empty space, which is what is in our hearts without Him. This fact escapes us because of the great deception that has been placed in our minds, a blindfold of doubt that prevents us from seeing the pure light of God's love for us. Peter, John and the other disciples that day on the beach were looking into the eyes of the eternal love of God manifest in the form of a Man, sacrificed for our every offence. He was and is, and will always be the eternal light of God's love that has shone down on humanity, that purifies the heart of every man and woman for all that are willing to accept Him as truth.

John 1: 4 & 5

In Him was life, and that life was the light of men. And the light shines in the darkness, and the darkness did not comprehend it. That was the true light which gives light to every man coming into the world.

John 8: 12

Then Jesus spoke to them again, saying, "I am the light of the world. He that follows Me shall not walk in darkness, but have the light of life."

John 9: 5 & 12: 46

"I am the Light of the world."

"I have come as a light into the world, that whoever believes in Me should not abide in darkness."

The true Light, by which we may see God, is Jesus Christ, as He is the expressed image of God, the purest manifestation of God that we can presently know. Moreover, since He alone is the payment for all our sin, by the sacrifice of His blood on the cross, He is the only way that we may journey home into the eternal presence of the Almighty.

2nd Peter 1: 19, Hebrews 13: 20

And so we have the prophetic word confirmed, which you do well to heed as a light that shines in a dark place, until the day dawns and the morning star rises in your hearts.

Now may the God of peace who brought up our Lord Jesus from the dead, that great Shepherd of the sheep, through the blood of the everlasting covenant, make you complete in every good work to do His will, working in you what is pleasing in His sight, through Jesus Christ, to whom be glory forever and ever. Amen.